A SECRET SURRENDER

DARCY BURKE

For Linda and Toni,
quite simply because they are awesome

A SECRET SURRENDER

The Pretenders

Set in the world of The Untouchables, indulge in the saga of a trio of siblings who excel at being something they're not. Can a dauntless Bow Street Runner, a devastated viscount, and a disillusioned Society miss unravel their secrets?

A Secret Surrender

A survivor of the mean streets of London's East End, Selina Blackwell has learned to be a chameleon, and in her current iteration as a fortune-teller, she's able to provide a Season for her sister. Only, Madame Sybila can't be a chaperone, so Selina takes on another identity as the proper Lady Gresham. But when a Bow Street Runner takes too much of an interest in her business, it seems the crimes of her past will finally come to light.

Determined to prove that Madame Sybila is a fraud bent on fleecing London's elite, Harry Sheffield enlists the help of the alluring Lady Gresham in exchange for introducing her to Society's best. With his busy career and aspirations for the future, Harry has no time for marriage, but an affair is just right—until he discovers the lady's disarming secret. Whatever his feelings for her, he can't ignore who she is and who she's been. And when she holds the key to the one case he couldn't solve, he must choose justice or love.

Don't miss the rest of *The Pretenders* trilogy!

Love romance? Have a free book (or two or three) on me!

Sign up at http://www.darcyburke.com/readerclub for members-only exclusives, including advance notice of pre-orders and insider scoop, as well as contests, giveaways, freebies, and 99 cent deals!

Want to share your love of my books with like-minded readers? Want to hang with me and get inside scoop? Then don't miss my exclusive Facebook groups!

Darcy's Duchesses for historical readers
Burke's Book Lovers for contemporary readers

A Secret Surrender
Copyright © 2020 Darcy Burke
All rights reserved.

ISBN: 9781944576875

Book design: © Darcy Burke.
Book Cover Design © The Midnight Muse.
Cover image © Period Images.
Darcy Burke Font Design © Carrie Divine/Seductive Designs
Editing: Linda Ingmanson.

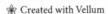 Created with Vellum

PROLOGUE

EAST LONDON, 1801

"More gin, girl!"

Selina Blackwell moved to the table where the bottle of gin stood next to the man's empty cup. He could have poured it himself, of course, but her boss, who was downstairs in the tavern, had told her to serve him up here in one of the private dining rooms. And no one went against Samuel Partridge.

As she poured, the strong scent of the alcohol filled her nose. She forced air out to push the smell away. Unlike some of the other children, she didn't drink the stuff. Her older brother Rafe wouldn't allow it, even if she'd wanted to.

After setting the half-empty bottle back on the table, Selina stepped back.

"Where ye goin'?" The man, old enough to be her father, was filthy with bloodshot eyes and a crooked nose. He clasped Selina's arm and pulled her back to the table. Though she wanted to jerk away, Selina knew better than to cause trouble.

"Nowhere," she replied quietly.

"Stay where I can see ye," he growled before

taking a long drink of gin. Wiping his hand over his mouth, his small, dark eyes didn't leave her. "Ye're a pretty thing. How old are ye?" He picked up his goose pie and took a large bite.

Selina shifted her weight, wishing she could at least move around to the other side of the table, but she didn't dare. Her brother always told her to follow directions, stay quiet, and hopefully escape notice.

"Eleven."

The man's eyes widened. "That can't be right. Ye look older than that. Don't lie to me, girl."

Everyone assumed Selina was older than her years. She was tall for her age—much taller than any of the other girls in Partridge's gang. She also had curves, primarily a bosom, that the other girls didn't.

"I don't lie, sir. Mr. Partridge don't allow it."

The man sat back in his chair and watched her as he used his tongue to try and clean the food from his yellowed teeth. His gaze raked over her crudely.

Selina's stomach turned.

"Eleven, eh? Ye look fifteen, so I'm sure ye're closer to that. Yer mama probably lied about yer age." He squinted at her. "Do ye even have a mama?"

Selina didn't remember her or their father, but she'd been just two when they'd died. Rafe had been five, so he recalled small things, like the color of their mother's hair and the kindness of their father's voice. Selina only knew the man who'd claimed to be their uncle. He'd turned her and Rafe over to Partridge several years ago and disappeared.

"My mother died a long time ago," Selina said, keeping her voice soft but steady despite the fear racing through her. "It's just me and my older brother." She hoped mentioning him might make the man think twice about trying anything. Then for good measure, she said her boss's name. "And Mr. Partridge. He takes care of us."

The man snorted with laughter. "Partridge don't care for no one but hisself." He pushed back from the table, the chair's legs scraping against the battered wood floor.

Selina's body twitched with the urge to run. Hopefully he would just walk away. So far, they always had, even after staring at her the way he was. "It's Partridge's tavern," she said, as if that would get the man to leave her alone.

The man stood. Owing to Selina's height, he was barely taller than her. "And Partridge sent ye up here to serve me."

"To serve dinner." Selina tensed.

"Ye know it'll be more than that." His thin lips spread in a grin, showing his disgusting teeth again.

He stood between her and the door. She looked in that direction, her heart thudding. Mayhap she could shove him hard enough to get by and leave before he could catch her. Why had Partridge sent her up here with him? She'd served other men, but they'd always been more interested in the gin than her. Had Partridge set her up for something more? Her stomach twisted again.

The man grabbed her bicep. "Don't think about it." He pulled her toward him until she crashed against his chest. Blowing out a fetid breath that made her gag, he lowered his head.

Sweat broke out on her nape and back as she reached for the bottle on the table. She didn't think as her hand closed around the neck, and she smashed it against his head. The glass shattered and noxious alcohol splashed over both of them.

Instead of letting her go, he shoved her backward, groaning as one hand went up to his head. "Silly bitch!"

Off balance, Selina staggered as she tried to maintain her footing. The wall was just behind her. She was trapped. Except for the window, which was to her left. She glanced out past the crack that ran from one corner of the pane to the other. It was a long drop to the cobblestones below.

The man moved toward her, his gaze menacing. "That's right, back up against the wall, ye little whore. Lift yer skirts."

Her vision blurred. There was no one here to save her—no Rafe, none of the other children who might help her. Just this man who would take her and do as he pleased.

She'd die before she let him do that. She shot another look at the window. Perhaps the fall would kill her. That would surely be better than the life she was living. No more hunger, no more fear, no more being forced to steal and scheme.

"Do you mind if I open the window?" she asked calmly, even though her heart was pounding and she still couldn't see right.

He sneered. "Why, so ye can scream for help?"

"No." Screams were normal in this neighborhood, and no one cared. "I'd like some air. You smell."

The back of his hand stung against her cheek making her gasp. "Up against the wall now!" He reached for her, but she bent and dashed under his outstretched arms. She probably wasn't going to make it, but if she didn't try… She let out a sob.

His hand grasped the back of her gown, pulling the fabric so that it rent down her back. Terror exploded inside her. She shrieked. He held onto the garment, but she reached wildly for the tabletop. If only she could find the knife.

The man pushed her so that she bent over the table then stood behind her, pinning her so she couldn't move her lower half. Frantic, she put her hands out in the hope of finding anything to use against him.

"No, ye don't." He scattered the dishes from the table but not before she clasped the fork. Her palms were slick with sweat, but she closed her hand around the metal and stabbed him hard in the forearm below the edge of his rolled-up sleeve. He yowled and jumped back, the fork sticking from his flesh.

She dove for the rickety chair, and swung it up then crashed it against him. The chair broke, and he fell back, teetering. Then his balance gave out.

So did the window.

The glass, already badly cracked, broke, and he fell. Selina raced to the window and watched as his arms and legs flailed briefly before he hit the cobblestones with a horrid snap. Dark blood oozed from the back of his head.

Selina froze as the door behind her opened. Before she could turn, comforting hands were on her shoulders. She began to shake.

"Shit," Rafe breathed as he moved past her and looked down. He turned to face her. "I heard the noise, and I knew you were in here, so I came to check. Come on, we need to move." He ushered her from the room, up a narrow staircase, then up another toward the tiny room they shared.

"Partridge knows I was there too." She was so cold, and it wasn't just the fact that her gown was gaping in the back. The ice permeated to the very marrow of her bones. She doubted she would ever be warm again. "He sent me up to serve." Quivering, she turned to face her brother as he guided her into their room. "Does he want me to whore?"

"No," Rafe said firmly as he pulled out the solitary bag they owned and began shoving her meager belongings into it. "He knows you're too young."

"That man didn't think so. I told him how old I was. He said it only mattered how old I looked."

Selina wrapped her arms around herself. "Partridge will expect me to whore someday. Mayhap today is that day."

Rafe, who at fourteen was somewhere between child and man, swore. He stopped and stared at her. "You can't stay."

"Where will we go?" Her teeth were chattering.

"Not we—you. I've been saving money. Partridge doesn't know. I knew this day would come. I just didn't realize it would be so soon." He swore again.

"What day?"

"When you would have to leave."

She slowly shook her head and took a deep breath, trying to calm the shaking. "No. I won't do that." He was all she had.

Rafe put the bag on her narrow cot and took her hands. Several inches taller, he towered over her as his eyes bored into hers. "Yes, you will. Forget what will happen to you if you stay, what almost happened to you downstairs, you just killed that man. Partridge may not be able to protect you from retribution."

"Partridge may be the one to seek it," she whispered.

Rafe's lips pressed together. "There's a school about fifty miles from here. I'm putting you on a mail coach. I already sent a deposit to save you a spot after the new year. Hopefully, they'll admit you now." He let go of her hands and went back to filling the bag. "Change your dress, Lina."

Feeling as though she moved in half-time, Selina drew the ruined garment over her head and donned the only other gown she owned. Then she tied her only bonnet beneath her chin.

By the time she finished, Rafe had completed his task of packing her things and was now kneeling beside the dresser. He reached up under it and brought out a purse, which he handed to her. "Hide this—it's the rest of what I saved."

Selina hefted the purse. "You said you'd hoped to save more."

"I'll send more when I can. Or you can...you know." He lifted a shoulder.

She could steal. That was one of the few things she could do well.

Like any good thief, she'd sewn secret pockets into her gown. Stashing the purse, she watched as Rafe swept his hat from a hook on the wall and crushed it over his bright blond hair.

"Come, we must get you away quickly." He reached for her, his hand closing around hers.

"I don't know if I can leave you." Unshed tears burned her eyes.

"Don't cry, my sweet sister." He smiled at her. "We'll be together again. You'll see. For now, this is safest for you. You trust me, don't you?"

She nodded, unable to speak past the knot of fear and grief in her throat. He was the *only* person she trusted.

He stroked away the single tear that slipped down her cheek. "Please don't cry. I can't bear your sadness. It's past time for you to be happy, and to do that, you must be far away from this life."

Selina took a deep breath and swallowed her tears. She followed him from the room, and they rushed down the back stairs as the alarm was raised about the dead man.

They escaped into the narrow alley and raced through the slums they'd called home the past several years. Fifty miles away from here...Selina could scarcely imagine it. What would the air smell like?

When they were a good distance from the tavern, she slowed to catch her breath. Rafe did the same, looking furtively behind them. "We must hurry," he urged.

"Why can't you come with me?" Selina asked.

"It's a ladies' seminary." Rafe chuckled. "Pretty as I am, they won't accept me."

She wanted to smile but couldn't. "Then why can't we go somewhere together?"

"Where would we go? What would we do? At the school, you will learn. Perhaps you will become a governess even." His tone had grown harsh, but now he lightened it once more. "Can you imagine that, Lina? You'd have a nice room, regular food, and a family to care for."

No, she couldn't really imagine it. "That's a dream, Rafe."

"Mayhap, but I've always told you that I would try to make your dreams come true, haven't I?"

"What about yours?"

He shook his head and fixed her with a fierce stare. "I have a plan. Don't you worry about me. Ever. Promise?"

She hesitated, and he squeezed her hand until it hurt. "Promise me, Lina."

"I promise I won't worry," she lied. If she couldn't worry about her brother, what did she have left?

He nodded encouragingly. "You're stronger than you realize. You just protected yourself without my help. Don't fret."

Yes, she had. And she'd killed a man. The persistent cold intensified.

"We'll be together again," he repeated. "Sooner than you think."

Selina would look forward to that day, and until then, she'd do whatever she must to survive.

CHAPTER 1

*H*arry Sheffield, constable for Bow Street, opened the door of The Ardent Rose on The Strand near Drury Lane. He'd been told he would find Madame Sybila at a perfume shop in this area, and since he didn't know of any others, this had to be the place.

A myriad of scents assailed Harry as he walked into the shop. There was definitely rose, but also other floral fragrances, as well as spice and a variety of smells he couldn't quite identify. It was a bit like listening to a quartet warm their instruments before playing an actual song. It wasn't terrible, but the cacophony wasn't entirely pleasing either.

The shop was relatively small compared to its neighbors, but well-appointed. A handful or so of patrons milled about, with a pair standing at the counter speaking with a woman of middle age. A gentleman approached Harry.

"May I be of assistance, sir?" the man asked while adjusting his gold-rimmed spectacles. He was also of middle age, with an average frame and a dearth of hair. He gazed at Harry with a benign expression.

"I came to see Madame Sybila."

"This way." The man pivoted and led Harry to the back corner of the shop and through a curtain. To the left was a corridor, and to the right, a wall. Directly across from the curtain was a door.

The gentleman rapped softly on the wood, then turned back to Harry. "She'll be with you soon, I'm sure. I do hope you'll browse the shop before you go." He offered a genial smile before returning to the store past the curtain.

Harry studied the dim corridor, which appeared to lead to a staircase. Did Madame Sybila live upstairs?

The door opened to reveal a tall figure dressed entirely in black—from the heavy veil covering the woman's face to the boots peeking out from the hem of her gown. At least, Harry assumed it was a woman. It was impossible to tell.

Except it wasn't. The veil didn't cover the swell of her breasts beneath the black muslin or the hint of her waist, just barely suggested by the drape of her gown.

"Good afternoon, Madame Sybila," he greeted her.

She did not open the door wider. "You don't have an appointment." Her French accent was soft but impossible to miss.

"My apologies. I'd be happy to pay extra if you're able to meet with me now."

"I don't see male clients."

"I'm surprised you can see anyone through that veil," Harry quipped. He could see the bare outline of her face, but nothing of her expression. So there was no way to gauge her reaction.

He cleared his throat. "I have the same coin as anyone else. I'd like you to tell me my future."

A lilting laugh soared through the air between them. "I do not tell the future," she said. "I read the cards or the palm and share what I see. What the client takes from that is up to them."

"You make no prophetic promises, then?" He found that hard to believe. Hearing such mystic non-sense was the reason his mother had come to see the fortune-teller. While she refused to disclose what was said at their meetings, whatever Madame Sybila was peddling had drawn his mother to return several times, as well as donate to a new charity, about which Harry's father was dubious. "How are your clients satisfied?"

"I help them look at things in a new way. It is my understanding they are quite pleased with my ser-vices." She cocked her head to the side. "Why are you here, Mister…?"

"Sheffield." He didn't hesitate to give his name, doubting there was any way the fortune-teller would realize he was the son of her client, Lady Aylesbury.

Harry offered his hand, and she took it without wavering. Because hers was cloaked in a thick black glove, he had no inkling of the age of the appendage; however, her grip was strong and sure.

He repeated why he'd come. Or, more accurately, the reason he was using for his visit. "I am here to have you tell me my future." In reality, he wanted to see what rubbish she was—successfully, apparently—selling to kindhearted, trusting women like his mother.

"As I said, I do not do that."

He looked past her into the room. The space was small, perhaps the size of the silver closet at Ayles-bury Hall, his childhood home. There was no win-dow, but several candles illuminated the space, as well as a pair of sconces on the wall opposite the door. The flickering flames conveyed an aura of mystery, or maybe even something more sinister. Her criminal behavior, perhaps.

Near the center of the room sat a small round table, covered with a dark red cloth. A deck of cards sat to one side.

He returned his gaze to her veiled face. "You won't tell me the future?"

She shook her head gently, causing the edge of the veil to sweep against her collarbone. "I cannot. And, as I also said, I do not provide services for gentlemen."

Harry found he was curious—not just about her business, but about her. "Why not?"

She lifted a shoulder. "I find most men are untrustworthy. Given the opportunity to meet with a woman alone, they take advantage. Forgive me if I don't invite you in."

Reaching into his pocket, Harry withdrew a purse with a substantial weight of coins. He jingled the lot. "Not even for a goodly sum?"

Though he couldn't see her features, he believed she was staring him straight in the eye. "Not for twice that."

Surprise, an emotion he rarely experienced, coursed through him. Everyone had a price. Except for Madame Sybila when it came to men. His curiosity about her grew.

He put the purse back into his coat and exhaled. "This is disappointing, Madame Sybila. I had heard your talents were unmatched."

She scoffed, and he had the sense that she was smiling. "You are an excellent liar, Mr. Sheffield, but not quite good enough."

Unable to deny that he was intrigued, Harry leaned against the doorframe. "Why do you say that?"

"You seemed to believe that I could tell your future and that I would help you, a gentleman. I can't believe you spoke to any of my clientele. They would have disabused you of both of those notions."

She was clever, he'd give her that. A smile teased his mouth. "You have caught me. I merely heard that a woman of your...abilities had taken up here in the back of the perfumery. I need to understand what my future holds, and I thought you could help me."

"Forgive me, sir, but I am not convinced you think that's possible."

"Why would I come here if I didn't believe that?"

"That is the question I would like to have answered, but I am not sure you will give me an honest response."

Far too bloody clever. "How about if I tell you why I've come? Of course, I would have done so eventually, but I wasn't sure if you wanted to know before you performed your services."

She crossed her arms over her chest in a pose of grave expectation. But she said nothing.

Harry said the first thing that came to mind. "My family wishes me to marry. I was hoping you could tell me when that might happen."

"When, but not to whom?" She chuckled. "Most people would want to know to whom."

"I suppose that too, but I'm more concerned with the timing." Because the truth of the matter was that Harry's father, the Earl of Aylesbury, had been pressing him to wed for some time now. It wasn't that Harry didn't want to; it was that he hadn't met anyone who remotely interested him as a wife. But then he was far too engrossed in his work, a fact his father—and mother and sisters—pointed out at every possible opportunity.

"I see. But I cannot help you."

"So you've said." He infused his tone with disappointment. "Is there nothing that will change your mind?"

"No, and anyway, I can't tell you what you wish to know. All I can do is look at your palm and reveal what I see. The same with the cards."

"I would accept that," he said, fixing her with a stare. He wanted to see what she could do, how she'd twisted this occupation into something that had captured the attention of women who ought to know better than to trust someone like her. Women like his mother.

"A pity I am not offering that," she said, putting her hand on the door. "Now, if you'll excuse me, my next appointment will be here shortly."

"Do you lift your veil when you see a client?" he asked, wondering if he should disguise himself as a woman and return. He was suddenly desperate to see her face. Was she young, old, somewhere in between? Not too old. Her voice hadn't yet weathered with age.

"I do not."

"That's a shame." Harry accepted that he'd learned all he could today. He'd have to find a way for someone—a woman—to visit her and report back to him on precisely what Madame Sybila did. In addition to reading fortunes, she was rumored to sell tonics for a variety of purposes, though he didn't think his mother had purchased any. If she had, he would have investigated it already.

Whether tonics or false futures, Harry had no doubt everything Madame Sybila did was fraudulent. Women like her would be better served on the stage, performing their act for precisely what it was meant to be—entertainment. Instead, she preyed on the innocent and easily charmed, giving them false hope and impossible dreams, perhaps even causing them to lose things that were very dear to them. His mother hadn't lost a great deal yet, just whatever sum she'd paid for the fortune-teller's "services" and perhaps a donation to the mysterious charity. Father had asked her to reconsider this "hobby," and when she'd refused, he'd asked Harry to look into Madame Sybila.

"I'm afraid you must go," she urged, closing the door.

He stuck his boot next to the jamb to halt her progress. "I'm sorry you couldn't help me. I may come again—in the hope that you will change your mind."

"I would expect nothing less." From the sound of her voice, he was certain she was smiling. "Besides, Bow Street isn't far."

Once again, he felt a jolt of surprise, this one even stronger than the last. He didn't bother prevaricating. "How did you know?"

She shrugged, stirring the veil gently against her neck and shoulders.

He narrowed his eyes slightly, then smiled as he withdrew his foot from the threshold. "Maybe you do have certain…abilities. I will consider it my *misfortune* that you weren't able to help me."

"Good day, Mr. Sheffield." She closed the door in his face, just as he stepped back.

Disappointment curled through him, and not because he hadn't found evidence of a crime. Madame Sybila had surprised him. Twice. She wasn't at all what he'd expected, and that was a bloody feat.

Turning, he pushed through the curtain and went back into the shop. As a courtesy, he browsed the perfumes before nodding toward the gentleman who'd showed him back to Madame Sybila.

Harry departed the shop and stepped into the overcast afternoon. Turning to the right, he made his way back to Bow Street, pausing a few times to converse with acquaintances. As a constable, he knew many people of all walks of life. It was one of the things he liked best about his job.

How had the fortune-teller bloody known he worked for Bow Street? He went back over what he'd said. Perhaps he should not have asked how her clients could be satisfied without having their future read. However, that could also have simply been interpreted as his disappointment. Which had been real.

Ah well, he'd find another way to get to the heart of her business. And he was quite looking forward to it. There was a shocking air of integrity about Madame Sybila. Oh, he still believed she was a fraud, but perhaps she truly thought she was helping people. The fact that she'd refused his considerable sum —double what he'd offered, even—was positively fascinating.

Did money not drive her? If not, was it possible she *wasn't* a fraud?

Harry didn't go to the magistrates' court at number four. Instead, he went across the street to the Brown Bear. As soon as he entered, he was greeted by numerous people, a few of whom were fellow constables. He paused to exchange pleasantries before making his way to a table near the wide front window where two other constables were seated. Harry called out a greeting before sliding into an empty chair.

"What news, Sheff?" John Remington asked before taking a drink of ale. A decade or so older than Harry's thirty-one years, Remy was, in Harry's opinion, the best constable Bow Street had to offer.

"Just came from the perfumery."

The other constable, Clive Dearborn, a younger man who'd come to Bow Street perhaps three months prior, nodded. "Investigating the fortune-teller?"

"Trying to. What are you fellows up to?" A serving

maid deposited a tankard of ale on the table for Harry. He thanked her before taking a long pull.

"We just ran into each other outside," Dearborn said.

Remy fixed his dark eyes on Harry. "I've just come from Blackfriars. Heard the Vicar might be lending money out of St. Dunstan-in-the-West again."

Bloody hell. An old apprehension raced along Harry's flesh, quickening his pulse.

Dearborn swung his head toward Remy. "Who's the Vicar?"

"An arsonist and a murderer," Harry answered, gritting his teeth. "Who has yet to pay for his crimes."

"How is that?" Dearborn asked.

Remy cupped his hands around his tankard. "Harry is referring to a fire four years ago that destroyed a flash house on Saffron Hill and killed several people inside, including the leader of a large gang of thieves."

"Along with many innocents." Harry hated that no one had paid for the deaths of several children and young women. "The Vicar started the fire, so he could take over the gang."

Dearborn looked between them. "Why wasn't he arrested and tried for the crime?"

"He's a bloody ghost," Harry spat before taking another drink.

"We couldn't find him," Remy said. "He's exceptionally good at being evasive—we don't even know what he looks like for certain."

Dearborn's brow creased with confusion. "But you know he's leading this gang in Saffron Hill? And lending money in Blackfriars?"

"We can't confirm either, unfortunately. The moneylending came to our attention last year, but then he went underground again," Harry explained before leaning toward Remy. "How do you know he's back?"

"One of my informers. I knew you would want to know."

"I appreciate that," Harry said. The fire had been one of Harry's first investigations after becoming a constable. That it remained unsolved had always unsettled him. It wasn't that there weren't other unsolved cases, but this one was different. He'd established an informer in the Saffron Hill neighborhood, a sweet young woman who'd been hoping to change her life. Harry had been trying to help her. Then she'd died in that fire. He clenched his jaw. "Looks like I'll be paying a visit to St. Dunstan-in-the-West."

"Just know the Vicar's as guarded as ever," Remy warned.

"Of that I have no doubt. This time, however, I'm going to catch him."

"For a four-year-old crime?" Dearborn asked. "Will he actually be convicted?"

Remy chuckled. "You forget that Harry here used to be a barrister. He'll ensure he has the evidence necessary for a conviction."

"I did forget." Dearborn looked to Harry. "Why'd you make the change? I'd think being a barrister would be a more comfortable occupation." He snorted. "Certainly more profitable."

It was a question Harry was asked rather often. "I wanted to get out on the street and ensure justice." It wasn't that he hadn't liked being a barrister. He'd just found it...boring. He'd considered purchasing a commission and going to war, but his father had convinced him to stay and make a difference here at home.

Remy took a drink and set his tankard on the

table with a clack. "What evidence do you have, Harry?"

"We know it was arson—the circumstances of how it started are documented, if you recall." At Remy's nod, Harry continued, "Every person we interviewed said the Vicar started the fire."

"Sounds like you've got him," Dearborn said with a grin.

"Except no one could provide a consistent description of the Vicar. They didn't *see* him. They just reported they knew it was him, meaning they were probably repeating a rumor."

That had frustrated Harry most of all. It had also troubled him. Why could no two people describe him the same way? He was tall. Or of average height. Oddly, he was never short. He had blue eyes. Or brown. Or gray. He wore a patch on one eye. His hair was dark or fair. Or he was bald. He had a scar. He had a tattoo. He walked with a limp and used a walking stick.

"The Vicar is a powerful figure," Remy said darkly. "It wouldn't surprise me if those people didn't describe him out of fear."

Dearborn frowned. "But they name him, so that doesn't seem to make sense."

No, it didn't, which was another reason the crime had lived in Harry's mind. There was just something *wrong* with it. Now that the Vicar had reemerged, perhaps Harry could finally put it to rest.

"Why is he called the Vicar?" Dearborn asked.

"It's a nickname," Remy said. "Some say he listened to the confessions of his fellow criminals before putting them out of their misery."

Dearborn blew out a whistle. "So he's a murderer beyond just starting that fire?"

"It's more than likely," Harry said. "Men like him have no moral code." Instead of making him angry, that made Harry sad. What had happened to them to make them that way?

"So you'll try to catch him?" Remy asked. Harry nodded, and Remy went on, "I'll assist you in whatever way I can—just say the word." He leaned back and crossed his arms. "Now tell us about the fortune-teller."

Harry thought back over his unproductive meeting with Madame Sybila. "There isn't much to report yet."

"Did she discern your future?" Dearborn asked. "Will you be head of Bow Street one day?" He grinned.

Harry shook his head. "She refused to provide her services. Seems she'll only help women, so I either need to dress as a woman or find a woman to see her and report back to me."

"There is no chance you could pass for a woman." Remy laughed, and Dearborn joined in.

Harry cracked a smile as he nodded. "Which means I'll find someone to help me. Furthermore, she insisted she doesn't tell the future."

Remy snorted. "Well, that's hogwash. What else does a fortune-teller do?"

"Precisely," Harry said. "But I'll get to the bottom of her scheme. Then I'll put a stop to it."

"I've no doubt." Remy lifted his tankard. "To honesty and lawfulness."

Harry and Dearborn joined him and repeated the toast.

Yes, he'd find out precisely what Madame Sybila was up to, and then he'd shut her down before she could do real harm to his mother or anyone else. Hopefully, she hadn't already.

CHAPTER 2

"*H*e's been over in front of Somerset House for more than an hour." Mrs. Kinnon, the owner of The Ardent Rose perfumery, closed the door of Madame Sybila's small room after stepping inside.

"Thank you for being so observant." Selina Blackwell set the bonnet over her honey-brown hair and tied the lavender bow beneath her chin.

Mrs. Kinnon blinked, her age-heavy lids briefly obscuring her dark eyes. "What kind of friend would I be if I didn't?"

Selina smiled at the woman she'd known as long as she could remember. "You have always been—and will always be—a wonderful friend."

Mrs. Kinnon came forward and gently pushed Selina's hands away from the ribbon. "It's not straight." She'd always tried to be a mothering influence since Selina didn't have one.

"Was he alone?" Selina asked. She'd recognized him from the numerous times she'd walked along Bow Street on her way between her house and the perfumery. He was often in the company of other Runners—either outside the magistrates' court or in the window of the Brown Bear pub across the street.

"As far as I could tell. But you never know with those Runners. Far too cunning for their own good."

Indeed, and Selina suspected Harry Sheffield was shrewder than most. She'd expected him to return, though maybe not as quickly as the *day after* he'd come to see her, and was grateful to have friends looking out for her. It was a strange feeling after so many years of just her and Beatrix, a luxury really.

Apprehension roiled through Selina. She wanted to get out to The Strand and see him for herself. It wasn't that she didn't trust Mrs. Kinnon... Well, maybe it was that, at least a little. With the exception of Beatrix, trusting people was hard.

"There." Mrs. Kinnon stepped back with a satisfied nod. It was astonishing how elegant and respectable she looked now compared with the woman Selina remembered from her youth. Gone was Mrs. Kinnon's wild, dark hair, replaced by a smooth silver that was always coiled neatly into a knot. And her clothing was impeccable and modest, a far cry from the cheap, coarse gowns she'd sewn for herself, along with the few gowns Selina had owned as a child. "Now you look like the proper lady you're supposed to be."

Selina was absolutely not a lady, and she had no notion what she was *supposed* to be. Dead, probably. The dark turn of her thoughts threatened to paralyze her. But she wouldn't fall. She couldn't. She mentally chided herself. Returning to London after so many years was playing havoc with her equilibrium.

As if that's all it is.

Selina ignored the voice in her head as she picked up her gloves from the table. Her Madame Sybila costume was safely stowed behind the hidden door in the corner that opened to a tiny closet. She'd also draped a curtain over it just to be sure it remained hidden. "Thank you, Mrs. Kinnon. I'll see you tomorrow."

"And Mr. Sheffield as well, I imagine."

"Probably," Selina agreed. "I'm not entirely sure what he's after."

"His kind don't like ours."

"How would he know what 'kind' we are?" Selina asked. It wasn't as if they wore their rookery origins on a sign around their necks.

"As I said, far too cunning." Mrs. Kinnon tapped her temple with her fingertip.

Perhaps. Selina often attracted skepticism when she portrayed the fortune-teller, but that hadn't stopped the scheme from being incredibly profitable. Which was precisely what she needed right now if Beatrix was to be a success.

"Be careful when you leave," Mrs. Kinnon said as Selina went to the door.

She flashed the older woman a smile. "Always."

Turning to the right, Selina walked down the corridor, then took a doorway to the right into a small chamber before opening a door that led into the alley behind the shop. Surreptitiously surveying her surroundings, she moved cautiously along the alley. A few minutes later, she turned left onto The Strand. It wasn't her normal route, but she wanted to see if Sheffield was still across the street.

A quick examination of Somerset House did not reveal the Bow Street Runner. Perhaps he'd grown tired of his surveillance.

Or not.

As Selina approached the front of The Ardent Rose, two things happened at almost the same moment: she saw the tall, hulking figure of Harry Sheffield just past the perfumery, and someone to her right—in a doorway two shops down from The Ardent Rose—cried, "Stop, thief!"

A blur of gray and brown darted past Selina just as she saw Sheffield start to run. Without consideration, Selina pretended to trip and put herself directly in his path. He was either going to catch her, or she was going to get a face full of pavement.

Thankfully, it was the former.

His strong arms swept her up before she hit the ground. Selina wrapped herself around him, clutching at his arms and neck with a loud cry.

"Are you all right?" he asked with great concern even as his gaze followed the fleeing child.

Selina could see the boy—or girl, it was impossible to tell—from the corner of her eye and was glad to see he—or she—was fast.

Even so, Selina wasn't going to let the Runner go after the child. "I'm afraid I twisted my ankle a bit," she said with an apologetic smile. "My apologies for falling in such an ungracious manner."

"Is there a gracious way to fall?" he asked with a hint of a wry smile.

She'd expected him to be annoyed that she'd foiled his pursuit. "I suppose not. Unless one is *trying* to fall." Which she absolutely had. "And look good doing it." Which she had not.

"Can you stand?" he asked.

"Let me try," she said and, as he lowered her to the pavement, added, "slowly, if you please." She'd buy as much time as possible for the child to escape.

Sheffield set her gingerly upon the ground, and Selina was careful to put all her weight on her right foot. Then she tested her left, wincing as she did so.

"Does it hurt?" His eyes crinkled at the edge as he asked, and Selina thought he was rather handsome in his concern.

No, a Bow Street Runner is not handsome.

Even if he possessed eyes the color of a warm

tawny port and the clear ability to show humor, which only accentuated his good looks. Or that he was quite possibly the most muscular man she'd ever seen.

"It's a little tender," she said, ignoring Sheffield's physical...attributes. She clutched his forearms as she balanced on one foot. "Would you mind giving me a moment?"

His gaze swept beyond her once more, and this time she followed his line of sight. The child had disappeared, likely heading toward the Thames where he or she would almost certainly turn east toward Blackfriars.

Sheffield exhaled, his disappointment palpable.

"Is there something amiss?" Selina asked. She wasn't sure what made her ask the question, but she was incredibly curious for his answer. Would he tell her the truth?

"I was going to run after a suspected thief." His use of the word "suspected" was not lost on Selina.

"So I did hear someone yell about a thief." She looked up at him and tried not to be drawn into his captivating gaze. "You were going to chase him down?"

"I work for Bow Street."

She feigned surprise. "Oh! And here I got in your way. My apologies." She let go of his arms and stepped back, wobbling for effect. "Perhaps you can still catch him and make an arrest."

His auburn brows pitched into a V as his magnificent eyes narrowed. "I wasn't going to arrest him—or her. It was a child."

Selina's breath snagged. "What would you have done?"

"Questioned the miscreant. The child stole from a bakery, so I presume he was hungry. A child like that isn't a criminal." His voice dipped. "No child is a criminal, at least not on purpose."

Now Selina's lungs utterly arrested. So much so that she had to remind herself to breathe. Mr. Sheffield was not what she'd presumed. And that made him even more dangerous than she'd originally thought. A person she couldn't anticipate meant higher risk.

As if her life wasn't already risky enough.

She'd prefer to avoid Mr. Sheffield completely, but it didn't seem that would be possible given his attention toward Madame Sybila. Which meant she'd have to return the favor and keep a close watch on *him*.

"You truly believe that?" she asked. "That no child is a criminal?"

"They must be taught, and that isn't their fault. They can also be taught to be law-abiding citizens."

"You see to that personally, Mister...?"

His gaze snapped to hers, and Selina realized—too late—that she'd said something very similar to him yesterday as Madame Sybila. Damn, she was usually far more careful. Hopefully he wouldn't notice the similarity since she used an accent when she was in disguise.

She held her breath until he blinked. "Sheffield." He bowed. "At your service, Miss? Missus?"

"Lady Gresham."

Surprise flashed in his eyes. "Lady Gresham. I'm pleased to make your acquaintance." He glanced around. "No groom?"

She shook her head. "I don't see a need." She also didn't have the budget for one. Her "retainers" were few and had been recommended by Mrs. Kinnon. Only two lived in the small house Selina had rented on Queen Anne Street: the housekeeper—who also served as a cook—and her daughter, who performed the duties of maid. The housekeeper's nephew occasionally filled the role of groom or coachman when they rented a coach.

Sheffield cocked his head slightly. "How interesting. What does your husband think of that?"

She gave him a mild smile. "My poor deceased husband would have approved. He saw no need for things that aren't absolutely necessary."

"I see." Did he? Since meeting Harry Sheffield the day before, Selina had made inquiries about him. She'd been surprised to learn he was the son of an earl, and as such, he was likely used to a bevy of footmen. The fact that he was a Bow Street Runner only added to his enigmatic aura—another reason she couldn't afford to lower her guard around him. Especially since he was also the son of one of her clients.

That made Selina wonder if she'd somehow upset Lady Aylesbury so that she'd asked her son to investigate. Selina found that surprising since the countess was one of her most charming clients and always seemed quite happy after their meetings.

"I probably *should* have brought a groom." She wanted to see what he would say. It was imperative she carry on like a respectable lady, and if she had to employ a groom to needlessly follow her around in order to sell the lie, she would. She'd do whatever it took to ensure Beatrix accomplished her goal of conquering London.

He shrugged. "If you don't need one, I see no reason. But then, I am not particularly adept at Society's rules." His tone was cool, and she recalled what she knew of him from Lady Aylesbury. When she mentioned her second son, which was often, it was to ponder how different he was from the rest of the family, how he shunned Society and sought an occupation dealing with criminals and degenerates. Selina wondered what had prompted him to take that path.

"Well, that makes two of us," Selina said with a light laugh. "I'm fairly new to town, and I'm afraid my country manners aren't enough to launch my sister in Society."

"That is no easy feat, even if you aren't new to town," he said with more of the warmth he'd demonstrated after she'd fallen into his arms.

"I'm glad to hear it isn't just me." Selina put her foot more firmly on the ground. "I think my ankle will be fine. I should be on my way."

"Shall I call you a hack? Or are you on a local errand?" He glanced about. "Perhaps you're going to see the fortune-teller."

"The what?" Selina was eager to hear what he might say about Madame Sybila.

He waved his hand dismissively. "It was my pleasure to save you from certain disaster. Perhaps we'll meet again."

"I can't imagine how, but that would be nice." Selina could *well* imagine how. In fact, she was already formulating plans to do so. Sheffield bore watching. "Actually, I will take that hack, if you don't mind." She didn't really want to spend the funds, but it would look odd if she didn't, given that she was supposed to be a lady and she'd just injured herself.

"Of course."

While Sheffield went to the street to hail a vehicle, Selina glanced toward the perfumery. Mrs. Kinnon stood watching them in the window. She inclined her head slightly, then turned.

"Here you are, my lady," Sheffield said, gesturing to the hack that had pulled to the side.

Selina limped toward him. "Thank you."

"Are you certain I can't see you home?" he asked.

The thought of sharing the confined space of the hack with his large, handsome form sent a bothersome shock of heat through her. "No, thank you. But I do appreciate your assistance. Again, I'm sorry for the trouble."

"It was no trouble at all." He helped her up into the hack. "Your destination?"

"Queen Anne Street." Now he knew where she lived. Not that it wouldn't have been hard for him, a Runner, to find out. She was quite open about her life as Lady Gresham. She had to be for Beatrix. The rest of her life, however, was not to be seen.

He gave the direction to the driver and looked back to Selina. "Good afternoon, Lady Gresham."

"Mr. Sheffield." She smiled as he closed the door.

Then she looked out the window at him as the hack drove away. When he faded from sight, she settled back against the squab. A ripple of unease twitched through her.

What exactly was Sheffield up to? Was he merely trying to ascertain if Madame Sybila was an innocent fortune-teller and nothing more? Or had he somehow uncovered the things Selina meant to keep hidden?

She ought to keep a distant eye on him, just to make sure he didn't get too close. However, something about him said she should do more than that. And if she'd learned anything in the past eighteen years, it was that she had no one to look out for her but herself. Yes, she had Beatrix, but Selina was the planner and the protector. She'd taken on the role her brother had played for her before he'd sent her away.

Pain weighted her chest. It was growing less, but the loss would always be there. She'd spent those eighteen years working to get back to him, only to learn he was dead. To find the goal she'd worked so hard to reach was nothing but a ghost had been utterly devastating. Achieving Beatrix's goal was all she had left.

Selina would deliver it at any cost.

wo days later, Selina strolled along Mount Street, her gaze covertly taking in every aspect of the imposing house that belonged to Sheffield's father, the Earl of Aylesbury. The Palladian-faced structure was wider than those on either side, and Selina glimpsed the lavish window hangings in what was probably their formal drawing room on the first floor. She imagined Sheffield growing up in such a place and again wondered how he'd ended up chasing criminals. As a second son, shouldn't he have been an officer in the army or a rector on the path to perhaps becoming a bishop?

She didn't pause as she continued toward Berkeley Square. Today was simply a reconnaissance mission. She didn't plan to stand across from the house—or from Sheffield's house on Rupert Street, which she'd walked past earlier—as Sheffield had done again the day before, situating himself in front of Somerset House once more so he could watch The Ardent Rose. What did he think about Madame Sybila never emerging from the perfumery?

Because Selina never, ever entered or left in costume, nor did she use the front entrance to the shop.

Perhaps he would next try to watch the alley. He was becoming a nuisance.

"Lady Gresham."

Hell and the devil. Selina had been so wrapped up in her thoughts that she hadn't seen her quarry coming straight for her. Anger—at herself—churned in her gut. She was never this careless. Forget nuisance, Sheffield was rapidly becoming a bloody menace.

Pasting a cheerful smile on her face, she reacted with surprise. "Mr. Sheffield, good afternoon. How astonishing to see you again so soon."

"Indeed. This is most welcome." His gaze dipped to the hem of her gown. "How is your ankle?"

"Quite well, thank you. You are my hero."

He laughed softly. "I hardly think so. What brings you to this neighborhood?"

"After browsing on Bond Street, I decided to take a short stroll. I am now, guiltily, on my way to Gunter's for an ice." The lie fell from her tongue as easily as spring rain.

"Would it be too forward of me to offer to escort you?" Sheffield bent in a slight bow.

"Not at all. I would be delighted for the company. My sister would have accompanied me today, but she was feeling a trifle under the weather." Another lie.

Mr. Sheffield pivoted and offered his arm. "I hope she is feeling better by the time you return home."

"I'm sure she will. Just a mild headache." Selina curled her hand around his arm and quashed her re-action. He felt as muscular as he looked, and she honestly couldn't remember ever touching a man and feeling a sense of…pleasure.

They walked toward Berkeley Square, which wasn't far ahead. "What brings *you* to this neighborhood?" Selina asked. "Do you live nearby?"

"My father does. Just across the street back there, in fact."

She looked over her shoulder. "These are rather grand houses."

"My father is the Earl of Aylesbury." He winced as he said it, almost as if he were embarrassed.

"My goodness, how prestigious. And how curious that you work for Bow Street."

He chuckled softly. "If I had a shilling for every time someone reacted in precisely that way, I'd be able to buy my father's house. Not that I want it."

"Why wouldn't you want it?"

"Too extravagant. I'm quite content in my small terrace on Rupert Street."

Compared to his father's house, it was *very* small. And simple, as far as she'd been able to tell. But it was still nice and in a good neighborhood. Did someone like him even understand what it meant to live in poverty? Of course not. Why would she think he would? Furthermore, it didn't matter. He didn't have to understand her.

"So you don't aspire to have wealth and luxury?"

"Do they bring happiness? Not to me."

Though she didn't want to be, Selina found herself fascinated. "Being a constable brings you happiness?"

"It does. More than being a barrister did."

"You were a barrister?" Selina hadn't known that, but then she hadn't asked for information on what Sheffield had done in the past, and Lady Aylesbury had never mentioned it.

He nodded as they made their way into Berkeley Square toward Gunter's on the east side. "I found it a trifle boring. So I became a constable instead. I quite enjoy what I do."

Another strike against him. Not because he loved the law, but because he was probably very good at it, and *that* was a problem for Selina. "What do you like most about it?"

He opened the door to Gunter's for her, and she preceded him inside. "Helping people."

"Not arresting them?" she asked wryly as they approached the counter.

He smiled briefly. "No. I must admit, I'm intrigued by what draws people to crime. As I told you the other day, no one is born a criminal."

"Perhaps not, but some are certainly more inclined, don't you think? If only because of their circumstance?"

He turned toward her, his tawny gaze lighting with appreciation. "Precisely. Circumstances make us, or at least contribute to, who we are, and if someone is born into a disadvantaged situation, is that really their fault?"

She didn't have a chance to answer as it was their turn to order ices. He requested elderflower, while Selina asked for lavender. When Sheffield paid for both, she looked at him in surprise. As they awaited their ices, she thanked him. "That wasn't necessary," she said.

"Perhaps not, but I insist." He flashed her a smile that rooted itself in her chest with a persistent and welcome heat.

They took their ices and sat at a table near the window but not directly beside it. After they each took a few bites, Sheffield addressed her. "You are a widow. Do you have children?"

"I do not. Just my younger sister, but she is far from a child. Still, I am responsible for her. We came to London so she could have a Season." Beatrix was twenty-six, far past the age for a Season as far as Selina could tell, but she looked younger, so they simply pretended that she was.

"That's right. You mentioned that the other day. Is she enjoying herself?"

"Somewhat. I'm afraid there's more to engaging in a Season than I'd anticipated." She glanced down at her ice. "We don't know many people here."

"That would make it difficult. Probably. I admit I don't rightly know."

She studied him a moment. "How can that be when your father is an earl?"

"I pay little attention to the Season or any Society nonsense. I'm far too busy anyway." He pressed his lips together. "Forgive me. I didn't mean to imply that your errand here is nonsense. Of course your sister should have a Season. It's wonderful that you could bring her here for that."

Selina laughed softly, deeply appreciating his opinion. "I can't disagree that it's nonsense. Even so, it's Beatrix's best chance for securing a husband. We came from a rather rural village, and there were no prospects for her there."

"Will you return there after your sister is settled?" He spooned some ice into his mouth, and she caught a brief glimpse of his tongue.

Readjusting her seat, Selina took a bite of her ice before she answered. "Probably," she lied. There was no village, just as there was no husband. "Unless I find a charity to support here in London. Like you, I am committed to helping others, and I'm keen to provide assistance to women in particular. If I find myself dedicated to such an endeavor, I may stay."

"How fortunate for that endeavor," he said warmly.

"First, however, I must see my sister wed."

"Yes, to that end, I wonder if I may be of assistance." He set his spoon down. "My parents are hosting a soiree on Saturday. If you don't have another engagement, I'd be delighted to ensure you're invited."

A rush of anticipation swept over Selina. This was precisely what Beatrix needed. "My goodness, Mr. Sheffield. That's incredibly kind of you. It isn't too much trouble?"

"I wouldn't have offered if it was."

"Then, yes, thank you. That would be wonderful. You'll be there?"

"Normally, I wouldn't. However, since I'm inviting you, I probably should be." He shook his head in a self-deprecating manner. "I'll be there."

She tried not to smile and failed. "Since I now know that isn't your favorite activity, I shall take it as a compliment that you would attend on our behalf. Thank you."

Satisfaction curled around Selina. Now for the next objective. "Tell me, what are you investigating now?"

"A variety of things." His brow furrowed, and his gaze drifted past her.

Selina turned her head to follow his line of sight. "Is there something amiss?"

"No." He shook his head. "I was just thinking about an old investigation. I wasn't able to bring the perpetrator to justice."

She could see that it burdened him from the creases furrowing his forehead and around the edges of his mouth and eyes. "It still troubles you?"

His gaze met hers. "Yes. Recent developments have brought it back to the forefront of my mind. It was a tragedy, and the man behind it is out there committing crimes even now."

"How can that be?" Selina asked, truly curious.

His gaze turned hard, his lip curling slightly. "I wasn't able to catch him four years ago—that was just after I became a constable. He started a fire in Saffron Hill, burning down a house owned by an infamous criminal just so he could take over the man's organization."

Selina's blood went cold. Four years ago... A fire... Saffron Hill...

"More than a dozen people died, including children." Sheffield's jaw clenched. "He disappeared, and the investigation was closed as arson wasn't proven."

"Who is he?" She couldn't have stopped the question even if she'd tried. Which she hadn't. Selina's pulse thrummed with apprehension.

"The Vicar." Sheffield blinked at her, then took a bite of his ice. "You wouldn't have heard of him, of course. He's a moneylender over in Blackfriars."

It took everything in Selina to remain in her chair and not race out to catch a hack to Blackfriars immediately. She was nothing if not a master at schooling her reactions and emotions.

"He's a criminal, and he calls himself a vicar?" she asked, keeping her tone light before taking a bite of lavender ice.

"He meets with people in St. Dunstan-in-the-West."

"Is he an actual clergyman?"

Sheffield made a guttural sound deep in his throat. "No, he's a murderer."

He was indeed. And Selina was going to find him.

"Enough of that," Sheffield said. "I didn't mean to speak of such things. I told you, I'm bad at adhering to Society's rules."

Selina met his gaze. "You seem a man of fierce commitment and honesty. That's rather commendable," she added softly.

His eyes held hers for a moment, and she had the unnerving sense that they shared the ferocity, if not the honesty.

They finished their ices, and he escorted her from the tea shop. "Where are you off to next?" he asked.

"Home. I'll catch a hack."

"Allow me." He hailed one for her and, as on the other day, helped her into the vehicle.

"This is becoming a routine," Selina said with a smile.

He held on to her hand a trifle longer than necessary. "A pleasant one, if I may say."

Heat flashed over Selina. She should stay far away from Sheffield, but she couldn't—for now. Aside from keeping watch over him and the fact that he was going to invite them to a soiree, she now also had to consider how to obtain more information from him about this "vicar" and the fire in Saffron Hill. More than ever, Harry Sheffield was a very important person.

He was also intriguing, and she found herself liking him.

"I look forward to seeing you Saturday," she said.

"I will do the same. Expect the invitation tomorrow. I'll speak with my parents now. I hope your sister is improved."

"Thank you, I'm sure she is."

He bowed and closed the door, then walked to the front of the hack, presumably to give her direction to the driver.

Selina arrived at her small rented house on Queen Anne Street a short while later. Her mind raced with thoughts and plans as she let herself in the front door. The housekeeper was almost certainly preparing dinner just now.

After removing her hat and gloves and setting them on a narrow table, Selina walked past the stairs to the small sitting room where she and Beatrix spent most of their time.

Beatrix looked up from the newspaper she was

reading, her light hazel eyes fixing on Selina and then narrowing slightly. "What's wrong?"

Of course Beatrix would see the turmoil inside Selina. Though they weren't related by blood at all, they were as close as true sisters and had been for over fifteen years. "Tomorrow, we will receive an invitation to a soiree given by the Earl of Aylesbury."

Beatrix's eyes widened, and her lips parted in surprise. "Sheffield's father?" She knew everything Selina did about the Bow Street Runner. Except for the peculiar way he made Selina feel.

"I ran into him on Mount Street just now."

"He didn't suspect why you were there?"

Selina went to the hearth. "Not at all."

"That's *good* news, which means you aren't telling me what's wrong. I can see something is troubling you."

Of course she could. They were as good as sisters, having met at Mrs. Goodwin's Ladies' Seminary when Selina was thirteen and Beatrix just ten. Beatrix's mother had recently died and her father had sent her to the school without even telling her in person. That her father was a duke and Beatrix a bastard hadn't ever mattered to Beatrix—until she'd arrived at the seminary, where the other girls had made sure it had mattered. Selina had taken Beatrix under her wing, and they'd formed a bond that persisted.

Pivoting, Selina walked to the door that led out to the small enclosed garden. She stared outside for a moment before turning to face Beatrix, who waited patiently with the newspaper resting on her lap.

"I know who started the fire in Saffron Hill." The words slid from Selina's lips on a throaty rasp.

Beatrix stood abruptly, the newspaper falling to the floor unheeded. "How? Who?"

"A man called the Vicar. It's a crime Sheffield wasn't able to solve."

Selina's body quivered as much as when he'd told her about this at Gunter's. "Sheffield wasn't able to catch him, and he—*the Vicar*—is still out there, lending money in Blackfriars." She spat the last out on a hiss.

"We'll find him," Beatrix said with cold certainty.

"Yes, and when I do, he'll pay for killing my brother."

Beatrix came to Selina and took her hand in a fierce grip. "We'll go to Blackfriars tomorrow."

"He lends money from St. Dunstan-in-the-West," Selina said coldly, her rage buried beneath a myriad of other emotions she fought to keep hidden: grief, regret, despair. "We'll start there."

"What will you do when we find him?"

Selina blinked and looked into Beatrix's familiar eyes, felt the warmth of her support and love in the grip of her hand. Loosening her shoulders, Selina forced herself to relax. "I don't know yet." Whatever she did, she'd have to do it under the nose of a Bow Street Runner who was both scrutinizing Selina as Madame Sybila and desperate to catch the Vicar.

"Come, let's decide what to wear for your first major Society event on Saturday evening," Selina said with more enthusiasm than she felt.

Beatrix pivoted toward the door, but cast a side-long glance toward Selina. "Don't put on an act for me. I know you'll be preoccupied with finding the Vicar until it's done."

"Yes, but I won't let it take away from our objective. We're so close—the Earl of Aylesbury is incredibly well connected. You'll be presented to the Duke of Ramsgate in no time, and he'll see what he's missed all these years after abandoning you at Mrs. Goodwin's."

Eyes narrowing with purpose, Beatrix held her

head high. "It seems we're both going to get what we want very soon."

No, Selina would never get what she wanted—a reunion with her beloved brother, the boy who'd kept her safe for years on the streets of London after they'd been orphaned. Then he'd sent her away to Mrs. Goodwin's Ladies' Seminary to keep her even safer and to ensure she had a better chance at a future than she would have had in the East End.

How wrong he'd been.

Mayhap her life *had* been better. There was no way to know. Either way, here she was, nearly right back where she started. And Rafe was gone.

So while she might not get what she wanted, she'd seize the next best thing: revenge.

CHAPTER 4

*H*arry slipped his finger between his neck and his overly starched collar and cravat and gave the fabric a gentle tug. His valet had gone to excess with his costume this evening, but then it had been a while since Harry had attended anything but a family dinner at his parents' house.

The discomfort of his overly elegant clothing extended to his mood—he didn't like these kinds of events. Pomp, fabrication, and *excess*. Though his parents did better than most as far as whom they invited and the expense they laid out, it was still far and beyond what Harry thought was necessary. Why not just invite a handful of friends over to play cards?

Because there will be dancing!

Harry heard his mother's dissenting opinion in his head along with her effusive laugh and couldn't help but smile. Yes, dancing, and he'd avoid it like the bloody plague.

Settling back against the squab and dropping his hand to his side as the hack turned onto Bond Street, he thought back on another pointless afternoon watching The Ardent Rose. The past five days, he'd either stationed himself across the street or observed the alley, onto which the back entrance opened. He had yet to see Madame Sybila leave the perfumery. She was either watching him and adjusting her departure, or he was incredibly unlucky.

Four days, actually, since he'd deduced that she hadn't been there on Thursday. He'd paid someone to go in and ask about the fortune-teller's schedule. She didn't make appointments on Thursdays—or of course Sundays.

What he really needed, however, was to learn what she did during her appointments. He supposed it was possible she wasn't up to anything fraudulent, but he wasn't going to wait for her to cheat his mother or one of her friends to know for certain.

His mind turned to the other investigation weighing on him: that of the Vicar. Harry had visited St. Dunstan-in-the-West and asked to see the Vicar only to be told there was no person by that name, just the *actual* vicar of the church. So Harry had watched the church for hours at a time—and seen nothing. He'd also asked around Blackfriars and learned that there was still no one willing to discuss the Vicar, let alone give a description of what he looked like. The man either paid people well or inspired a deep loyalty.

The hack turned onto Grosvenor Street, and soon cut through Grosvenor Square before turning onto Charles Street, where Harry got out.

He strode into the mews behind his parents' house, where he greeted one of the grooms. "Good evening, Barker."

"'Evening, sir," Barker said. "Surprised to see you here tonight. But not surprised you're stealing in the back." He chuckled.

"You know me well." Harry winked at the groom, then took himself to the house, entering through the back door that the servants used.

Sounds from the kitchen carried up the backstairs, giving indication of how busy they all were for the soiree. It was early yet, and Harry could only hope Lady Gresham and her sister arrived near the start so he could leave as soon as possible.

Harry opened a door and stepped into the corridor that led to the library at the back of the house, where his family typically gathered before dinner—and before events such as this. He heard their voices before he stepped inside.

His brother Jeremy, Viscount Northwood, and whom everyone but Harry called North, stood just over the threshold and noticed him immediately, his dark auburn brows climbing his forehead in a combination of surprise and amusement.

Harry put his finger to his lips. He wanted to see how long it took before anyone else noticed he was there.

"That's a beautiful color on you," his youngest sister, Imogen, was saying to the oldest of his three sisters, Delia. "And the drape is perfection. It's hardly possible to tell you're increasing."

"That can't be true," Delia said. "I feel as large as Lord Blakesley's ridiculous new coach."

"An absolute monstrosity," Delia's husband, Edward, Baron Moreton, said with a sniff.

Delia arched a chestnut brow at him. "You say that, but we will need one that big if we're to cart four children about."

"What a marvelous idea," Imogen said, her dark brown eyes lighting with inspiration. "A vehicle for an entire family. One would think those would be readily available."

"I believe that's called a caravan, darling," Imogen's husband, Sir Kenneth, said with a smile from beside her.

"Well, that's the definition of such a thing, and it involves multiple vehicles. Perhaps someone should design a family-sized vehicle called a caravan, so the whole family could travel together," Imogen suggested. She cocked her head to the side. "Whom do we know who could do that?" Glancing about the room as if she'd find such a person within their family, she settled her gaze on Harry. "Well, look who's here." Her lips spread in a wide grin.

Every head in the library turned toward Harry. His mother gasped.

"Harry!" She came forward, her arms outstretched so that she took his hands when she reached him. "You came!"

"I said I probably would."

"You always say that." Her tone was wry, but her eyes were alight with pleasure. Letting go of one of his hands, she kept hold of the other and turned to face everyone. "Everyone is here—save the grandchildren, of course. How lovely."

Harry's middle sister, Rachel, narrowed her eyes at him. "Why *are* you here? Is there an investigation afoot? Have Mama and Papa invited a criminal to the soiree?"

"Goodness, I hope not." Harry's mother sounded scandalized. She grimaced at Harry. "*Is* that why you're here?"

"No, Mother." He exhaled. "I finally come to a soiree, and everyone thinks I have an ulterior motive."

Jeremy clapped his shoulder. "Because they know you." He laughed. "Brandy?"

Harry nodded. A smile crept over his lips in spite of himself.

Their father walked to Harry with an approving look. "It's good to see you here. I'm glad you came, whatever the reason."

Harry knew the sentiment was genuine. "Since I

asked you to add a pair of guests, I thought it only right I attend."

"So you *do* have an ulterior motive," Rachel said with a touch of triumph. Of his three younger sisters, she'd always teased him the most, and he expected nothing less since he'd been the one to teach her how to do it effectively.

"Not really. Mother and Father were delighted to welcome these guests as they are new to town. Since when is helping someone an ulterior motive?" Harry accepted the glass of brandy from his brother.

"And who are these guests?" Imogen asked.

Mother answered before Harry could. "Lady Gresham and her sister, Miss Beatrix Whitford."

Jeremy stared at Harry. "They're women? How on earth did you meet women who are new to town? They weren't brought in front of the magistrate, were they?"

Several people in the library chuckled. Harry rolled his eyes. "No. I met Lady Gresham the other day. It's a long story."

"Please tell it," Delia said with an eager smile.

"Later," Mother said. "Guests will be arriving shortly. Come, girls." She gestured for her daughters to join her. "Let us make one last pass through the main rooms to ensure all is ready."

Harry's sisters began to file past him. First was Delia, who paused briefly as she walked by. "I'm going to hear this story if I have to hunt you down later."

"I'm sure you will." Harry could only hope he was gone by then. If he told them the truth—that he'd nearly run the woman down while in pursuit of a child thief—they'd say it was a sign that he should marry her immediately. Trying to find wives for him and Jeremy was their chief objective.

After Delia came Imogen. "Shall we arrange for you to be alone with her?"

Rachel joined her. "But which one? Lady Gresham or Miss Whitford?" She scrutinized Harry as if she could divine the answer from his unamused face.

Harry lifted his glass and sipped his brandy without a word.

Imogen looped her arm through Rachel's. "This soiree has suddenly become very interesting."

Hell. Harry wished he'd never said anything. Or invited Lady Gresham and her sister.

No, he wouldn't regret that. He *was* only trying to help. And Lady Gresham was…intriguing.

After the ladies had gone, Jeremy moved closer. "There isn't any truth to any of that, is there?"

"Of course not," Harry said. "I really was just trying to help Lady Gresham. Her sister is having her first Season. You may wish to steer clear of her."

As heir to an earldom, Jeremy was a sought-after match. But, regardless of what their mother thought about him doing his duty, he had no desire to wed at present, especially to a young lady on the Marriage Mart. He'd been to Almack's once and swore he'd never return. Which was once more than Harry had gone.

"I appreciate the warning." Jeremy took a drink of brandy, and they went to join the other gentleman.

Their father broke away and came to Harry. He was a few inches shorter than Harry, and his dark hair, liberally streaked with gray, was beginning to thin. He possessed a warm smile and demeanor, both of which were on full display as he spoke. "I'm pleased you came. It makes your mother happy."

"I know it does." Harry should probably do it more often.

Father lowered his voice and leaned close. "Do you have any news about the fortune-teller? Your mother didn't see her this week, as far as I know, but I don't think she's given her up, despite my insistence."

Harry almost smiled. "The more you insist, the more she will cling to the woman. Perhaps if you leave the subject alone, Mother will simply lose interest."

"Not bloody likely." Father snorted softly before sipping his brandy.

"Well, I have nothing to report, unfortunately. Madame Sybila refuses to read the fortune of a gentleman, so I'm developing another plan. And no, don't ask for details, because I won't give them. Please let me do my job."

Father held up his hand, his dark brown eyes flashing with irritation and then determination. "I do have information to share, however. Would you like to hear it?"

Harry kept the exasperation out of his voice. "Of course. Information is always helpful."

"Lord Balcombe told me his wife donated a considerable sum to that charity suggested by the charlatan. He's livid."

"Do you know if Lady Balcombe gave the money to Madame Sybila or to the charity directly?"

"I don't." Father blinked, his gaze intent. "Does that matter?"

"Yes." If Lady Balcombe had given the money to Madame Sybila, it could be theft—*if* the fortune-teller hadn't given it to the charity as intended. "May I speak with Lord Balcombe, or are you still demanding I keep this investigation a secret for now?" Not that Harry hadn't shared it with some of his fellow constables, such as Remy.

Father winced. "I don't want your mother finding out I asked you to investigate."

"She won't know it was you. This is what I *do*, after all."

"Then yes, you may speak with him. He should be here later."

Harry groaned inwardly. He didn't want to be here *later*. If he didn't see the earl tonight, he'd pay him a visit tomorrow or the next day. "I'll get to the bottom of this. I promise this woman will not swindle Mother."

"Thank you. I trust you to take care of this matter." He lifted his glass in a silent toast before taking another drink.

A short time later, Harry and the others left the library to join the soiree as the first guests were arriving. Their father took his place beside their mother to greet people, while Harry and Jeremy went directly to the card room.

"You playing?" Jeremy asked.

"Perhaps. I should probably look for Lady Gresham and Miss Whitford first."

"Careful, Harry, or I'll think our sisters are right about your potential interest in one of them."

Harry gave his brother a light shove that did nothing to move him, nor was it meant to. Then he turned and left the card room without a word, intent on going up to the drawing room, where he'd find a cozy corner to inhabit until Lady Gresham arrived. Hopefully, that would be very soon.

Luck was smiling upon him, for just after he'd taken up his position, Lady Gresham appeared in the doorway. Dressed in a stunning dark pink gown that seemed to shimmer in the candlelight, she was impossible to miss. Also because she was taller than most women, and tonight, with her golden-brown hair styled with a pair of white ostrich feathers, she seemed even more so. A single pearl rested against the hollow of her neck, and he found himself staring at the spot.

Forcing himself to look up, his gaze followed the graceful slope of her neck and the pert jut of her chin. He paused briefly on her mouth, a captivating bow, before moving even higher. She surveyed the room, and he imagined he could see the bright blue of her eyes—nearly the color of a robin's egg—from where he stood. He couldn't really, of course, so he pushed himself away from the corner and went to greet her.

"Good evening, Lady Gresham. I'm pleased to see you were able to attend." He forced his attention away from her, which he found strangely difficult, and smiled in greeting to the petite young woman at her side. "You must be Miss Whitford."

The younger lady curtsied, dropping her hazel gaze briefly before lifting it to meet his once more. Golden-blonde curls grazed her temples and cheeks. "I'm pleased to make your acquaintance, Mr. Sheffield. I just met Lord and Lady Aylesbury downstairs and thanked them for the invitation, but I understand I really have *you* to thank." Deep dimples formed when she smiled, giving her an aura of youthful exuberance.

"I'm happy to have helped. How are you enjoying London?" he asked politely. This sort of usually mundane social discourse was a primary reason he avoided these events. It was one thing to talk with people he knew or with just one other person away from a crush—such as he'd done with Lady Gresham on two occasions now, and another to make idle conversation with someone with whom he wasn't already acquainted. He glanced toward her and wondered at her almost surreal calmness. She wasn't like everyone else who attended these sorts of activi-

ties. They were typically humming with enthusiasm and glee.

"It's a lovely city," Miss Whitford said, her eyes
sparking with enthusiasm. "We've been to Hyde Park,
to Astley's, and of course shopping on Bond Street. I
am hoping to visit Vauxhall and that I might be fortunate enough to obtain a voucher to Almack's."

"I wish you luck with your endeavors." He caught
sight of his two younger sisters heading straight for
them. Blast, what were they about?

Rachel smiled wide in greeting. "Harry, are these
the ladies you invited this evening?"

"Allow me to present Lady Gresham and Miss
Whitford." He looked to their guests. "These are my
sisters, Lady Fitzwilliam and Mrs. Hayes." He gestured to Imogen first because her rank was higher
and then to Rachel, who'd married the second son of
a viscount. That made Harry wonder what Lady Gresham's rank was. He ought to look her deceased husband up in Debrett's, but probably wouldn't bother.

Everyone exchanged curtsies, and when both of
his sisters rose with broad, sparkling smiles, he grew
suspicious.

"Did I hear you mention Almack's?" Rachel asked
Miss Whitford.

"Yes. I was just telling Mr. Sheffield that I hope to
be fortunate enough to receive a voucher."

"That can be difficult," Imogen said. "But not impossible. We shall endeavor to assist you."

"Do you go to Almack's?" Lady Gresham asked
Harry.

"No."

"Not even once," Rachel clarified, as if it mattered.
"Our other brother at least did that."

"Neither one of them is on the Marriage Mart,
much to our parents' chagrin," Imogen said sweetly.

"I hardly think Lady Gresham and Miss Whitford

care to hear about our family, er, matters." He darted a look at Lady Gresham and saw that she was watching him with a bit of…humor?

Rachel and Imogen exchanged a look, and then Rachel spoke. "Lady Gresham, might we borrow Miss Whitford for a bit? It would be our pleasure to introduce her to some of the guests."

"We are excellent chaperones," Imogen assured her.

Harry coughed. Once, long before any of his sisters had wed, Delia had led all three of them on an excursion to Hyde Park *alone*. They'd made paper boats and had wanted to set them afloat on the Serpentine. Then they'd been seen by the bloody Duke of Holborn, of all people. A stickler for propriety, he'd marched them back home and given their father an earful. And that had been just the first of their unsupervised outings. Harry couldn't imagine them as chaperones, excellent or not.

Even so, he said nothing because he found he was quite content to have Lady Gresham to himself.

Hell, was he?

"That would be wonderful, thank you." Lady Gresham gave them an appreciative smile.

Imogen looped her arm through Miss Whitford's, and they pivoted. Rachel looked from Harry to Lady Gresham and back again. "You should take a stroll in the garden. It's a lovely evening." She narrowed her eyes almost imperceptibly and gave Harry a fleeting smirk before turning and following the others.

Bollocks. They were playing matchmaker, the shrews. They'd—rightly—assessed the situation and determined Lady Gresham would be of more interest to Harry. Because she *was* of interest to him.

"Why are you frowning?"

Harry blinked and turned his head toward Lady

Gresham once more. "I didn't mean to. My sisters can be vexing."

"I thought they were quite pleasant. Should I worry about Beatrix going off with them?"

"Not at all. Your sister will be fine. Tell me, does she have any tendencies toward independence or provocation?"

"Many." Her eyes glinted with amusement.

"Then they'll all get along quite famously."

Lady Gresham laughed softly. "I won't worry, then, while we're in the garden." Her gaze shot to his, and she seemed suddenly hesitant. "That is, if you wish to go."

"I would be honored to escort you." He presented his arm and was surprised to find he wasn't lying, which he would almost assuredly have been with anyone else.

She put her hand on his sleeve, and he escorted her through the growing throng in the drawing room to the doors that led to the terrace. From there, they descended to the garden, which was larger than one might have expected, owing to the larger width of the house.

"What a splendid garden," she said as they walked toward the path that snaked between the beds of flowers and shrubbery as well as his father's odd collection of statuary. "Is that a giant rabbit?"

"Yes. My father likes animals, and he commissioned a sculptor to design statues for the garden. Some of them are much larger than he anticipated—all of them, actually—but he ended up liking them. In addition, he didn't want to hurt the sculptor's feelings."

Lady Gresham lifted her hand to her mouth, but a giggle escaped nonetheless.

"You find that amusing?"

"And endearing. Your father sounds rather wonderful."

"He is likely better than most. What is your father like?"

Her expression, alight with humor a moment before, closed up like a flower retreating for the night. "He died so long ago that I don't remember him."

"I'm sorry to hear that." He was eager to learn more but wouldn't ask. What the devil was going on with him? He'd never taken an interest in a woman like this before. And she was a lady, definitely not the sort of woman he wanted to attach himself to.

Now he was thinking about attachment? *Get a grip, Harry.*

Yet, perhaps because she was a widow, she had no apparent interest in *attachment*. Maybe that was why he was intrigued. Yes, that was it. He'd simply never met anyone like her.

She cast him an uncertain glance. "I hope you don't think I'm too forward, but I wanted to ask you about your investigations."

He was grateful for the change in topic to distract his ridiculous thoughts. "Not at all. I'm happy to discuss my work, provided it doesn't interfere with an investigation. What do you want to know?"

"I couldn't help thinking about this Vicar you mentioned the other day. He sounds perfectly horrid. Do you think you'll ever find and arrest him?"

They rounded a corner, and Harry paused. A hedge partially obscured them from the house, and they stood in the shadows with just a hint of light finding its way to her eyes, firing them a brilliant blue.

"I hope so. In addition to arson, he's likely guilty of usury at least, given his practice of lending money at exorbitant rates. I suspect he also probably owns receiver shops and maybe even flash houses. We'll find him—and evidence of his crimes."

"I wonder if he would lend to a woman," she asked, cocking her head to the side. "Then I could help you catch him."

Harry stared at her. "You would do that?"

She lifted a shoulder. "Why not?"

"Because he's dangerous."

"Would it surprise you to know that I carry a pistol, Mr. Sheffield?" The corner of her mouth ticked up.

He laughed. "No, actually." Yes, he quite liked Lady Gresham. Why couldn't she just be plain old Mrs. Gresham? And without a sister she was trying to launch into Society? "I assume you know how to shoot it?"

"Quite well, in fact. My brother taught me years ago."

"Remarkable. I'd like to see that some time. Mayhap you're better than me."

She flashed a smile that lit her face to glorious effect. "Given your profession, I would doubt that."

A thought suddenly occurred to him. No, he couldn't ask her. And yet, she'd offered to help him. "While I don't think it would be wise for you to help with the Vicar, there is a way you could help me. If you're sure you want to."

"I think I do." She sounded almost as surprised as he'd been by her offer. "What would this assistance entail?"

"Nothing dangerous, I assure you. In fact, you could leave your pistol at home."

Her gorgeous eyes twinkled, and he was suddenly quite aware of her hand on his arm. "Never."

His gaze dipped to her reticule. "Not even now?"

"A lady must protect herself," she said. "Who else will?"

Something about the way she asked the question sent a chill down his spine. Had she been unprotected? What sort of man had her husband been? Harry had so many questions, and he wasn't going to ask a single one of them. Not tonight, anyway.

"You're an astonishing woman, Lady Gresham," he said softly. "What I require is someone of your intelligence—and discretion—to conduct a small investigation. I would like you to make an appointment with a fortune-teller."

She blinked at him. "Why?"

"I believe she's perpetrating some sort of swindle, but she won't read fortunes for men."

"Which is why you need me." She nodded once. "Where do I go? Wait, you mentioned a fortune-teller when we met."

"I did. She sees clients in a room at the back of The Ardent Rose perfumery. Near where we met on The Strand."

"You said swindle. What kind, exactly?" Her hold on his arm shifted, her fingers curling around his sleeve more securely. "I mean, what should I expect?"

"She sells tonics, apparently, and I suspect they are no more than flavored water. If you're able to purchase one, I'd like to see it and ascertain its contents. If she mentions any charities, I want to know which ones. Beyond that, she's probably just filling her clients' heads with enthralling nonsense so that they will return again and again, eager for her 'counsel.'" He rolled his eyes.

"You're skeptical of the mystic arts, then?"

He barked out a laugh. "There's no such thing. Don't tell me you believe in them?"

"Honestly, I've never given the topic much thought. I think I must now, however." She straightened. "So I will pay this fortune-teller—"

"Madame Sybila," he provided.

Lady Gresham smiled slyly. "Sybila—I believe that name means prophetess. How charming."

Harry snorted, then coughed. "Forgive me."

"I will visit Madame Sybila and ask her to read my fortune, and I will try to buy a tonic and ask about charities. Then I'll report to you what occurred?"

"Exactly. You are going to be rather adept at this, I see."

"Perhaps I'll start my own inquiry office after Beatrix is wed."

"You won't remarry?" The question leapt from his mouth before he could stop it. "That's none of my concern. You're just rather…young." And beautiful and intelligent. And far too engaging to be alone.

Who the hell was he to judge whether someone should be alone?

"I've been married, Mr. Sheffield. Once was quite enough, thank you."

"You weren't happy?"

"I wasn't *un*happy. But I find independence more to my liking."

He understood that more than she could know. Though he was content to remain in the shadows with Lady Gresham, he started along the path with her once more.

"I'll visit the perfumery to inquire about an appointment on Monday," she said.

"Thank you. I shall compensate you for your time."

"That isn't necessary."

"It is, and I insist." He winced inwardly. She was a lady and likely didn't need the funds. Furthermore, most people of her rank found working for hire to be beneath them. "If you'll allow it."

"I will," she said softly.

He slid a glance toward her and saw a smile

teasing her mouth. She continued to surprise him. He suppressed the urge to smile in return.

They walked for a moment, the sounds of the soiree drifting over the garden, before she asked, "How shall I advise you of my progress?"

He didn't want anyone at Bow Street to know he was employing a woman to help him, since some would not approve. "Send word to me at number seventeen Rupert Street."

"That is your residence?" she asked.

"Yes, now you know where I live, should you wish to pay a call." He steered her along the path back toward the house.

"Given our alliance, it seems I must."

"For propriety's sake, we should probably meet in public—such as at Gunter's."

She laughed. "Despite what you say, you are better at Society rules than I am. I don't give a fig about propriety, but I suppose I should for Beatrix's sake. I'll send word, and then we can meet."

He paused near the house. "Name the place and the time, and I'll be there."

Their gazes held for a moment, and he had the distinct impression they'd just been flirting. His sisters would be positively giddy if they knew. Hopefully, they never would.

"I hope I am able to be of assistance, Mr. Sheffield."

"I am certain of it, Lady Gresham, and I am most grateful." He took her hand and pressed a kiss to the back of her glove. "Thank you," he murmured.

"The pleasure is mine." She dipped a brief curtsey, which only emphasized the fact that she didn't really understand the rules at all, and turned to climb the stairs to the terrace.

Harry watched her go and wondered just where this partnership would take them.

CHAPTER 5

At least four of Madame Sybila's clients were at the Aylesbury soiree. Selina had just "met" Lady Rockbourne, whom she'd seen five or six times in the last month. Petite, with pale blonde hair and light blue eyes, she looked like an angel. However, she had the disposition of a demon. Her appointments with Madame Sybila were full of complaints about her husband and her lust for another man with whom she hoped to begin an affair.

It was a situation in which Selina strove not to provide an answer but to guide the client, in this case Lady Rockbourne, to reach her own decision. She was fairly certain the viscountess had engaged in the liaison, and having met Lord Rockbourne earlier, Selina hoped she would have the chance to counsel the woman to be faithful to her husband. The viscount had been charming and witty, and Selina didn't like thinking of the woman's betrayal.

Which was odd given that Selina betrayed people all the time. The hypocrisy stung, particularly in the case of Mr. Sheffield, whom she liked very much. He reminded her of Sir Barnabus Gresham, the man whom she'd tried to swindle, but who had found her out and still allowed her to "borrow" his name. She'd grown to like him and regretted her efforts to cheat him. Then he'd been kind and unbelievably generous. That had happened eighteen months ago, and since then, Selina had been slowly losing her ability to remain detached from her marks.

However, she didn't know how to support herself and Beatrix without their schemes. Hopefully, Beatrix would secure her father's support, and Selina would earn enough money during the Season to give up this life and live modestly somewhere. Legitimacy and security were so very close.

Her gaze fell on Harry's trio of sisters, who were once again squiring Beatrix about. They'd started the evening that way, and it appeared they'd end it in the same manner. In between, Beatrix had danced and conversed and seemed to have a wonderful time.

Good. That was the entire point of being here. She was well on her way to becoming precisely what she wanted: the toast of London.

"Are you enjoying yourself, Lady Gresham?"

Selina turned, and her pulse instantly quickened. But only for a moment, which was how long it took her to realize it wasn't Mr. Sheffield who'd spoken to her, but his brother, Lord Northwood. They were identical, and if it hadn't been for the difference in their attire, Selina wondered if she could tell them apart at all.

"I am, thank you. And you?"

"I always enjoy the parties my parents host. There is an advantage." He lowered his voice. "Because I can sneak away quite easily if I feel the need."

"I see. Does such a need arise for you frequently?"

"Not as much as it does for my brother. You're aware he left some time ago?"

At least two hours. After their stroll in the garden, he'd come back up to the drawing room, where he'd spoken to a few people. Then he'd come to tell Selina he was leaving, an event that still had her puzzled. It was as if they'd formed some sort of...attachment. But then, she supposed they had. She was working for him. To help him investigate herself. The thought made her simultaneously giddy with satisfaction and nervous with apprehension.

But it was perhaps more than business. There was something in the way he looked at her, the way he felt beneath her palm as they'd promenaded, the way he'd kissed her hand.

They way they'd almost flirted.

That's nothing new, she reminded herself. *You flirt when you have to.*

And given how things were working out with the Bow Street Runner, it had clearly been beneficial. Yet, she hadn't done it on purpose.

"Yes, he was kind enough to bid me good evening before he left," Selina said, answering the viscount.

Northwood's brows arched. "Did he? How fascinating. How is it you two met?"

Mr. Sheffield hadn't told him? "I tripped in front of him, actually. On The Strand. He caught me before I fell."

"How dashing." Northwood chuckled. "No wonder he didn't tell us. Delia will be delighted to hear the tale, unless she was able to pry it from him before he left. Somehow, I think she didn't. Harry is notoriously closemouthed."

"About everything?"

"Most things. Our family can be rather, ah, boisterous. Harry is probably the least so." He shook his head. "Not probably, definitely. Which isn't to say he doesn't get up to mischief. He's just incredibly subtle about it. What is your family like, Lady Gresham?"

"Small. It's only me and Beatrix." Her gaze went to where she stood with Northwood's sisters. "Your sisters have been very kind to her this evening."

"They love to help people, particularly young ladies trying to navigate London. And find husbands."

It seemed to Selina that Mr. Sheffield's family was perhaps playing matchmaker. She knew Lady Aylesbury wanted him—and his brother Northwood —to wed. It was almost all she talked about when she came to see Madame Sybila to discuss the future.

Selina was glad to see Beatrix, escorted by the sisters, coming toward her. After thanking Mr. Sheffield's siblings for a wonderful evening, Selina and Beatrix departed.

Once they were ensconced in the vehicle Selina had hired for the evening, she removed the ostrich feathers from her hair so she could sit without bowing her head. "That went well."

"It was better than well. It was *marvelous*." Beatrix positively beamed.

"You were quite popular this evening," Selina said.

"I was, wasn't I? I do think Mr. Sheffield's sisters will help me with a voucher for Almack's."

"That would be lovely. However, don't place all your faith in them. We must still cultivate other connections. Identifying such people is part of what I'm doing as Madame Sybila."

"I know it's your nature never to trust anyone, but I do believe they are earnest in their pledge to help. You should relax a bit, like you did around Mr. Sheffield."

Selina turned her head to stare at Beatrix. "What makes you say that?"

Beatrix shrugged. "Just something I noticed. And don't try to say I couldn't know. Of course I could. I know you better than anyone."

That was true. "I find it necessary to be as *relaxed* as possible around Mr. Sheffield. He is a means to an end—launching you successfully—and we are now working together."

Angling her body toward Selina, Beatrix gaped at her. "You're what?"

"I'm helping him investigate Madame Sybila."

Beatrix blinked. "You're helping him…investigate…you." She began to laugh, softly at first, and then her guffaws filled the coach.

Selina couldn't help but join in, even as she felt a slight discomfort. After a moment, she said, "I'm glad you find this amusing."

"How can I not? It's too perfect. However did you manage it?"

"Quite easily, actually."

Beatrix settled back against the seat. "I'm sure. You could talk the devil into handing you hell. How do you plan to work this situation?"

"I'll meet with Madame Sybila and then tell Mr. Sheffield what I've learned. I'm afraid he'll be disappointed to learn she's incredibly harmless." Selina ran her fingertips along one of the ostrich feathers. "We need to create the appearance of the charity for wayward children, as we've done in the past. Sheffield mentioned charities tonight in reference to Madame Sybila."

In the past, they'd collected funds for charities as a means of income. On occasion, they had to make the fake charity look real, and they hired someone to act as the proprietor of whatever endeavor they were "supporting." In this case, it was a home for wayward children.

"You already have someone in mind to help us."

"I do, and I'll visit him tomorrow." Selina didn't have very many connections in London after so much time away, but she had Mrs. Kinnon and a boy who'd been a good friend to her and Rafe. Of course, Luther was no longer a boy.

"Do you want me to come along?"

"No, I'll see him after I go to church, and I don't want you coming with me to St. Dunstan-in-the-West either."

"I understand you not wanting to endanger me," Beatrix said softly, "but I want to help." She put her hand on Selina's. "We're family, and I'm as committed to avenging your brother's death as you are."

So far, Selina hadn't been able to find the Vicar. She'd gone to the church the other day—in disguise in case Sheffield had been around—and requested a meeting, only to be told he wasn't available and that she shouldn't return. Of course she *would* return and planned to do so tomorrow to attend church. During the service, she would endeavor to search the building. At the very least, she hoped to encounter someone who could help her find the Vicar, if not at the church, then somewhere else.

"I appreciate that, truly." Selina smiled, and Beatrix withdrew her hand. "I promise I will ask for your help if I need it."

"I hope so," Beatrix said. "Sometimes I think you hold yourself back even from me."

The coach turned onto Queen Anne Street and drew to a stop in front of their small house. Selina stared at the façade, wondering if she'd ever think of any place as home again.

Home was the small pair of dingy rooms she'd inhabited with Rafe and their "uncle," who, like Beatrix, hadn't been a relative at all. Or the various spartan spaces she and Rafe had shared after they'd gone to work in Samuel Partridge's gang.

One would think those memories would have long faded from Selina's mind. But they were indelibly imprinted on her, as were the trying years at the boarding school and, even more so, the disastrous year that had followed.

Selina twitched as Beatrix departed the vehicle, and was glad she hadn't seen. Beatrix was too adept at sensing the darkness that resided deep inside Selina, even if she rarely said anything, as she had a few moments ago.

Yes, she held herself back—even from Beatrix. She was in too many pieces, had been too many people. In some ways, she wasn't even entirely sure who she truly was. Perhaps more troubling, she had no idea who she wanted to be.

~

"*W*hat do you wish to know today, Lady Aylesbury?" Selina asked from behind her veil. It was a bit odd seeing Mr. Sheffield's mother in this context after having been a guest at her house the other night, but Selina didn't worry the countess would discern her identity. Between the heavy veil and the French accent, Selina was confident in her disguise.

Lady Aylesbury leaned slightly over the small round table, her tawny gaze that was nearly identical to her sons' dipping to the cards sitting in front of Selina. "As I am a bit rushed today, I have just two questions. First, I would like to know about my son."

"Which one?" Selina asked serenely. Now that she'd met both of them, she pictured them in her mind.

"Harry, my younger son."

"How do you tell them apart?" Selina wanted to know if there was a secret to it or if she'd missed something obvious. She supposed Mr. Sheffield was slightly larger across the shoulders.

Realizing her question had no bearing on their meeting and could arouse suspicion despite the fact that Lady Aylesbury had told her they were twins,

Selina sought to explain. "Since you told me they are twins, I've been curious."

"Mostly by their demeanor. Harry is more serious. Northwood seems to always have a twinkle in his eye. Which isn't to say that Harry isn't capable of humor—or mischief. He was always the one I had to look out for when they were children." She laughed briefly, then pursed her lips. "I worry he's too serious. About his work. Although, I wonder if something hasn't finally distracted him. Rather, some*one*." The countess smiled and waggled her light red brows.

"You wish to ask about someone?" Selina asked, reaching for the cards.

Lady Aylesbury nodded. "My daughters suspect he may be interested in a woman who is new to town —Lady Gresham. I'd like to know if they will form an attachment and if that might proceed to courtship."

Bloody hell. Selina had been reading tarot cards for seven years and, she thought, had become rather good at it. But she never, ever read them for herself. Because in the end, she didn't believe any of this was actually true. And if she did, she wouldn't want to know her future. Sometimes, she wished she didn't know her past.

"You said you didn't have much time, so I'll do this more quickly than usual, with just three cards, if that's acceptable?" Selina had already shuffled the cards when Lady Aylesbury arrived.

"Yes, I do appreciate it."

Selina turned over the top card. The hair on her arms prickled, and she had a sudden urge to set the card on fire. "The Two of Cups."

"That looks like two people in love—perhaps toasting their nuptials!" Lady Aylesbury's glee lit the small room.

This card did, in fact, look like that, and because Lady Aylesbury was asking about a romantic relationship, it would typically mean exactly that. Which was why Selina wished it would spontaneously combust. Since that wasn't possible, she fibbed. "Because this card was drawn first, it tends to mean a partnership or alignment. Love *could* be present, but not necessarily." While Selina always tried to tell her clients what they wanted to hear, she did not want to encourage the countess to push her and Mr. Sheffield together. Ironically, the card as she read it was still accurate, since she and Mr. Sheffield *did* have a partnership.

Lady Aylesbury pursed her lips. "Go on."

Selina turned over the next card and felt a bit of relief. "The Ten of Wands. This is almost certainly about your son as it signifies a great burden or someone who is working too hard."

"That is definitely Harry. Could it also be Lady Gresham?"

Yes, it most certainly could. Selina's relief evaporated. She didn't like these cards today. They were far too accurate. "It could mean both of them, but we know it relates to your son, so let's assume it is him."

"That makes sense. Lady Gresham is focused on launching her sister in Society. Perhaps that is a burden to her since she is new to town. I shall endeavor to help her. My daughters quite liked her sister and are keen to provide assistance. They are trying to get her a voucher to Almack's. Perhaps you should read that next." Lady Aylesbury waved her hand. "No, no, I'm getting distracted, as I am wont to do." She laughed. "Please, continue."

Maybe this wasn't so bad after all, if it meant the countess would help Beatrix in her quest to become the most popular young lady in town. Selina took a deep breath and turned over the third and final card.

The Tower.

She liked this card least of all as it likely pertained

to her. Rather the woman, Lady Gresham, that Lady Aylesbury was inquiring about with regard to her son. It could mean many things—change, disruption, conflict, but inescapably, it represented a threat. Withdrawing her shaking hands from the table to her lap, Selina reminded herself that she didn't believe any of this.

"Well, that's a rather distressing-looking card," Lady Aylesbury said, frowning down at the figures who were falling from a flaming tower. "I was hoping for the Lovers."

Selina might have laughed if the Tower hadn't so unsettled her. The fire reminded her of the fire that had killed her brother. Was her life to come to an end soon too? She hadn't felt physically threatened in a very long time—not since after she'd left Mrs. Goodwin's seminary and taken that awful position as governess.

After that, she'd gone to great lengths to ensure that she and Beatrix would always be safe from harm. Nothing had changed on that front. She forced herself to take another, deeper breath.

No matter the cards she drew, Selina always strove to weave a story that would please her client. If she didn't, they wouldn't return, nor would they encourage their friends to come. She thought of what she could say about the Tower relative to Lady Aylesbury's question. "This could very well represent the change to both your son's and Lady Gresham's lives should they come together."

"Can you draw just one more?" Lady Aylesbury asked, her voice rife with concern. She put a great deal of trust in these pieces of paper.

"Yes, let's." Selina often did this when the final card drawn wasn't satisfactory. It made no difference to her, but today it did. She liked that Tower card even less than Lady Aylesbury did.

Dread mixed with anticipation as she turned over a fourth card.

The Star.

Lady Aylesbury smiled broadly. "That looks promising!"

"Illumination, hope, renewal. This card could signal a beginning for them." Selina forced the words out while her heart beat heavy in her chest. She knew this card was for her—except she didn't believe in this!

Maybe she *wanted* to believe it this time. The possibility of hope and light, for an unburdened future, was a heady thought. And one Selina oughtn't indulge in.

She swept up the cards. "What is your second question?"

Lady Aylesbury's gaze had settled on the wall behind Selina, and now she startled. Blinking, she refocused on Selina. "Oh yes, just a moment. So, it seems there is some sort of association between Harry and Lady Gresham, and perhaps the change of the Tower means Harry will stop working so hard—as seen in the Ten of Wands. Because he and Lady Gresham will start a new life together." The countess looked at Selina in question. She typically provided a summation of the reading for the client, but in her distress she hadn't. Thankfully, Lady Aylesbury had done a better job than Selina probably could have.

"I think that's exactly right." She smiled even though Lady Aylesbury couldn't see her do so. "Would you like to ask another question?" Selina rather hoped she didn't, but shuffled the cards anyway.

"Yes, please. I've lost my emerald necklace, which my husband just gave me for my birthday last month. I haven't told him because he'll be upset. Can you help me find it?"

Selina set the cards down on the table. "This is not something I usually do. It's very difficult to see something so precise as to where an object may be. When did you lose it?"

"I'm not sure, but I couldn't find it yesterday. I tore my entire dressing room apart." She grimaced. "And I'm certain it was there Saturday, because I considered wearing it at our soiree but chose pearls instead."

Suspicion curled through Selina. She might be wrong, but she was probably right, and if so, she knew precisely where Lady Aylesbury's necklace was. Unless Beatrix had already fenced it.

"Perhaps you could just tell me if I'll find it?" Lady Aylesbury asked hopefully.

"I can try. I'm going to lay down three cards at once."

Three of Wands. The Sun. The Nine of Cups.

The first card—the Three of Wands—was reversed, which signified patience and a wish fulfilled. Since Selina planned to ensure the necklace was returned, this was another alarmingly accurate card. The Nine of Cups was also a wish fulfillment card, and it carried the added "bonus" of indicating the wish might include a man, since the image was of a wealthy gentleman. Selina was strongly considering retiring this deck of cards.

"All these cards point toward success." She didn't even have to lie. "You will find your necklace, but the Three of Wands urges patience."

"Wonderful!" Lady Aylesbury leaned back in her chair in relief. Then she reached for her reticule and withdrew several notes.

Selina was surprised to see so much money. "That is too much," she said, picking up the cards.

"I was hoping you would take the extra and donate it to your friend's home for wayward children. Lady Balcombe and I agree it's an excellent cause."

Selina set the cards to the side of the table. She'd decided not to discuss her "charity" with Lady Aylesbury given that she was Mr. Sheffield's mother. It was too risky. But since Lady Balcombe had told her and the countess was bringing it up, Selina couldn't avoid telling her about it.

"Friends of mine started taking in wayward children —they haven't been blessed with children of their own —and the number has grown more than they can support without assistance. They do their best to provide a safe place for the children, but it's a very costly endeavor. I give what I can, and when my clients ask where they might help, I sometimes mention their home."

"I would be honored to provide assistance. Please give them the money, will you?"

Selina inclined her head. "I will. They will be most grateful."

Lady Aylesbury stood from the table. "Thank you so much for your insight and expertise. I look forward to our next meeting. May I return at the same time next week?"

Selina nodded. "Yes. Thank you, Lady Aylesbury." She rose, clasping her gloved hands together as Lady Aylesbury turned and took her leave.

The money lay on the table like a nauseating plate of liver when Selina had been young. She didn't want it, but was too hungry to decline it. Taking money from Sheffield's mother felt wrong. Because Selina had met her socially, and she and her daughters had been unbearably kind to her and, more importantly, to Beatrix.

Yes, *unbearably*. Kindness was not something Selina was used to, and it never failed to make her feel unsettled. Still, money was money, and Selina had learned long ago that, like the liver, you took it when you could and harbored no regrets.

Finished with Madame Sybila's appointments, Selina removed her veil and changed her clothing, carefully stowing her fortune-teller costume back in the closet. When she emerged from the small room, Mrs. Kinnon was just coming through the curtain from the shop.

"I presumed you were about to leave," she said. "Mr. Sheffield has been across the street the past quarter hour or so."

"Since before Lady Aylesbury left?"

"Yes, though watching him try to hide himself behind a street lamp as she departed was rather comical."

Selina wished she could have seen it. "I suppose I must wait awhile longer before leaving, then." She wanted him to think she'd been here waiting to see Madame Sybila after his mother. But then she'd have to say she hadn't seen his mother... She looked to Mrs. Kinnon. "I'm going to need a package of something—an excuse for not seeing Lady Aylesbury as she left. I was too busy making a purchase."

"Yes, of course. I'll wrap something up for you." She went back into the shop, leaving Selina lingering in the corridor.

Selina had told her about assisting Mr. Sheffield with his investigation. Mrs. Kinnon was an enormous help, and Selina simply couldn't manage the size and scope of her enterprise here in London without the woman's help.

A few minutes later, Mrs. Kinnon returned with a wrapped package. "Orange and honeysuckle soap. It will suit you well."

Selina had never indulged in the luxury of extravagantly scented soap. "Thank you."

"Luther stopped by earlier," Mrs. Kinnon said

with a smile. She, of course, knew him from when they were children. "He said you finally visited him yesterday."

"It was good to see him after so long." He'd been thrilled that she'd visited. In fact, his enveloping embrace had gone on a bit too long for Selina's comfort, prompting her to extricate herself. Then he'd offered his help in whatever way she required, and Selina had relaxed.

She'd barely recognized him after eighteen years. He was no longer the tall, skinny boy with the jet-black hair and onyx eyes. While he was still quite tall and his eyes and hair were still dark as pitch, he'd filled out into a handsome, athletic man. The crinkles around his mouth revealed that he must laugh as much as he'd done when they were children. He and Rafe had always been joking—a bright spot in their often harrowing lives working as thieves for Samuel Partridge.

The familiar stab of loss cleaved into her chest, but she'd become accustomed to ignoring it—mostly. She hadn't mentioned her brother to Luther and was glad he hadn't brought him up either.

"Luther said he's pretending to run your home for wayward children." She winked at Selina.

"Yes, he's doing me a great favor." Now she just needed Sheffield to visit the "home" and confirm it was real. Or appeared real, anyway. Selina looked toward the shop window. It was most fortuitous that he was waiting outside. She'd planned to tell him about the home after "learning about it" in her meeting with Madame Sybila. Selina looked to Mrs. Kinnon. "Will you send a message to Luther posthaste and tell him we are on our way?"

"Of course. I'll send Joseph at once." She took herself back through the curtain to direct the errand boy to accomplish the task.

Confident that enough time had elapsed for Selina to have had an appointment with Madame Sybila after Lady Aylesbury, Selina walked out into the bright afternoon. It was a glorious spring day with blue sky and puffy white clouds. Even so, it wasn't as pretty as the countryside. Selina doubted London ever could be. And yet there was a bustle and excitement to the city that she was surprised to find she enjoyed. Perhaps that was due to the way her mind never seemed to cease working.

She'd barely walked twenty steps before Mr. Sheffield intercepted her. Stopping short, she feigned surprise. "Good afternoon, Mr. Sheffield. I wasn't expecting to see you."

He took her hand and bestowed a kiss on the back of her glove. While it was more rapid than the one he'd delivered the other night, the result was the same—a frisson of anticipation raced up her arm. "Lady Gresham. I'm afraid I was impatient and decided to walk by in the event your inquiry for an appointment led to an actual meeting with Madame Sybila today. Were you able to see her?"

"I was, in fact."

"You must have encountered my mother. She came out a while ago."

"I did not, but then I was busy making a purchase." She held up the package. "I'm sorry I wasn't able to exchange pleasantries with her."

"It's just as well." He tipped his head to the side, his tawny eyes narrowing slightly. "Except, perhaps she would treat you as a confidante if she knew you were also seeing Madame Sybila."

"I'll look for her when next I visit." Selina tucked the package into her reticule.

"Splendid. May we walk for a bit while we discuss your meeting?" He offered her his arm.

"Certainly." She clasped his sleeve and ignored the

jolt of awareness that was not unlike what happened when he'd kissed her hand.

"Well?" he asked expectantly. "What did you learn about your future?"

"That Beatrix will marry exceptionally well."

"How wonderful to hear." He laughed. "If you believe that. Do you?" He turned his head to look at her as they made their way along the pavement.

"No, but I'd like to. For that reason, I will pretend Madame Sybila is actually capable of seeing the future."

"Pretending is fine, I suppose, but I can't see why anyone would pay money to do that."

Selina could. "People spend money on all manner of things that give them comfort. I imagine, for some, hearing about a future they want is incredibly reassuring."

"How insightful of you, Lady Gresham."

"Thank you. I didn't say I was one of those people, however."

He chuckled again. "No, you did not. Does that mean you didn't ask her about your future, just your sister's?"

"That's correct." Turning over the cards relative to her and the man whose arm she was currently clutching was as close as she ever meant to get. And that had been far too unnerving.

"Did she sell you any tonic?"

"No, but I mentioned that I'd heard she had some. She didn't offer any information." Selina preferred to avoid placing any of it directly in his hands. She sold them as sleeping aids or mood enhancements, but they were little more than flavored water with a dash of herbs that *might* help one sleep or calm one's nerves.

"A pity. What of the charities? Were you able to learn anything about them?"

"Yes, she was quite pleased to discuss the good works of the Magdalen Hospital in particular, in addition to a home for wayward children, which is apparently run by friends of hers."

He snorted. "I'm sure it is."

"She certainly had a great deal of information about it. A Mr. and Mrs. Winter opened their home to wayward children after not being blessed with any of their own," she explained. "They feed, clothe, and even teach the children. Like the Lambeth Asylum for Orphan Girls, they hope to train the children for domestic service. It's a far better place for them to be than on the streets or in a flash house."

He glanced at her in surprise. "You know what that is?"

"I am not ignorant of the world, Mr. Sheffield." She tried not to sound as indignant as she felt. Of course she knew what a flash house was. She'd narrowly escaped from one when she'd left London. And she might have ended up in the Lambeth Asylum if not for her brother.

"No, you are not," he murmured. There was a hint of admiration in his tone. Selina didn't quite know what to make of that. So she made nothing of it.

"Honestly, it sounds like a wonderful endeavor," she said. In truth, she wished she *could* help children in that way. Maybe someday. If she married a duke perhaps. The thought nearly made her laugh.

"Oh no, has she fooled you too?"

"No," Selina said calmly. "I'm merely repeating what she said, but yes, if it's real, it does sound wonderful. Surely you can agree with that."

"Of course, but it's not real."

"Shall we go and look? She said the house is over near St. Paul's."

Sheffield stopped abruptly then blinked at her. "You know where it is? Then yes, let us investigate."

He looked about. "As it happens, we are on our way in that direction." He smiled faintly. "I'm afraid I wasn't even paying attention to our direction. I was too distracted by your lovely company." His gaze met hers, and there was a rush of that same sensation as the kiss or the feel of his arm.

Selina didn't understand what was happening. No man had ever affected her in this manner. She didn't like it one bit.

Except that she rather did.

He'd clearly said "us" in reference to investigating, but Selina wanted to know for sure he meant that. "You wish for me to accompany you?"

"Yes, if you want to."

Of course she wanted to. This gave her the opportunity to ensure Luther and whomever he'd recruited to portray his wife behaved convincingly. She also couldn't deny that she was enjoying Mr. Sheffield's company too, but that wasn't the reason she wanted to go.

Of course it wasn't.

"I'd find it ever so fascinating. If you don't mind."

"Not at all. This is not a dangerous excursion." He gestured east. "Shall we?"

She nodded, and they started along the pavement once more. "Is your work usually dangerous?"

"I wouldn't say usually, but sometimes. This will be a straightforward discussion. If we even find this Mr. Winter. I suspect he doesn't actually exist." He cast her a glance. "I don't suppose Madame Sybila mentioned where near St. Paul's?"

"Just off Paternoster Row. She said there was a sign." Luther had chosen the location because the owner of the home had been looking for boarders.

"Excellent," Mr. Sheffield responded. "Though we won't find this charity," he added.

"At what point do you decide you've exhausted

every avenue of investigation? I mean, when will you conclude that he and the home don't exist?"

"Not today. I'm very thorough. So while I don't expect to find him, I will continue my search until I am confident there is no such person or home, and that this entire 'charitable' endeavor is a fraud."

"Will you tell your mother, or simply allow her to realize Madame Sybila has been arrested?" Selina slid him a guarded look. "I assume that would be the next step—arresting Madame Sybila for fraud."

He clenched his jaw. "I will be the one to tell my mother, and yes, once I can prove this Mr. Winter doesn't exist, I will determine whether Madame Sybila took money for this counterfeit charity, and then likely arrest her for fraud."

A chill raced down Selina's spine, but she didn't let it encompass her. She'd faced far greater risks in her life and almost certainly would again. "Will your mother be angry with you?"

He looked at Selina in surprise. "No, not when I can prove that she's been taken advantage of. She'll be angry with Madame Sybila. As she should be. I'm just trying to protect her."

"You're a good son," Selina said softly. The notion of a family who looked out for each other wasn't completely foreign—she'd had Rafe, and she had Beatrix—but to have parents... She couldn't imagine it.

She was intrigued by Mr. Sheffield's family and yet terrified of them at the same time. But when it came to Mr. Sheffield, she was simply intrigued. Well, not *simply*. She liked him, despite the fact he was intent on putting her out of business, and wondered if, in another life, things might have been different. She'd met so few kind men. Just him, really, and Sir Barnabus Gresham. And her brother. Not that Rafe had been a man when she'd last seen him.

Except in the East End, fourteen was generally regarded as manhood.

"I try to be," Mr. Sheffield said. "Although, my mother would probably argue that if I was truly a good son, I'd find a wife."

Selina smiled because he was absolutely right. She wished she could tell him how his mother's concern was truly rooted in her love for him, as was his desire to protect her. "I'm sure she just wants to see you settled and happy."

"I am happy. I don't need a wife to be so." He cast her a sidelong glance. "You were wed and now choose not to be, so surely you understand."

Though she hadn't actually been wed, she did understand. Happiness was what you made it.

She suddenly noticed St. Dunstan-in-the-West just up ahead. She'd been unable to learn anything about the Vicar when she'd gone to the service the day before, and she hadn't been allowed to search the corners of the church. Though they didn't identify themselves as his gang, the handful of boys and young men who had prevented her from investigating the building were clearly loyal to him.

Selina felt Mr. Sheffield's arm tense as they walked beneath the clock that extended over the street from the church. "Are you thinking of that other case?" she asked softly.

"Yes." He turned his head briefly toward the church. "If you weren't with me, I'd go inside and see if today might be different—perhaps the Vicar would agree to see me."

"Don't let me stop you," Selina said, nearly breathless with anticipation. If he thought there was a chance they would see the Vicar...

Then what? She couldn't very well interrogate him about her brother's death in front of Mr. Sheffield. To do so would be to reveal the secrets of her past, and she wouldn't. And she certainly couldn't *kill* him in front of a Bow Street Runner. She wasn't sure she could kill him at all, but that was what he deserved.

"Lady Gresham?"

Mr. Sheffield's voice broke through her thoughts. "Yes?"

"You slowed. Is everything all right?"

"Indeed. I didn't mean to lag. Let us hasten to St. Paul's so you can prove Madame Sybila is a fraud."

He gave her an appreciative look that would have warmed her if not for the fact that he was responding to their apparent shared goal of destroying Selina's life.

CHAPTER 6

*W*hat the hell was he doing bringing someone along on an investigation? Let alone a woman he liked and was attracted to?

How Harry wanted to deny the last, but he would admit—to himself at least—that he was past that. He admired her intellect, and he'd be damned if every time they touched he didn't have the urge to wrap his arms around her and see if her lips felt as soft as they looked.

Harry dragged his gaze from her mouth and tried to focus on the matter at hand as they arrived at St. Paul's.

"Such a beautiful cathedral," Lady Gresham said.

Tilting his head to look up at the dome, Harry said, "I've always preferred Westminster."

She smiled, her blue eyes glinting in the afternoon sunlight. It was difficult not to lose himself in her alluring gaze. "I do too. I think it's the history of it—all the monarchs being coronated there."

"Except Edward the Fifth."

"Because his uncle killed him. Now there's a crime that requires resolution."

Harry chuckled. "You aren't wrong about that, but I fear that's beyond my skill."

"Is it? You strike me as rather tenacious. Perhaps you should give it a try."

"Perhaps if you agreed to conduct the investigation with me, I might." Harry barely recognized himself. He didn't flirt. Yet he couldn't seem to stop himself with Lady Gresham.

Adopting a more modest tone, Harry gestured toward the south side of the cathedral. "Did you know Guy Fawkes and his coconspirators met in a tavern on Carter Lane?"

"I did not," Lady Gresham said, sounding impressed. "Shall we walk that way? Carter Lane sounds the perfect place for a criminal enterprise. Perhaps Mr. Winter and Madame Sybila are in that very tavern plotting their next scheme."

He grinned at her, seeing the amusement in her gaze. "Possibly. But I'd argue that Paternoster Row on the other side of the cathedral and where this supposed Home for Wayward Children is located might be even more conducive to crime." Still, he led her onto Carter Lane, which would increase their time together as they walked around the cathedral.

"And why is that?" Lady Gresham brought her other hand over to clasp the top of his arm.

"Are you familiar with the murder of Sir Thomas Overbury?"

"I am not. Did this crime happen recently?"

"No, two hundred years ago. Overbury was thrown in the Tower after trying to caution his friend, Lord Rochester, against marrying his lover, the already wed Countess of Essex."

Lady Gresham's brow creased. "How could he marry the countess if she was already wed?"

"Rochester was the king's favorite, and His Majesty supported the annulment of the Essexes' marriage on the basis that Essex was impotent."

Lady Gresham gasped. "Was he? How could they know?"

Harry shrugged. "There's no telling for certain, of course, but Lady Essex had friends who dabbled in magic and poison. It's assumed she made sure Essex took something that made him unable to perform in bed." He glanced at her as a rush of heat swept over him. "My apologies. This is a rather indelicate conversation to be having."

"Not at all. It's fascinating. And if you don't finish the tale, I shall never speak to you again."

"Well, I wouldn't want that." He was enjoying himself far too much.

She looked over at him. "It sounds as though this Overbury fellow was sent to the Tower for unlawful reasons."

"Indeed he was. He had the misfortune to anger the wrong people. Which was how he found himself murdered in the Tower."

"What has any of this to do with Paternoster Row?" Lady Gresham asked.

"I'll get there," he said, as they turned from Carter Lane onto The Old Change. "It's quite a convoluted story. Suffice to say that Overbury annoyed many people, including Rochester, who'd been his dear friend for quite some time. However, in the end, Rochester, sided with the manipulative woman who would eventually become his wife—"

"The former Countess of Essex."

"Yes, her," he said with a smile. "She and Rochester masterminded a plan to murder Overbury, and that planning took place—"

"In Paternoster Row," she finished, giving him an eager look. "Do you know exactly where?"

"I don't. It was the home of Anne Turner, the widow of a prominent doctor and supposed cunning woman. She dealt in potions and was, if you can believe it, a fortune-teller."

Lady Gresham tripped, and Harry clutched her forearm before she lost her balance. "Thank you," she said. "This is such a fantastical tale. I'm afraid I wasn't paying attention to where I was walking."

Harry cast a look back over his shoulder but didn't immediately see any impediment. "You're all right?"

"Quite. I promise I am not usually this clumsy."

"Just when I'm around?" he asked, not intending to make it sound flirtatious, and yet it did. Or perhaps that was only in his mind as he considered whether he might distract her the way she distracted him. Hell, where was he in his story? "We studied the trial when I was at the Inns of Court."

"The trial?"

"Two trials, actually. The first was regarding the annulment of Lord and Lady Essex, which involved the question of whether Essex was impotent. He was found to be, and the marriage was finally annulled after raising a considerable cloud of gossip."

"I should say," Lady Gresham murmured.

"The second trial, or trials, really, was regarding the murder of Overbury who was poisoned in the Tower. Lord and Lady Somerset—Rochester had been made Earl of Somerset upon his wedding to the former Lady Essex—and four conspirators, including Mrs. Turner and two employees at the Tower, were tried for a variety of crimes. It's a quite fascinating study, really."

"It sounds like it. Perhaps I'll look for a book to read on the subject."

"I have several, as well as my own treatise about it." He guided her to the end of The Old Change, which had been lined almost exclusively with merchants, and no signs about a home for wayward children, and came onto Cheapside, where he turned left toward Paternoster Row.

"What happened to the accused?" she asked.

"All the coconspirators were hanged, including Mrs. Turner, who was in possession of wax figures that she apparently used in sorcery. She was found guilty of poisoning."

"What a horrid affair."

"It was, particularly when you consider the evidence presented and, in some cases, lack thereof." Harry lifted a shoulder. "The trials of two hundred years ago were not as fair as they are today. If one was arrested at that time, he or she was almost universally found guilty. The process of the law has improved greatly."

"I should hope so. Were Lord and Lady Somerset also hanged?"

"They were tried by their peers, and while Lady Somerset pled guilty, her husband did not. Nevertheless, both were convicted. However, they were not executed and instead lived in the Tower for seven years before they were released to live quietly in the countryside—without their titles or holdings, of course."

"That punishment hardly seems fair. They organized the entire crime, did they not?"

"Yes."

She scoffed. "People with wealth and privilege are held to different standards."

Startled by the bitterness in her voice, Harry snapped his head to look at her. She looked as serene as ever, so perhaps he'd imagined the emotion in her tone. "You're correct. And in this particular case, it served Lord and Lady Essex well. I'm sure a couple of Henry the Eighth's wives would argue their privilege didn't help them." He said the last to provoke humor, just in case Lady Gresham *had* been angry. Did she dislike inequity as much as Harry did?

As they reached Ivy Lane, Lady Gresham pointed up the narrow street. "There's the sign."

His pulse quickening, Harry guided Lady Gresham around the corner. The house was across the lane and bore a small sign that read House for Waywerd Children. "I hope they aren't teaching the children to spell."

"At least they can write," Lady Gresham said. "Many people in this area cannot. It's terrible that not everyone can learn to read and write."

He pivoted toward her. "Lady Gresham, you are a woman of singular thoughts and opinions when it comes to the less fortunate. How did you arrive at these sentiments?"

She hesitated briefly before answering. "I came from a poor family, Mr. Sheffield. I was fortunate to have caught the eye of my husband. I shall always care greatly for those in poverty."

"How astonishing." Harry would have wagered she'd been educated—and maybe she had been. "Was your father a vicar, perhaps?"

"No, he was not." When she didn't offer any other information, Harry was disappointed. He didn't, however, pursue the issue since it seemed to make her uncomfortable. And why wouldn't it? She was talking to the son of a bloody earl.

"Shall we go and speak with Mr. Winter? Assuming he's actually there. I suspect the sign is meant to ward anyone off who might go in search of the home."

"That seems like a great deal of trouble just to make something look real. Unless Madame Sybila expects someone will seek to verify the home's existence."

"In fact, I think she does. When I visited her last

week, she correctly—and surprisingly—deduced I was from Bow Street. I think she absolutely expects someone—me, in fact—to investigate her and her fraudulent charity." He inclined his head across the lane. "Shall we?"

She nodded, and they crossed the street to the home. Harry lifted his hand and pounded lightly on the door. The sound of a child shrieking answered the summons, and Harry frowned. Was there a chance this *was* real? No, it couldn't be.

Footsteps preceded the door opening. A woman, her dark brown hair pulled on top of her head with wisps grazing her cheeks and neck as if the entirety simply could not be contained, looked at them warily.

"Good afternoon," Harry said formally. "I'm here to see Mr. Winter."

"Mr. Winter!" the woman shouted, her eyes never leaving Harry and Lady Gresham.

A child darted out from behind the woman's legs, her dark hair a wild mop above the roundest blue eyes Harry had ever seen. She stared up at him with a mixture of fear and curiosity. "Who're you?" she asked.

The woman turned on her and snapped, "Don't be rude."

The girl didn't react, but Harry said, "There's no need to speak to her like that. I took no offense."

Blanching, the woman looked to Harry with an apologetic stare. She opened her mouth, but before she could speak, a masculine voice filled the corridor stretching behind her.

"Who's there, Mrs. Winter?" A tall, dark-haired man came up behind her. He smiled broadly, his dark eyes twinkling in the light filtering into the entry from the parlor to the left of the front door. The man didn't look like the sort who would run a home for wayward children. In fact, if his hair had been cropped a bit shorter and his clothing upgraded, Harry might have expected to see him at Brooks's.

"Someone to see you," the woman said.

Mr. Winter slid his arm around Mrs. Winter and drew her against his side. "How can I be of service?" He looked from Harry to Lady Gresham, and it seemed his smile widened even more.

Harry felt a pang of…something. Stifling a frown, he addressed the man. "I'm Harry Sheffield from Bow Street. May I come in to speak with you?"

"Certainly." Mr. Winter moved away from his wife and gestured for them to enter.

Lady Gresham took her hand from Harry's arm, and he found he missed the contact immediately. She preceded him into the narrow house, and Harry followed her.

"This way," Mr. Winter said, indicating the parlor. He crooked his finger at the little girl, and she went to stand before him. Winter crouched down. "Will you go back to the sitting room until we're finished?"

She nodded, and Winter rose, patting her head with a "Good girl." Her face split into a smile revealing missing front teeth, and she skipped toward the back of the house.

Harry continued into the parlor, where Lady Gresham stood with her hands clasped near a battered settee. One of the legs didn't match the others.

"Pardon our intrusion," Harry began as Mr. and Mrs. Winter came into the parlor. Winter's gaze fell on Lady Gresham, and one of his brows arched. Yes, this man could definitely pass for an aristocrat.

"And who is this?" Mr. Winter asked, his mouth spreading into another smile. He certainly seemed a jovial fellow.

"My associate, Lady Gresham," Harry said. "We

came to inquire about your Home for Wayward Children. That is what you do here?"

"We live here," Winter said. "And yes, we take in wayward children. Don't we, my dear?" He looked down at his wife, whose gaze held a rather blank quality. Harry would have guessed she was drunk on gin, or perhaps she'd taken opium.

Mrs. Winter nodded. "Yes, wayward children. Those that need homes. It's a bit like an orphanage." She smiled expectantly at Lady Gresham.

"How wonderful of you," Lady Gresham said softly. "How many children do you currently have with you?" She looked to Mr. Winter.

"Eighteen at present. That may not seem like a great number, but we can't afford to take any more on just yet. We have to rely on the generous charity of others to support so many children. Fortunately, we have a kind benefactor, and we sometimes get donations from people in the neighborhood or the parish church."

This was beginning to look like a legitimate charity, or at least a home with a couple who were trying to do good. "Do you keep records of these contributions to your cause? If you don't, you should."

"I do, in fact." He went to a small desk set back in the corner of the room. Opening the drawer, he withdrew a ledger and brought it back to give to Harry. "Everything's marked in here, going back six months or so, when we really started taking children in earnest. It started with just three—orphaned siblings—but we haven't been able to stop." He laughed, then put his arm around Mrs. Winter once more. She blinked, then cozied up next to him, snaking her arm around his waist.

"I can't have children of my own," Mrs. Winter said, looking forlorn. Perhaps that deep sadness was the reason for the vacancy in her eyes.

"I'm sorry," Lady Gresham said with considerable warmth.

Harry opened the ledger and perused the entries. The dates did indeed start about six months prior. The handwriting was atrocious, but Harry could make out at least one name: Madame S. He looked up from the ledger at Mr. Winter. "Who is Madame S?"

"Madame Sybila," Winter answered cheerfully. "She's French, but we don't let that get in the way." He chuckled, and Mrs. Winter laughed along with him.

"How do you know her?" Harry asked, glancing down at the ledger, unable to make out any other names apart from Mister Th and Mrs. Cro. It was as if Winter was incapable of finishing the last word.

He lowered his voice. "She's a fortune-teller. Mrs. Winter here went to see her to ask about having children. It was she who gave Mrs. Winter the idea to take in a few children. She's a kind sort, heart as big as the moon."

Utterly thwarted in his quest to prove this charity didn't exist, Harry found himself a bit speechless. He frowned down at the ledger before snapping it shut and handing it back to Winter. "Do you mind showing me the house?"

Mrs. Winter turned to her husband and looked up at him, her lips parted, her brows pitched in distress. "He'll wake the children that are sleeping."

Lady Gresham touched Harry's arm. "Is it really necessary to search the house?" she asked softly. "I realize you like to be thorough, but surely you've seen enough?"

Winter whispered something to his wife, and she cast a disgruntled look toward Harry before taking herself from the parlor. "I've asked Mrs. Winter to fetch the children who are awake and, ah, presentable. A few of them need baths, and Mrs. Winter is adamant you don't meet them. It's a matter of pride for her, you understand. We do our best with just the pair of us and the lot of them."

"I'm sure you do a wonderful job," Lady Gresham said.

This was not going at all as Harry had anticipated. Was it possible Madame Sybila supported a legitimate charity and wasn't actually stealing from the ladies whose fortunes she told? And if that part was true, was she also just a fortune-teller who made a living making wealthy ladies feel good? Was there any harm in that?

His father was never going to believe it, but Harry didn't think there was anything he could say or do that would convince him to support his mother's desire to see Madame Sybila.

Children began to file into the room. After several minutes, there were twelve of them of varying ages. The youngest was perhaps four and the oldest maybe ten. They looked relatively clean, and their clothing was in fair to good condition and, like them, also clean.

"Good afternoon, children," Harry said with a smile. He walked to the tallest of them, a girl with wheat-blonde hair and freckles on her nose. "I'm Mr. Sheffield. I am looking into your home here. You live here with Mr. and Mrs. Winter?"

"Aye, sir."

"You're well cared for?"

"Aye, sir. We aren't hungry anymore." She looked to the girl next to her, who appeared to be a smaller version of herself. "Are we, May?"

May shook her head. "No, sir. And we get baths!"

Two of the boys made faces, while a third standing between them elbowed each in the side.

Resigned, Harry turned to Mr. Winter. "Well, you seem to be exactly what you purport to be."

Lady Gresham came forward and pressed some coins into Mr. Winter's hand. "Thank you for your kindness. I hope you'll allow me to contribute to your cause."

"Thank *you* for your generosity, my lady." He smiled at Lady Gresham with a rather charming twinkle in his eye, and he gave her hand a squeeze as he accepted the coin.

Harry felt another pang of that something he didn't want to identify.

Mrs. Winter came back into the parlor then, carrying another child on her hip. The toddler had stuffed his entire fist in his mouth. Drool ran down his chin as he stared at Harry. He pulled his hand free and looked at Mrs. Winter. "Mama?"

Harry narrowed his eyes. "I thought you didn't have any children."

"We don't," Winter answered. "But Jacob here thinks Mrs. Winter is his mother. We don't know where his went," he added quietly, his eyes downcast. He reached over and ruffled the boy's light brown hair.

Lady Gresham curled her hand around Harry's arm. "We won't keep you any longer. Thank you for your time."

Harry walked from the parlor with her, his mind churning at this astonishing turn. Winter rushed to open the door for them, and Harry bid him good day.

Once they were outside, he turned and frowned at the house. "Maybe they're all paid actors."

Lady Gresham laughed, and he turned to look at her, his frown still in place.

She quieted. "You're serious." Alarm lit her gaze. "You can't really think that. That would cost quite a bit of money, I'd think. If this were some sort of scam, how much money could Madame Sybila really be making?"

"You'd be surprised how cheaply people will work, and those children likely aren't getting paid. They probably happily agreed to pretend to live there in exchange for good clean clothing, and food. And baths."

"You are quite cynical." There was an edge of frost to her tone that Harry didn't like. Or maybe he didn't like that she was right.

He turned with her toward the cathedral and exhaled. "I can be, yes. It's a fault I endeavor to overcome."

"And if you think those boys willingly took baths, you are being disagreeable on purpose."

Now he laughed. "You're right, of course—that they wouldn't have wanted to take baths. I am not, however, trying to be disagreeable." He glanced back at the house. "I'll pay another visit in a week or so just to make sure today wasn't some sort of performance."

"Please tell me when you do, because I'd like to send more money. I didn't have enough with me today to give them what I'd like."

He looked at her as they walked through the churchyard, feeling anything but cynical about her generosity and kindheartedness. "You really do care about the less fortunate. It's not just a fashionable thing to do."

"There's your cynicism again."

"Perhaps, but I also know the people of the ton, and many of them care only how charity makes them look."

"How sad," Lady Gresham said. "Are you terribly upset that your expectations were not met?"

"Yes and no. Mostly no." How could he be when it seemed children were being helped and he'd spent a lovely afternoon with Lady Gresham?

"I admit I rather enjoyed this endeavor today,"

Lady Gresham said as they left the churchyard and walked along Ludgate. "If you ever require an associate in the future, I hope you'll think of me."

He looked over at her elegant profile. "I shall think of you as far more than an associate."

"Will you?" Her eyes met his, and Harry felt the connection deep in the pit of his belly. Did she feel the same as he did?

In front of them, a hack was just letting someone out. "I should be on my way home," she said, disrupting the moment between them.

Disappointed their time was at an end, Harry hailed the driver and guided Lady Gresham to the vehicle. She gave her direction to the coachman, and Harry held the door for her as she climbed inside.

"I'll see you soon, Lady Gresham."

"I hope so."

Their gazes held a moment before he closed the door. His blood thrummed as the hack departed.

CHAPTER 7

*S*elina tossed her hat and gloves on the small console table in the entry hall and nearly collided with the housekeeper, one of the few women who were actually taller than Selina.

"I thought I heard you come in," Mrs. Vining said. "You've been gone quite a while."

"Yes, you have," Beatrix said from the stairs. She was already dressed in her smartest walking outfit, ready for the park.

"I'm sorry," Selina said. "But I've had an extraordinary afternoon."

"I can see that," Beatrix said, her brow creasing. "Let us take refreshment before you change."

Grateful for Beatrix's concern—and understanding—Selina nodded.

"I'll bring lemonade," Mrs. Vining offered, pivoting toward the back of the house.

"That won't be necessary," Selina said. "I require something a bit stronger."

Mrs. Vining nodded, then took herself off.

Beatrix came down the stairs and followed Selina into the sitting room, closing the door behind them. Selina went directly to the bottles of brandy and Madeira sitting on a square table in the corner. "Do you want anything?" Selina asked, pouring a glass of brandy.

"I don't wish to be left out," Beatrix said.

Selina poured Madeira, which Beatrix preferred, and handed her the glass. After downing half her brandy, Selina began to prowl the room as nervous anticipatory energy coursed through her.

"You seem agitated. Did something happen?" Beatrix asked. She stood near the settee but didn't sit, likely because she didn't want to crease her gown. The coach ride to Hyde Park would add enough wrinkles as it was.

"I spent the last couple of hours in the company of Mr. Sheffield." Selina sipped her brandy. "We went to Ivy Lane."

"Ah, and how did Luther do?"

"Better than I could have anticipated. I wasn't sure his 'wife' was going to meet the demands at first, but she came through. They gathered an astonishing number of children, who performed as if they were on the stage," Selina said with admiration. "I wish I had more coin to give them."

"Perhaps you'll receive enough donations to do so."

Selina pressed her lips together. "We can barely cover all our expenses." She saw the crease in Beatrix's brow and sought to soothe her concerns. "Don't worry, your Season—your goal—is happening." She began pacing again and tossed back the rest of her brandy. Then she diverted her course and went back to the bottle in the corner. They were in danger of running out of funds, but she wouldn't tell Beatrix. Not yet.

"It sounds as if your afternoon went well, and yet you're upset," Beatrix said. "What aren't you telling me?"

Selina refilled her glass and turned to Beatrix. "I'd

hoped to learn something about the Vicar, but despite being a Bow Street Runner, Sheffield seems no closer to finding the Vicar than I am."

"It's rather difficult when no one knows what he looks like," Beatrix said.

And how frustrating that was. Anytime Selina had asked someone about the Vicar, they simply ended the conversation and walked away. "I'll find out—*we'll* find out. We are formidable when we want something."

Beatrix chuckled. "That much is true. If we do find him, what then? Are you going to kill him on the spot? You've never killed anyone, Selina." She fell quiet, and the air in the room crackled with old secrets and terrible lies. "Have you?" The question was so small that Selina might not have heard it if she hadn't seen Beatrix's lips move.

Not on purpose. Selina sipped the brandy, seeking a fortitude she wasn't sure she could ever find. The memory of that day at the tavern had faded to the corners of her mind, pushed to the side so often that she could almost convince herself it wasn't real. Why hadn't that happened with the other memory from after she'd left school? That one rose in her thoughts unbidden, crippling her in odd moments, when she least expected it.

Because in the first memory, you saved yourself, and in the second, you allowed yourself to be violated.

"Why not let Sheffield handle him?" Beatrix asked, thankfully oblivious to Selina's dark thoughts. "You could tell Sheffield why you want to find the Vicar. I'm sure it would only strengthen his resolve to know the blackguard killed your brother."

It would not be difficult to unburden herself, and then they could share their antagonism toward the Vicar. Moreover, she *wanted* to tell him at least this small truth. But there was too much at stake.

"No," Selina said. "Then I'd have to explain how my brother was even involved with that band of criminals, and that would expose us needlessly."

"Don't you even want to tell Sheffield? It seemed you and he had established a rapport. I thought you could perhaps tell him what you needed to without disclosing your secrets. You're rather good at that. So good that you still keep some from me."

Selina felt bad, because they *had* established a rapport. And her current unease was as much due to her growing friendship with him as it was to her frustration over not finding the Vicar. But she didn't want to admit that, especially when she wasn't the only one keeping secrets. "Is there something you want to tell me about an emerald necklace that belongs to Lady Aylesbury?"

Beatrix briefly averted her gaze. "What can I tell you that you don't already know? I like pretty things."

"And you just happened to find your way to Lady Aylesbury's dressing chamber—during the soiree which she was kind enough to invite us to—and accidentally pilfer her jewels?"

Her blonde brows pitching low over her narrowed eyes, Beatrix put a hand on her hip. "You act as if we don't routinely swindle people who are kind to us."

Selina flinched. Yes, this was becoming more difficult. Almost untenable. She honestly didn't know how much longer she could endure this duplicitous life. "And you act as though your stealing things isn't a problem."

Selina had taught her to steal after rescuing her from the seminary. Beatrix had proven to be more skilled than Selina had been as a child on the streets of East London. A few years ago, Selina realized Beatrix stole even when it wasn't necessary. It was a compulsion she couldn't seem to control.

Beatrix's shoulders twitched. "You know it is," she said quietly.

"I do." Just as she knew how Beatrix had suffered after her beloved mother had died and her father had sent her to the seminary without telling her in person. He hadn't visited or written, and despite the fact that he was a duke and hadn't claimed her as his daughter, Beatrix had spoken of a family life Selina could only dream of—parents who adored each other and her. Beatrix had felt utterly abandoned, and the heartless girls at the school had only made things worse with their taunts that Beatrix was an unwanted bastard.

Selina set her brandy glass down and went to Beatrix, putting her hands on her shoulders. "I know you don't mean to do it, but we must be especially careful now. When your father embraces you, things will change. You can't be stealing from these people who will be your friends and neighbors."

Beatrix exhaled heavily. "I know. Are you really going to leave after the Season?" Her eyes met Selina's, and the apprehension in their depths made Selina pull her close. Beatrix embraced her in return.

"You know I won't be able to afford to live here," Selina said.

"My father will give me enough money so that you can."

Selina didn't believe that, but Beatrix sometimes nurtured impossible dreams. "We will always be sisters. I love you, Trix."

Beatrix held her tightly. "I love you. I'm sorry for causing trouble."

"It's all right. We'll fix it." Selina already had a plan.

～

*T*he following day, Selina closed the door on Madame Sybila's small room and made her way from the back of the perfumery. The door opened to a narrow alley, which was empty as usual at this hour. Still, Selina was careful to survey the surroundings, lest someone, such as Mr. Sheffield, was watching for Madame Sybila to leave.

Selina took a variety of routes home, one of which was along Bow Street. She avoided that course now.

The journey allowed her to reflect upon her day's appointments. Today, however, she was thinking of Mr. Sheffield and their pleasant excursion the day before.

Pleasant. How could spending the afternoon with a Bow Street Runner who was eager to charge her, rather Madame Sybila, with a crime be pleasant?

Because she'd enjoyed his company far more than she wanted to. She glanced toward Bow Street and wondered where he was now. Hopefully not patrolling the area so that she might run into him. Due to that risk, she'd become even more attentive about her surroundings since meeting him a week ago.

Which was how she knew with certainty that she was being followed.

She'd suspected someone was trailing her on Friday, but had convinced herself she'd been mistaken. Had Mr. Sheffield worked out the truth? Did he know she was Madame Sybila? Perhaps he and other Runners were even now closing in.

Trepidation raced up her spine, and she quickened her pace, skirting Covent Garden. The man she'd identified, an exceptionally tall fellow, was still behind her—but across the street.

She turned up Bedford Street, knowing there was an alley she could duck into. Hastening her steps, she dashed across the lane just before a coach passed and used the vehicle to block the man's sight of her darting into the alley.

Chest heaving, Selina moved into a doorway and pressed herself back into the nook so that he couldn't see her if he glanced this way. She reached into her reticule and withdrew her pistol. After a few minutes, she heard a boot on the cobblestones.

Her heart hammered. She held her breath and waited until she could see him. The moment she verified it was the same man, she moved out from the doorway, pistol raised.

"Why are you following me?"

"Damn, Selina, don't shoot."

The man knew her. But it wasn't Mr. Sheffield. This man was taller, and his shoulders weren't as broad.

He stepped toward her, and Selina barely kept herself from pulling the trigger. "Don't come any closer, or I *will* shoot you. Who the devil are you?"

The man exhaled, and there was something eerily familiar about the tone of it. In a flash, he disarmed her with a tsk. "You let me get too close, Lina."

Lina.

The only people who called her that were Luther and…Rafe. This wasn't Luther.

"Rafe?"

He swept his hat off, revealing light blond hair. Edging closer, he nodded slightly.

Selina couldn't help but stare at the nasty scar on his chin. But she forced herself to look up, her gaze settling on his eyes—brilliant blue except for the orange spot in the right one, which she could barely make out in the dim light of the alley. "Is it really you?"

Eighteen years was an awfully long time, and

they'd been barely more than children the last time they'd seen each other.

"Yes, it's me, Lina."

She kicked him hard in the shin. "That's for following me." Next, she punched him in the gut, drawing a loud grunt from his throat. He bent at the middle. "And that's for letting me think you were dead!"

Shaking out her fist, she glared at him as he straightened.

He held up the hand that wasn't holding her pistol. "Truce."

"Give me back my gun."

"Only if you promise to wield it properly. I taught you better than that."

He had. She *had* let him get too close. "It's been some time since I've had to protect myself like that."

"I'm glad." He handed her the pistol, butt first.

She took it with a scowl and dropped it back into her reticule.

"Will you get an ale with me?" he asked.

"Only because I want to know why you let me think you were dead." He was alive! She was torn between hugging him and hitting him again. In the end, she did neither.

"I will tell you anything you wish to know. And perhaps a thing or two you don't," he said rather ominously. But then he smiled faintly and offered his arm. "There's a tavern around the corner."

Tentatively, she put her hand on his sleeve. He led her from the alley, and they didn't speak again until they were seated at a table tucked into the corner of the tavern's common room.

The serving maid brought two tankards of ale, which Rafe had called for when they'd entered, and quickly departed. Rafe took a long drink before fixing his familiar gaze on hers.

Familiar and not. Though he looked somewhat like her brother, and his eyes confirmed it, she realized they were strangers. All this time, she'd been searching for an ideal. The brother she'd known when they were children was gone. Just as the girl she'd been had long since disappeared.

"I knew almost the moment you returned to London," he said. "As soon as you showed up in Whitechapel."

That had been weeks ago. Selina's insides contracted. "Why are you following me and not welcoming me to town?" She didn't wait for him to respond. "Do you have any idea how it felt when I was told you died?"

"I can imagine, and I'm sorry. I was trying to keep you safe—away from me. But you're working with that goddamned Runner now, so I've been keeping an eye on you to make sure you're safe from him." He leaned slightly forward, his brows pushing down over his narrowed eyes. "Why are you entangled with him?"

"I'm not 'entangled' with him."

"I heard you were traipsing all over Cheapside on his arm yesterday."

"That is my business." She took several sips of ale, hoping to calm her ire.

"The fake home for wayward children. Yes, I know all about that, and about your ruse peddling fortunes."

He knew all about her while she thought he was dead? "If you must know, I was working with Sheffield to protect myself," she spat. "And to find the man I thought had killed you. I wanted to avenge you, but now I wonder why I should care."

"The Vicar," he said quietly, glancing down at his tankard.

Selina exhaled some of the anger from her frame. "Yes."

He gave her a lopsided smile that was absolutely the boy she'd known. Her heart twisted, and her breath caught. "*I* am the Vicar."

"What?" Selina had picked up her mug again, but now set it hard upon the table with a thud.

"It's an identity I created to get away from Partridge. Surely you understand the importance of creating identities."

She stared at him, then shook her head gently. "Very amusing. I take it your plan didn't work since the Vicar killed Partridge?"

"That's correct. But even though Partridge was dead, it suited me to kill Rafe Blackwell too."

Selina was working to process everything he was saying. "If you know about my business, you must know that I'm working with Luther. Does he know you're alive? And Mrs. Kinnon?"

Rafe grimaced apologetically. "Don't be angry with them. I made them promise to keep my secret. Rafe Blackwell *needed* to die."

Selina sat back and crossed her arms. "Even for his sister?"

"As I said, I was trying to protect you." He pierced her with a dark glower. "This is a dangerous life here —one I worked hard to escape. You may not remember just how terrible it was."

"Oh, I do, brother. I do." Her tone was soft, but the memories were hard. "How could I ever forget when that was why you sent me away, separating me from the only family I knew? Is that why you stopped responding to my letters? To protect me?" Hurt threaded through every part of her so that tears should have streamed down her face. But she didn't cry. Not since he'd told her not to that long ago day.

"Somewhat." He wrapped his hands around the

tankard and briefly squeezed as if he was trying to release some of the tension between them. "I know you wanted to come back here. You wrote that in every letter. I didn't want to encourage that."

"So you stopped writing altogether." That had been about the time that Beatrix had come to the seminary. "Even though I kept writing to you." Right up until she'd left her governess position. After that horrid event, she'd wanted to put every part of the past behind her except for Beatrix. It was several years before she'd decided she wanted to find her brother.

"You'd found Beatrix, and it was obvious from your letters that you were close. You're still close—she's your bloody sister." He picked up his tankard and took another drink.

Was that jealousy in his tone? Good. "In every way that matters," Selina said.

He set his tankard down, and his eyes softened to a warmth that eased the remnants of her anger. "I'm glad. Once I read about her in your letters, I knew you'd be all right. Better than you could ever be here. With me."

The sadness in his voice bent her even further. Her safety had always been paramount to him. That was why he'd sent her away in the first place. And apparently why he'd kept himself from her until now.

She could never tell him what had happened to her when she left the school.

Selina sipped her ale. "So you're worried about Sheffield?"

"He's a danger to your enterprise. And, to be honest, to mine."

"Why, because he wants to see you hanged for killing children?"

"Yes, but I didn't start that fire at the flash house. It was Partridge's place." His eyes turned so frigid,

Selina nearly shivered. "You wouldn't have remembered it. That was after you left London."

"Why did you kill Partridge?" There were so many reasons to do so, and that was only what Selina remembered from her time in his service. She had to think there was something more, something that pushed Rafe over the edge.

"I had to, but not for his business, which Sheffield and others assumed. I wanted out. I'd started up my own enterprise, loaning money, mostly, as the Vicar. In those days, I didn't show my face, so no one would know it was me. It was the only way I could leave—if I became someone else."

"How close were you to Partridge, then?" Selina and Rafe had started thieving for him when she was eight. Samuel Partridge had taken a liking to them, and Rafe had become one of his favored lads, earning positions of increasing importance. By the time Selina had left London, Rafe had been in charge of several gangs of child thieves and had begun working in one of the receiver shops. His success had given him the financial means to send her away. He hadn't thought twice about continuing his life as a criminal, even as he protected Selina from the same.

"His right hand—or I had been until I asked to leave. I didn't want to work for him any longer."

"We never wanted to work for him." They hadn't had a choice at all. Well, she supposed she had. She could have been a prostitute instead.

"No, we didn't. And I'm trying very hard not to be a criminal at all, which is why I don't need Sheffield on my arse."

He was trying not to be a criminal? Perhaps he'd found financial security. Selina hadn't—not yet. But hopefully after this stint as Madame Sybila here in London, she'd be in a position to finally secure her and Beatrix's futures. Though if Beatrix got what she came here for, she wouldn't need Selina's help.

"Why not just kill the Vicar now?" Selina asked.

Rafe cracked a small smile. "Because he runs a very lucrative moneylending business."

"An illegal one, from what I hear."

He cocked his head, his hand gripping his tankard. "Not anymore. I used to charge higher interest than the banks, but I've lowered my rates in the past several months. None of that matters at the present. I don't need Sheffield breathing down my neck as I try to transition to a respectable life. As you have on Queen Anne Street. Lady Gresham, eh? Did you actually marry?"

"No. Sir Barnabus Gresham was kind enough to allow me to use his name, despite the fact that I'd stolen a hundred pounds from him."

Rafe blew out a whistle. "Did he not know?"

"Oh, he knew. And he let me keep it. Barney is a nice man." Selina winced through the regret piercing her chest. "Was. I'm sure he's passed on by now. He became rather ill."

"Here I thought you were an accomplished charlatan." His smirk told her he was jesting, but Selina wanted to make sure he knew exactly who she was.

"I am Selina Blackwell and Lady Gresham *and* Madame Sybila, and anyone else I need to be. That Sir Barnabus learned I'd stolen from him was entirely my choice, and it's worked out rather well, thank you." That wasn't exactly the truth, but Selina had learned long ago that the truth was vastly overrated. And almost always unnecessary. Furthermore, the truth made one vulnerable. Selina would avoid that at all costs.

He surveyed her with admiration. "See? I knew you understood the importance of identities."

She began to feel more comfortable with him, but

there was still so much they needed to share if they were going to regain their bond. She wondered if he would reveal his secrets, or if, like her, he'd learned to bury himself so deep that sometimes even he wasn't sure where to find his true self. "Why did you kill Partridge?"

"Because he was a vile, evil man." The hatred in his eyes sparked a fear Selina had rarely encountered.

She knew when not to prod a sleeping beast. "So you want to straddle the polite world and that of the Vicar. I have earned Sheffield's trust—in my endeavors to protect my interests. If you didn't set the flash house on fire, all we have to do is find out who did, and he'll leave you alone. He wants justice for that crime. I don't suppose you know who did it?"

Rafe shook his head. "Honestly, I didn't really care. I killed Partridge, but the building was quite intact when I stole away from the back. When I learned it burned down, it gave me the opportunity to kill Rafe. I would have been the presumptive leader of Partridge's gang. I didn't want that. Whoever set that fire made it easy for me to leave. Why does Sheffield care so much about an old fire?"

"Because innocents died," she said quietly, thinking that could so easily have been her and Rafe years ago.

Rafe sat back, sprawling in the chair. It was a familiar position he'd often adopted in their youth. Selina couldn't help smiling.

"What?" Rafe asked.

Selina shook her head. "It's odd being with you. You're a stranger, and yet familiar."

"I was thinking the same." His eyes found hers, that orange blemish—no, not a blemish, that mark of fire she'd always thought had given him his courage —burning as he looked at her. "You still have that mole behind your ear along your hairline."

Lifting her hand behind her left ear, she stroked the location of the mole. "How can you see that?"

"I looked very closely as we walked here."

"Confirming I was really me?"

His lips spread in a grin that she'd longed to see for eighteen years. "Perhaps."

"So, let's find out who set that fire. Then Sheffield will leave you alone."

"I'll look into it." His eyes narrowed slightly, and she could tell he was thinking.

"What?"

He shook his head, blinking. "Nothing, just contemplating."

"Conspiring," she said.

He didn't respond to her comment. "How will you get him to leave you, or rather Madame Sybila, alone?" He straightened and leaned slightly toward her.

"I'm taking care of that." She suddenly realized part of coming back to London to find Rafe had been to show him that she'd managed quite well on her own—much as Beatrix was trying to do with her estranged father.

"If I can help you in any way, I hope you'll tell me." He seemed earnest, but Selina didn't need his help. She had things well in hand.

"Is it all right if Mrs. Kinnon and Luther know I'm aware you're not really dead?"

"Yes. I really was just trying to protect you, Lina. When I heard you were back, and I saw how lovely and refined you'd grown up to be…" He smiled, but there was sadness behind it. Perhaps even regret. Selina felt both those emotions too. "I thought it best if I remained dead to you."

"And yet, if you become respectable, we could be what we always dreamed. We'd both be secure. No more begging or scraping or hating our lot in life."

That sensation was still so familiar, even after years of being "safe." Was that because she actually still hated her lot? Or that she hated the lies she was forced to tell—to others and to herself?

Rafe reached across the table for her hand. She placed her palm in his. "I'd like that more than anything. I'll let you know what I find out about the fire."

"I can't tell Sheffield what you learn—we'll have to find another way to convey the information."

"Of course." He gave her a wolfish grin. "I already have a plan."

CHAPTER 8

On Thursday evening, Harry walked up the short flight of steps to his parents' house on Mount Street. The butler opened the door before Harry reached the stoop and welcomed him inside.

"Your father would like to see you in his study." The butler, Tallent, was somewhat new to the position as their longtime butler had retired last year. Tallent had been promoted from footman and by all accounts was doing an excellent job. Harry particularly liked him because he'd helped him and Jeremy out of a few scrapes in their younger years.

Harry handed him his hat and gloves. "Thank you, Tallent. How is his mood this evening?"

"Let us hope you have good news for him, sir." Tallent pressed his lips together and gave his head a light shake.

Exhaling, Harry made his way through a sitting room to the study. His father was seated in a wingback chair in front of the hearth where a few coals burned.

"'Evening, Father," Harry said. "Do you need a refill of brandy?"

The earl glanced toward the glass in his hand. "Not at the moment, thank you."

Harry went to the sideboard and poured himself a glass, then took the other chair situated in front of the fire. After sitting and sipping his brandy, he leaned back in the chair and awaited his father's interrogation.

"What news?" Father asked.

"I assume you're asking about the fortune-teller, or are you perchance interested in me?"

His father snorted softly. "I am always interested in you. However, everything you discuss involves work. Your investigation into the fortune-teller serves both of us."

"I suppose that's true." Harry took another drink of his brandy. "I regret to inform you that it appears Madame Sybila's charity—the Home for Wayward Children—is, in fact, a legitimate operation.

Father thumped his palm—the one that wasn't holding his brandy—on the arm of the chair. "Damn and blast! How can that be?" He speared Harry with a dark, angry stare.

"I went to the home, and everything seemed as it should. I'll return next week, but I can't say I expect to find anything different. That doesn't mean Madame Sybila isn't executing some other fraud." There was still the matter of the tonics. Harry meant to obtain her offerings to determine if they were anything other than water or something equally innocuous.

Scowling, Father lifted his glass and polished off the contents. He rose from the chair and took the empty vessel to the sideboard. Turning back to Harry, he exhaled. "I appreciate you looking into this. I just can't see why your mother believes in such nonsense."

"It could be that Madame Sybila simply comforts her. Would that be so bad?" Harry didn't mean it as a defense of the fortune-teller, but of his mother. Even so, he realized how it sounded to his father, who despised the fact that his wife was seeking the counsel of what he perceived to be a charlatan.

"Of course it is!" Father frowned. "You aren't giving up, are you?"

Harry rose from the chair. "No. I'll continue to supervise the fortune-teller's activities. I won't let her take advantage of Mother."

"Good." Father straightened his coat. "We should join the others in the library."

"After you." Harry gestured to the door.

His father departed the study, and Harry followed behind. They entered the library a few minutes later, where everyone was gathered with the exception of Jeremy. Harry wondered if his twin would come—he didn't attend every week. In fact, he attended less often than Harry, who always strove to be present unless his work interfered, which happened on occasion.

Rachel strolled toward him, an auburn brow arched saucily. "You're here."

"You doubted it?"

She shrugged. "Your presence isn't guaranteed. But tonight of all nights, I was really hoping you would be here."

Instantly, Harry's neck pricked. He looked from one sister to the other. Every single one had an anticipatory sheen to their expression—that and an irritating smugness. What the hell was going on? He shot a look toward his mother. She had that same sense of anticipation about her, along with something else: giddiness.

Bloody hell, what were they planning?

"Lady Gresham and Miss Whitford," Tallent announced, drawing Harry to turn.

Standing just over the threshold was Lady Gresham and her sister. Probably her sister—because

Tallent had said so. Harry couldn't confirm her presence because he couldn't tear his gaze from Lady Gresham.

But he did. Because he knew what this was: an unabashed attempt at matchmaking. How the hell had they—his sisters and mother—correctly determined that Lady Gresham was special? That he was, *perhaps*, interested in her?

Because they weren't stupid, apparently.

Harry cast a narrow-eyed glare at Rachel. She barely lifted a shoulder in response as her lips almost curved into a smile. Almost. The wretch.

Except was he upset that Lady Gresham was here? Not at all. And maybe *that* disturbed him more than his family's machinations.

Harry took in the ivory gown with its red and dark orange embroidery that perfectly draped Lady Gresham's tall, elegant form. She looked like she belonged in London's best drawing rooms, which, he supposed, she was—the Earl of Aylesbury's library was as fashionable as any in the upper crust. He suddenly felt a great divide between them. She was a woman at home in this environment, while he was more comfortable working.

Except she'd seemed quite well adapted to assisting him with and accompanying him on investigations. He ought to be careful not to make assumptions about her. Perhaps that was why he found himself so attracted to her—she did not fit any particular mold.

Miss Whitford curtsied to the room at large. "Good evening."

Lady Gresham also dipped a brief curtsey, her gaze going to Harry's father. "Good evening, my lord. Thank you so much for your kind invitation to dinner this evening."

"It is our pleasure to welcome you," Harry's

mother answered, moving toward Lady Gresham and drawing her into the room.

Rachel went to Miss Whitford, smiling, and escorted her to sit on the settee next to Delia.

Harry resisted the urge to go directly to Lady Gresham. That would only encourage his family's efforts to pair them off.

Would that be so bad?

Yes. He wasn't seeking a wife, and she wasn't planning to remarry. He'd made himself quite clear on that topic to his entire family. Perhaps he ought to suggest to Lady Gresham that she do the same.

Instead, Harry simply looked in her direction. Their eyes locked, and her lips curved into a slight smile, as if they shared a secret. He supposed they did. His family had no idea they'd spent an afternoon together—two if he counted their previous visit to Gunter's—and he certainly wasn't going to tell them.

He went to stand behind the settee where his brother-in-law Nathaniel Hayes, an MP, stood with his other brother-in-law, Sir Kenneth. "We were just discussing the need for greater governance regarding child labor. Limiting hours and ages for those working only in cotton mills isn't enough," Hayes said with a frown.

"I couldn't agree more." Harry thought of the children at Mr. Winter's home the other day. They could all be working in a textile mill for far too many hours and even overnight. Too many of them suffered those conditions and were exposed to environmental dangers. "You're fighting for this in the Commons, I expect."

Hayes nodded. "Of course, though I've not nearly enough support."

Harry appreciated that Rachel's husband fought so hard for others. That made Harry think of Lady Gresham's concern for the less fortunate. She would undoubtedly support Hayes's efforts too. Harry's gaze strayed toward her, but she was focused on his mother. Were they discussing Madame Sybila? That was actually a good idea. Perhaps Lady Gresham, as a woman who had also seen the fortune-teller, could dissuade his mother from seeing her.

But no, he wouldn't ask her to do that. It wasn't fair—to her or his mother. His father might just have to accept that his wife enjoyed seeing Madame Sybila. So long as the woman wasn't fleecing Mother, what harm did it truly cause?

"We're still working on your voucher for Almack's," Delia was telling Miss Whitford. "I expect we'll be able to accomplish it within the month for certain. Mark my words, you will be presented there before the Season draws to a close."

Miss Whitford had charming dimples when she smiled, as she was doing now. "I deeply appreciate your assistance. I'm having a dress made especially for the occasion."

Imogen sat down on Miss Whitford's other side and asked about the dress. As Miss Whitford described the costume in excruciating detail, Harry wondered where Rachel had gone only to see her standing with his mother and Lady Gresham. Rachel was angled toward Lady Gresham, her gaze darting toward Harry as she spoke.

What on earth was she saying to poor Lady Gresham in her effort to make a match? Hell, was that a pained expression in Lady Gresham's eyes?

Knowing the need for a rescue when he saw one, Harry excused himself from his brothers-in-law and circuited the seating area on his way to reach Lady Gresham.

"Oh, Harry, how nice of you to finally join us and welcome Lady Gresham," Rachel said, pulling him into their half circle so that he was between her and Lady Gresham.

Harry quashed the urge to glare at his meddling sister. "Good evening, Lady Gresham."

"We were just telling Lady Gresham how the entire family meets for dinner most Thursdays during the Season," his mother said. "I feel so fortunate to have everyone so close." She looked to Lady Gresham. "And every other Sunday, my grandchildren come over after church to spend the day. They're such a delight." Her gaze shot briefly to Delia on the settee. "And we are soon to have another."

"How many grandchildren do you have?" Lady Gresham asked.

"Seven. Delia has three already, as does Rachel. Imogen has but one so far, but I suspect there may be another soon." She arched her brows briefly and smiled.

Rachel pursed her lips. "Mama, you shouldn't speculate about such things. You don't want to curse anything."

"Nonsense. I'm not speculating. A mother knows things. Besides, Madame Sybila told me recently that there would soon be even more additions to our family. The cards never lie."

Rachel rolled her eyes, which Harry found amusing. "Let me understand, Rachel. You believe in curses, but not the forecast of a fortune-teller?" He laughed softly and had the strong impression Lady Gresham was doing her best not to smile.

"Oh, laugh all you please. I don't like to speculate about babies—too many things can go wrong."

"That is very true," Lady Gresham agreed. Once again, Harry wondered if she'd lost a child.

"Not wanting to discuss whether someone will increase is not at all related to fortune-telling."

Rachel turned her head to their mother. "You're still seeing Madame Sybila? I thought Papa forbade you."

Mother waved her hand and scoffed. "Your father doesn't *forbid* me to do anything. He strongly suggested I find another hobby, as he called it, but I enjoy seeing Madame Sybila. She's a lovely woman with a kind heart. Did you know she supports several charitable endeavors, such as the Magdalen Hospital?"

"Unless she showed you receipts for her donations or personally visited the hospital with you, I'm not sure I'd believe that," Rachel said wryly.

Harry hadn't realized his sister possessed such a cynical opinion on the matter. If she'd tried and hadn't been able to persuade their mother to give up the fortune-teller, he didn't think Lady Gresham could.

"I saw Madame Sybila just the other day," Lady Gresham said, clearly surprising his mother. "I also found her to be very kindhearted. In fact, I visited one of the charities she supports and was delighted to donate to their cause."

Looking very pleased, Harry's mother grinned at Lady Gresham. "Which one was that?"

"The Home for Wayward Children. A wonderful couple has taken in many children and are doing their best to provide a home and comfort so the children do not fall victim to the streets."

"Good for you for going to visit," Harry's mother said. "Perhaps we should coordinate an excursion to this home with Madame Sybila. Several of my friends see her and donate to her causes, and I know they'd love to contribute more." Enthusiasm gleamed in her tawny-brown eyes. "I'll speak to Madame Sybila when next I see her." She inclined her head to Lady Gresham. "You should do the same."

Lady Gresham looked briefly at Harry. "I'll do that."

Harry's father was going to be furious. But if this was a legitimate endeavor that was about to be further legitimized by a group of Society ladies, what could he do? It seemed Harry was going to have to talk to his father about this—but not tonight.

Turning his head, Harry smiled at his mother. "Perhaps I'll come along."

Mother's brow creased, and she blinked in surprise. "Will you?"

"Probably, to make sure it's not a fraud," Rachel said.

Harry slid a look toward Lady Gresham, who seemed to be taking care not to make eye contact with him. It would become apparent the moment he —and Lady Gresham—went to Winter's that they'd been before, because the Winters would surely say something about them having already paid a visit.

Which meant he ought to just admit it right now, but then he'd have to explain why he'd gone there. Not to mention his sister would take great delight in the fact that he'd gone with Lady Gresham.

No, he wasn't sharing that now, and maybe not ever. He'd talk to Lady Gresham about them both not joining this excursion. What a bloody tangle it was to keep secrets, especially in this family.

Rachel abruptly turned to Lady Gresham. "Excuse me, I've just remembered I wanted to tell Miss Whitford something."

"And I need to speak with Delia," Harry's mother said.

They both extricated themselves and went to the settee. Harry stared after them, nonplussed by their lack of subtlety.

"Your family is very…large," Lady Gresham noted.

He turned to her. "I thought you were going to say obvious."

She laughed softly, the light of amusement dancing in her eyes. "You seemed surprised when we arrived. The countess didn't tell you we'd been invited?"

"No."

"Would you not have come?"

His family probably thought so, and if they'd invited any other woman, he would not have. "My attendance would not have changed."

She just barely nodded, and the light from the chandelier above caught on the jeweled comb tucked into her honey-brown hair. "That's...nice."

Looking about, Harry saw his sisters pairing off with their husbands, while his father offered his arm to Miss Whitford. Mother left the library first, leading the procession, which meant Harry was to escort Lady Gresham. That was, of course, not an accident.

Resigning himself to his family's manipulations, he offered Lady Gresham his arm. "May I escort you to dinner?"

The barest smile flitted across her lips. "It seems you must."

Harry would be annoyed with his family's efforts if he didn't like Lady Gresham so much. And what did that say?

~

"*W*here might I find the retiring room?" Beatrix asked as the ladies gathered upstairs in the drawing room after dinner.

"Go on upstairs and turn to the right," Lady Aylesbury said. "Follow the short corridor, and my personal dressing chamber is just through the door on the left."

Well, that was too perfect. Selina gave Beatrix a stare that—she hoped—clearly conveyed *Don't steal anything else!*

With the barest inclination of her head, Beatrix departed the drawing room with Lady Aylesbury's emerald necklace tucked safely into a hidden pocket in her gown. Beatrix had continued to express remorse for stealing the jewelry, which always happened after she stole something. She promised she would work harder to rein her bad habit under control.

Besides, if she took something else, Selina wasn't certain she could garner another invitation to the Aylesburys' in order to return it. Selina had facilitated that by sending a thank-you for the invitation to the soiree, stating what a wonderful time they'd had, especially Beatrix. Selina had also noted how lovely it had been to be so welcomed by their family and that she and Beatrix looked forward to seeing them again soon.

The invitation to dinner tonight had arrived a few hours later.

As if Lady Aylesbury were a party to Selina's thoughts, she said, "I'm so pleased you and your sister could come tonight."

Selina took a vacant chair. "We were elated to be invited, thank you."

"Of course!" Lady Aylesbury glanced at her daughters, who sat lined up on a settee. "Lady Gresham sent the most charming missive complimenting our family." She looked back to Selina. "It's always good to hear that we haven't driven people away. We can be rather, ah, raucous."

"Harry and North can be raucous," Rachel said.

"We're far too refined for that." She winked at her sisters, who smiled in return.

Selina tried to imagine Mr. Sheffield as raucous and found she couldn't. "You're referring to when they were younger, I presume?"

Imogen laughed. "Goodness, no. They are incredibly competitive. You should come for card night sometime. It can get positively ruthless around the table." She waggled her red brows and grinned.

"Oh yes, you must come for that," Delia said, stroking her belly. "Before I have the babe."

Rachel patted her arm. "You've a few months yet. Plenty of time for Lady Gresham, and Miss Whitford, of course, to come for cards."

"We just need to make sure North will be here."

Selina had realized during dinner that North was the nickname the Aylesbury sisters called their eldest brother. That they'd mentioned him after Beatrix made Selina wonder if they were trying to match the two of them as they were clearly trying to do with her and Mr. Sheffield.

Selina considered how she might let them know that neither she nor Beatrix were interested in being paired off. However, before she could find the right words, Imogen spoke.

"Do you ride, Lady Gresham? Harry is an excellent horseman."

"No, I do not." Selina had never even owned a horse. She had, out of necessity, learned to drive about ten years before.

"What a shame," Delia said. "Do you have an aversion to it?"

"No. I just never learned." Selina tried not to lie when it wasn't necessary. That only complicated matters. She also endeavored not to offer information, just in case a lie *became* necessary. "I take it you all ride?"

"We do," Rachel said. "It's never too late to learn, you know. Perhaps Harry would give you a lesson."

Their efforts were shameless. It was almost enough to make Selina laugh. And she might have if not for the ever-present pull she felt toward Mr. Sheffield. Because of that, there was no humor but an apprehension of where that might lead. Not to horse riding—of that she was certain. "I don't think that's necessary."

"He'd be happy to teach you," Lady Aylesbury said enthusiastically.

"What about chess?" Rachel asked. "Do you play? Harry is quite accomplished at that."

"Rarely," Selina said. Sir Barnabus had taught her, but she hadn't had time to master the skill needed to win.

"When you come for card night, you can play with Harry," Imogen suggested as a maid entered with a tray of Madeira.

Selina gratefully took a glass and prayed Beatrix would return soon. Perhaps then they could divert the conversation from Mr. Sheffield and what he liked to do. After sipping her wine, Selina said, "It is my impression that Mr. Sheffield's favorite pastime is his work."

"Not necessarily," Lady Aylesbury began. Before she could continue, Rachel waved her hand.

"No need to make it seem otherwise, Mama. Lady Gresham's impression is dead accurate, as we all well know." Rachel winked at Selina.

Now Selina did smile. She was torn between enjoying Mr. Sheffield's family and succumbing to the urge to flee from their presence. She realized their closeness was incredibly unnerving. She didn't share that with anyone beyond Beatrix, and even then, as Beatrix had pointed out, Selina still kept some things to herself.

"What do you think of that?" Lady Aylesbury asked.

Selina wasn't entirely sure what the countess was getting at. "Of what?"

"Of Harry having an occupation. Some women, a great many, actually, find that bothersome."

That was their loss. A man who knew himself and possessed the drive to pursue what he wanted and help others in the process was a man worth admiring. "How unfortunate for them. I think it's commendable."

It was as if a firework had gone off in the room. The Aylesbury ladies all exchanged looks warmed with enthusiasm and hope. Selina felt heat rise in her face. She rarely bungled things that badly. Now they would be absolutely relentless.

"Are you all right, Lady Gresham?" Delia asked. "You look a bit warm."

"I am, actually. If you'll excuse me, I'll just step outside for some air." Selina knew precisely how to find her way to the back garden, since she'd accompanied Mr. Sheffield there on her last visit.

"Just through there." Lady Aylesbury gestured to the closed doors, and Selina realized the large drawing room had been opened into another room at the back of the house for the soiree to provide more space.

"Thank you." Selina went through the doors and continued on until she was outside on the terrace. From there, she went down the stairs to the garden, where she took a deep breath.

"Lady Gresham."

The familiar sound of Mr. Sheffield's voice caressing her name drew her to turn. He stood just under the stairs, his eyes gleaming in the light from the torch burning near the house.

"Mr. Sheffield." Selina had been looking for

respite, but she suddenly felt even more heated than she had upstairs. Her heart beat a fast rhythm as her blood rushed briefly through her ears.

He stepped out from beneath the stairs and walked toward her. He held his hat and gloves as if he were on his way out. "Is everything all right?"

She didn't hesitate to respond. "Yes, thank you."

His gaze found hers, and she felt the intensity of his stare deep in the pit of her belly. No, lower than that. "I must apologize," he said, his voice low and hypnotic, the resonance thrumming in Selina's chest. "For my family trying to match us."

She took a step toward him, leaving a bare foot between them. "I'm afraid I had to escape their machinations. They suggested you give me riding lessons or teach me to play chess."

A faint smile teased his lips. She loved that smile, for it was a combination of mirth, flirtation, and something unknown, something yet to be revealed.

"You don't know how to do either?"

"I play chess passably, but I have never learned to ride."

"I would be delighted to teach you." He grimaced. "Except my family will think they've succeeded in their efforts to pair us off. This is how I spend much of my time with them. If it wasn't you, it would be someone else."

"You've given riding lessons to other ladies? Or taught them chess?"

His gaze settled on hers with a smoldering intensity. "Not once."

A shiver raced down her spine. "Well then, that *would* be quite troublesome for you. Why don't you wish to marry?"

"I'm busy." He flicked a glance at the terrace above, scowled, then drew her back under the stairs from whence he'd come. "I am fairly certain I saw at least one of my sisters up there spying."

Selina looked up even though she wouldn't be able to see anything from here. "They're merciless." She kept her voice low in case they were trying to eavesdrop.

"Shameless too." He shook his head, but there was humor in it. "To answer your question, I don't want to marry just now. I suppose my family pushing me in that direction makes me want it even less. I'm contrary like that."

A smile split Selina's mouth unbidden. "I completely understand. I'm contrary too." She hated being told what to do—or what she *couldn't* do.

He stared at her a long moment. "Perhaps that's why I like you so much. That, and I needn't worry you are trying to ensnare me in the parson's trap because you don't want that either. You've already wed, and for whatever reason—which I would actually love to know—you don't seek to enter that state again."

The torchlight made his eyes glow and his dark lashes seem impossibly long. Selina felt a bit breathless and found the sensation wholly unnerving. But also intoxicating.

"No, I do not."

"Will you tell me why?" he whispered, close enough that she could feel his breath.

"I see no benefit in marriage."

He lifted his free hand and gently caressed her cheek with his bare knuckles. "None?"

Selina couldn't answer. She knew what he was referring to, but since she hadn't really ever been married, she couldn't say. And her one experience…well, that was nothing like this.

"I'm attracted to you, Lady Gresham."

"Selina," she breathed.

His knuckles moved against her jaw. "I'm attracted to you, Selina. If I *did* want to marry, you would be my first choice."

She couldn't see beyond him, couldn't hear anything but the beating of their hearts. She couldn't breathe. Nor did she want to, for it would surely devastate this moment.

You would also be mine.

The thought alarmed her. His hand moved back behind her ear, and he drew her toward him.

"Why?" she asked, captivated by his touch and his words.

"You're intelligent, independent, thoughtful, caring, fascinating, and I desperately want to know how your mouth feels beneath mine." Then his lips were against hers, soft and sure, restoring her breath if not her sanity.

He dragged his thumb gently along the base of her jaw and pulled back slightly to look into her eyes. He was so close, she could see the thin rims of gold edging his tawny irises.

"What does this mean?" she asked, still not completely regaining her breath.

"Whatever we want it to."

Selina couldn't quite make sense of anything. So she gave up trying. "Oh." She slipped her hands beneath his coat and slid her palms along his waist until she reached his back. Then she tipped her head to the side and kissed him.

The first kiss had been a question, a curiosity. This was an exploration, a search for...something. Selina had kissed several men, starting with Luther when they'd been little more than children.

But none of them had ever felt like this. Like something she'd never been able to attain—a sense of belonging, of rightness, of everything leading to this particular moment.

His lips brushed and moved across hers, teasing and enticing. Sensation built, and the connections grew longer until his mouth molded against hers, and he held her in his arms, one hand cupping her nape. Then his tongue slid along her lips, and she invited him inside.

Selina clutched at his back, her fingertips digging into his waistcoat. She kissed him back with what little skill she felt she possessed. He, however, was not remotely deficient. Desire—at least she thought it was desire, because she had nothing to compare this sensation to—streaked through her. It would be so easy to lose herself on this tide.

Selina brought her hands around him and slid them up his chest. Then she closed her lips against his, giving him one last kiss before she stepped back. Now he was breathless too—if the rapid rise and fall of his chest meant anything, and of course, it did.

"I need to get back upstairs," she said. "Beatrix will wonder where I've gone."

"I'm surprised she didn't accompany you. And glad." He bent to retrieve his hat and gloves, which he'd apparently tossed aside at some point. Selina had been completely unaware. "Forgive me for not escorting you back to the drawing room. I was just on my way to the mews."

"You're leaving?"

He cracked a small smile. "It seemed best given my family's behavior this evening, don't you think?"

She couldn't disagree. "Yes." His family thought they would make a good match, and if things were different, they actually might. But things weren't different. He was who he was, and she was...not worthy.

The sensation of not being able to breathe returned, but for a wholly different reason. Selina fought to calm herself before he noticed her agitation. "Well, good evening, then." She pivoted and went back to the stairs leading up to the terrace.

She didn't look down until she reached the top. He'd made his way to the gate that presumably led to the mews. He hadn't left, though. She could make him out in the shadows standing there. Looking up at her.

Turning swiftly, she went into the house, her hand shaking as she opened the door. Once inside, she finally drew a deep breath.

That couldn't ever happen again. It was one thing to keep him—her enemy—close. It was quite another to let down her guard and invite him into her life.

That she must never do.

CHAPTER 9

*E*very time Harry closed his eyes, he smelled
Selina's fragrance—orange and honeysuckle—
and he tasted her lips, more succulent than any fruit.
He opened his eyes and took another drink of ale. He'd
been walking around all day like an enamored fool.

"Sheff!" Remy called out as he and Dearborn
made their way to Harry's table in the Brown Bear.

The two constables sat down, and almost immediately, the serving maid brought them tankards. She
also brought a fresh one for Harry and scooped his
nearly empty one away.

"Haven't seen you in a few days," Dearborn said as
he lifted his tankard.

"He's probably been spending all his time around
St. Dunstan-in-the-West," Remy said. "Or investigating his fortune-teller."

"Not *all* my time. And she's not *my* fortune-teller."
Harry snorted before taking a drink of the fresh ale.
He set his tankard down and looked to Remy. "As you
said, the Vicar's being as elusive as ever. I don't expect to find him there. I've decided to go back to Saffron Hill to investigate the fire and ask about the
Vicar. Maybe a new clue will allow me to find him."

Remy narrowed his eyes slightly for a brief moment. "Don't get too caught in the past." He knew that Harry had begun to care for one of the young women who'd died.

"I'm not."

Remy gave Harry a look that clearly said he thought that was twaddle, but he wasn't going to pursue the issue in front of Dearborn. "Do you want help?"

"I'd be glad to help too," Dearborn offered, seemingly oblivious to what Harry and Remy weren't saying. Or perhaps he was ignoring it on purpose as a matter of deference.

"Thank you," Harry said, relaxing somewhat. "I appreciate that." He took another drink, then set his tankard down with a light clack. "I must be off."

"Where to?" Remy asked.

"Things to do." Harry wouldn't tell them he was going to The Strand to check in on Madame Sybila. Not after the comment Remy had made.

With a nod, Harry turned and left. His walk to The Ardent Rose was brisk, and not just because a light rain had started to fall. He'd decided it was time to speak with Madame Sybila again, and he was eager to do so.

Or perhaps he was eager to get to the errand he planned afterward.

Harry went into the shop just as the rain began to pick up. Instead of the gentleman greeting him as he'd done last time, the woman who'd also been working on his first visit approached him.

"Good afternoon," she said, her brow creasing gently. "You've been in here before, yes?"

"I have. To see Madame Sybila. I'd like to do so again, please."

"She is busy, I'm afraid."

Harry offered a benign smile. "I'll wait until she's finished."

The shopkeeper, an attractive woman of perhaps sixty with bold features, held his gaze. "I believe she will be busy the rest of the day."

"I require only a few minutes of her time. Perhaps you could tell her I will compensate her handsomely. And you, if that would help." He pivoted toward a display of perfume. "I'll just take a look around while you go and speak with her." Harry took himself off before she could refuse him.

He went to a table where scents were arranged. Picking up a bottle labeled rosy peach, he held it near his nose and inhaled. The woman hesitated, watching him a moment, before finally turning and going back through the curtain to Madame Sybila's closet.

Wrinkling his nose, Harry set the bottle back down. Moving from bottle to bottle, he sampled them all, not liking a one, until he reached the last. The scent was familiar and more than a bit disarming.

Selina.

He looked at the label—fruit and floral. He smelled it again, wondering if he had it right. Yes, that was her.

Had she purchased it here? She must have. The other day, she'd had a package when they'd met. Harry didn't like that another woman could purchase *her* scent. Frowning, he set it back down. He was now in even more of a hurry for his next errand.

The shopkeeper came toward him. "Madame Sybila is just finishing with her client and said you may speak with her for five minutes." The woman didn't look as if she approved. Harry wondered why.

"You seem protective of Madame Sybila. Is she a friend of yours?" Harry could perhaps find out the true identity of the heavily veiled fortune-teller, or at least where she lived.

"We have a business arrangement," the shop-keeper said rather tersely, as if she didn't want to be linked to the fortune-teller in that way. But if Madame Sybila bothered her, why let her use the back of the perfumery?

"What sort of business arrangement?" Harry began to speculate that there was a reason for this association beyond financial. When the shopkeeper's brows drew together and her lips pressed into an irritated line, he added, "I'm Mr. Sheffield, and I work for Bow Street."

The woman's dark eyes flashed with surprise. Her features relaxed from annoyance into wariness. "She pays rent on her space, and my husband and I help with the people who come to see her."

"Do you help keep the gentlemen away?" Harry asked this given her behavior and despite the fact that her husband had taken Harry to see the fortune-teller on his last visit. Perhaps that incident had prompted Madame Sybila to ask the proprietors to decline gentlemen access.

One of her silver brows arched. "You, sir, are the only gentleman who has come to see her."

A woman bustled through the curtain from the back corner into the shop. Harry recognized her immediately. Just as she did him.

"Mr. Sheffield?" She was another of his mother's friends. Harry had known her for years.

"Good afternoon, Mrs. Mapleton-Lowther."

Her eyes sparkled as she glanced about the shop before settling on him. "I wonder whom you might be buying perfume for." She smiled expectantly, as if she'd asked a question she wanted him to answer.

"Just browsing," he said with the same mild smile he'd given the shopkeeper earlier.

"I shall have to tell your mother I saw you here." Of course she would. Dammit. He couldn't say he was here to see Madame Sybila, so the assumption was that he was here buying perfume. For whom? None of his sisters, nor his mother, had a birthday coming up soon. *Hell and the devil.*

"I shall do the same," Harry said, cursing his luck. This would only add fuel to the fire of his family's matchmaking endeavors. Rachel in particular would nag him incessantly about why he was here. "Good to see you, Mrs. Mapleton-Lowther."

"And you, Mr. Sheffield." She smiled again, then left the shop, standing just outside the door as her groom approached, carrying an umbrella.

Harry turned to the shopkeeper. "Mrs.?"

"Kinnon," she provided.

"Mrs. Kinnon, I assume you sell fragrances for gentlemen?"

"We do."

"Will you package a bottle for me, and I will purchase it before I go?" Harry didn't want to miss any of his five minutes with Madame Sybila.

"Certainly. What scent do you prefer?"

He hadn't the faintest bloody idea, nor did he care. "I trust you to select something appropriate. Better yet, make it soap."

Her silver brow arched again. "You can find your way to Madame Sybila?"

"Yes, thank you." Moving swiftly, Harry took himself behind the curtain and saw that the fortune-teller's door was ajar. He rapped his knuckles on the wood before pushing it wider.

"Come in," Madame Sybila said in her warm French accent.

Harry stepped inside and saw that she was still seated at her table. She finished shuffling the cards and set them to one side.

"You've returned," she said. "I have only a few minutes to spare as I am expecting another client shortly. How can I help you today, Mr. Sheffield?"

"You still won't read for me, I presume?"

She hesitated the barest moment, and Harry wondered if she would. More than that, he wondered if he wanted her to. He found himself wanting to ask if there was anything between him and Lady Gresham to which he could look forward.

Preposterous.

"No," she said, effectively shutting down his folly, thank goodness.

Harry exhaled. Why had he even asked? Because if she'd said yes, he would have done it—not because he believed she'd tell him anything of value or import, but in the hope of learning something about her and the "services" she provided. Yes, that was the *only* reason.

"I had to ask." He looked around her small room. Besides a round table with two chairs, one of which she occupied, there was a narrow dresser in the corner. A high, rectangular window was cloaked with a white, mostly opaque drape. Candles burned on the dresser and on the table. A dark curtain hung against the back wall. The atmosphere carried a hint of mystery and serenity. Why serenity? He attributed it to the scent in the room—a fresh, outdoor smell. He looked toward the dresser again and realized in addition to the two candles, incense was burning.

"Did you just come to look?" she asked, reminding him that his time was short.

He cleared his throat and fixed on her dark veil, wishing he could see beneath the covering. "No. I came to say I think I may have been wrong about you, Madame Sybila. I visited Mr. Winter's home— the charity you have been encouraging others to support."

He stepped closer to the table and pulled the chair back. He hadn't meant to sit since she was only giving him a few minutes, but he found he couldn't resist being on her level. Sometimes that encouraged people to relax rather than see him as an authority figure, and when they relaxed, they were inclined to be more forthcoming. He lowered himself to the chair.

"You heard of Mr. Winter's home?"

He imagined she was staring at him. What did she think of him learning this information and ensuring it was true? He hated that bloody veil that hid so much from him. "I did. It was exactly as described to me—a home for wayward children, some of whom I met."

"And were you impressed, Mr. Sheffield?" she sounded as if she genuinely wanted to know.

"I was...satisfied." Impressed was not the word. Because he still wasn't entirely certain he believed it. Perhaps after his mother visited, he would feel differently. That would be quite an endeavor to set up such an elaborate fraud. Madame Sybila needed people to accomplish such a feat—and funds to pay them, probably. Or perhaps she had a network of supporters. Criminals often worked together if it benefited them to do so. Which took him back to funds. How profitable was fortune-telling?

"Well, that is something," she said, and he heard a hint of amusement in her tone.

"How did you come to support Mr. Winter's home?"

She folded her hands in her lap. "Before I moved here to The Ardent Rose, I had a room near Cornhill. Mrs. Winter came to see me. She can't have children and hoped I could help her."

"With one of your tonics, maybe?" Harry was glad for the opportunity to ask about them.

"No," she said coolly. "I don't offer such things. She wanted to know if the future held children for her. The cards said yes, and I suggested she help some of the lost children in the neighborhood."

"Lost children?"

"Those without parents or a means to support themselves. Those who, without love and kindness, would be forced along a path that could end prematurely. As a lost child myself, I understand their plight and do what I can to help."

A lost child who now told fortunes. Perhaps because she had no other way in life. It was certainly better than the choices many girls were forced to make if they had no family and no means. Harry couldn't help but think of Mercy. Yes, he could understand the fortune-teller's desire to provide support. If they were, in fact, doing as they purported. Which it seemed they were.

Still, Harry would investigate every piece, just as he'd told Selina he would. "Where was your room near Cornhill?"

"Finch Lane, but if your plan is to go and find my landlord, he'll pretend I never lived there. When he found out what I do, he insisted I leave."

That was bloody convenient. Harry would still poke around the neighborhood and see what he could learn. "Surely you realize your profession is questionable."

"Your repeated presence here supports that, yes." She sounded beleaguered.

"Forgive me, Madame Sybila, but in my experience, women like you are frauds at best and criminals at worst. I'm trying to determine which one you are."

"There is no room in your estimation for an honest woman simply trying to make her way? Or is prostitution the only acceptable choice for lost children like me?"

He heard the edge of a taunt in her voice and gritted his teeth. "Of course it isn't. If Mr. Winter is what he purports to be and you are earnestly supporting him, I would be delighted. But I will make sure that's what is happening." He leaned forward and could have sworn he smelled that orange-honeysuckle scent again, but it had to have lingered with him from before. Because Selina was ever present in his mind, even when he was bloody working.

Refocusing, he tried to see through the thick black veil, but couldn't. "If I find you are fleecing my mother or her friends, such as Mrs. Mapleton-Lowther, I'll make sure you're prosecuted and imprisoned."

"I happen to like your mother—and her friends. Your mother is particularly devoted to your happiness. I hope you realize and appreciate that. Family should never be taken for granted." Her words carved into him. Did he do that? She continued, "I provide a service to them that they desire. It is not harmful. On the contrary, I think it helps them in some way, and I am glad to do so."

Harry sat back in the chair, frustration roiling inside him. "Helps them how?"

"You'd have to ask them, and you should. Perhaps then you'll understand." Now she leaned forward, and he had the sense she was as agitated as he was. "And stop meddling in their affairs."

Meddling? He stood. It was time for authority. "I'm conducting an investigation, Madame Sybila, and I would appreciate your full cooperation. Where do you live now?"

She tipped her head back to look up at him. "I don't think I need to tell you that," she said softly. "For my personal safety, you understand."

She was afraid of him? He didn't believe that for a moment. For some reason, he believed Madame

Sybila was quite capable of taking care of herself. She'd survived this long. How long was that exactly? "How old are you, Madame Sybila?"

"Old enough to know I won't be intimidated by you, Mr. Sheffield." She picked up the cards and turned three over in quick succession. She gestured to the first one "The Hermit—this is you. It means you are contemplative and you seek truth, excellent traits for a man of investigation. However, this card is reversed." It was upside-down from his perspective, while the other two cards were not. "So instead, this means you are lonely, isolated." She looked up at him.

His entire body had tensed when she'd turned the cards over. He wanted to argue that wasn't true, but he couldn't. Because it was, at least partly.

"This card is me." She lightly touched the one in the center. "The Queen of Swords represents perception and a clear mind." Harry bit back a retort. She could tell him these cards meant anything she wanted him to think. How would he know?

"And this card, the Five of Wands, is conflict." She pushed it to the center of the table. "This is us. Shall I turn over a fourth card to see how this resolves?"

"No, thank you. Things will resolve exactly as they must—with the truth." From the position of her head, he believed she was staring at him, just as he was at her. "One day, I'd like to see you without your veil."

"That will never happen, Mr. Sheffield."

Her arrogance frustrated him. He gripped the back of the chair and pushed it into the table. Their five minutes had passed some time ago. "Until next time, Madame Sybila."

"Until then, Mr. Sheffield." She picked up two of the cards, but left the Hermit. "Maybe then you will have stepped outside yourself, and I will draw a different card."

Harry spun on his heel and left without a word. He was not a goddamned hermit.

"Mr. Sheffield?" Mrs. Kinnon startled him as he headed toward the door.

Hell, he'd forgotten about the perfume. And paying Madame Sybila for her time. He went to the counter and made the transaction for the perfume, then gave extra money to Mrs. Kinnon. "Give this to the fortune-teller."

Tucking the small package into his pocket, Harry turned and strode out into the gray day. The rain had stopped, but he would catch a hack anyway.

Now, he could go where he truly wanted. But given the interview he'd just had, he wasn't sure he should, not in his agitated state.

The fortune-teller was wrong. He'd already stepped outside himself. He wasn't isolated. And he'd bloody well prove it.

~

After paying the hack driver, Harry contemplated the house before him. Situated on Queen Anne Street, not far from the intersection with Portland Street, the residence was narrow, with three stories above ground. Small but neat, with three steps leading up to the front door, it was unassuming. Perhaps less than what one might expect of a baronet's widow. Rachel had informed Harry that Selina's deceased husband had been Sir Barnabus Gresham from some small town in northern England.

The distance from London invited many questions. Was she originally from there? Her accent didn't support that. So where was she from, then?

And how had she found herself in northern England, married to a baronet?

Harry wanted to know the answers to all that and so much more. Frustration from his appointment with Madame Sybila still rattled through him. He strove to push it away as he walked to the front door and rapped loudly on the wood.

After a long moment, a tall, thin woman with blonde hair and pale blue eyes that made him shiver answered the door. Harry couldn't quite discern her age—older than him, but not old enough to be his mother.

He gave her the best smile he could muster, considering his earlier agitation. "Good afternoon. I'm here to see Lady Gresham."

"She's not here." The woman started to close the door, but Harry put his hand on the wood.

"Do you know when she'll return?"

"Mrs. Vining, who's there?" a voice called from inside, which Harry recognized as belonging to Miss Whitford.

"It's Harry Sheffield," he called past the woman, who was perhaps the housekeeper. Did they not have a butler?

Miss Whitford appeared behind the tall, thin woman. "Let him in, Mrs. Vining." She gave Harry a welcoming smile. "Selina isn't here, but she should be home soon if you'd care to wait."

"I would, thank you."

Harry stepped into the small entry hall and took off his hat. The housekeeper gave him a bland stare, and Harry wondered if she was perhaps new to the position. Given the size of the house, he supposed a butler wasn't necessary. However, this housekeeper didn't seem to be up to the task either. At least she didn't exhibit the manner one might expect. Another thought occurred to Harry—what if a housekeeper who was somewhat lacking was all Lady Gresham could afford?

"Mrs. Vining, please bring refreshments to the sitting room." Miss Whitford looked to Harry before turning and walking past the narrow staircase to a room at the back of the house. He knew to follow.

The sitting room, like the rest of the house, was small. The furnishings were tidy but not extravagant, and there was little in the way of décor—a mirror over the fireplace and a wooden box with a carved lid that sat on the mantelpiece.

Miss Whitford sat in a simple chair with a deep-green-cushioned seat. "Will you sit, Mr. Sheffield?" She indicated the settee.

Harry situated himself, setting his hat down beside him, and a bare moment later, Mrs. Vining entered with a tray. She set it on a table next to Miss Whitford's chair. There were three glasses of some liquid and a plate of biscuits. He removed his gloves in anticipation of partaking and put them atop his hat.

"Thank you, Mrs. Vining, that will be all." Miss Whitford picked up one of the glasses and handed it to Harry. "Lemonade?"

He didn't particularly want any, but he also didn't wish to be rude. "Thank you." He took the glass and held on to it. "Where is Lady Gresham?"

"She had an errand to run, but I expect her back shortly." Picking up a biscuit, Miss Whitford took a nibble as she contemplated Harry. Harry sipped his lemonade and nearly spit it out. It was the worst lemonade he'd ever tasted.

"What brings you here, Mr. Sheffield? I wasn't aware you knew where we lived. But I suppose you would since your parents know our direction."

"Just so," he said, transferring the lemonade to his other hand when he really wanted to toss it into the hearth. "I came to invite Lady Gresham—and you, of course—to Spring Hollow. It's a pleasure garden in Clerkenwell."

"Why are you inviting her? And when? I mean, will we go in the afternoon or in the evening?"

"I thought the evening so we could see the fireworks. And I'm inviting both of you. Because I'd like to help you see London."

Miss Whitford narrowed her eyes slightly, and they took on a sheen of steel, making her look older than Harry had thought her to be. "You came to invite Selina and are including me because you must. I am not a fool, Mr. Sheffield. You like my sister."

Hell, if his family was frightening in their desire to match Harry, Selina's was equally so in her desire to… investigate. Harry knew that when he saw it. But was she hoping for a match as his sisters were?

"I do," he said cautiously. "I also like you."

"It would probably be better if one of your sisters and her husband came along—for appearances. Perhaps Rachel and her husband wouldn't mind joining us?"

Bloody hell. If Rachel came along, her efforts to push Harry and Selina together would be doubled. At least. And Harry didn't need her. He wanted Selina.

On the other hand, if Rachel and Nathaniel were to come, Harry could find himself alone with Selina —they could chaperone Miss Whitford. Which meant…

Harry looked sharply at Miss Whitford. "It seems Lady Gresham's family is as keen to play matchmaker as mine." He laughed softly and nearly took another sip of lemonade before recalling it tasted like the Thames.

The steel returned to Miss Whitford's gaze along with a chill. "My sister isn't looking for a match, and I certainly wouldn't presume to know her mind better than she. You would do well to remember that, Mr. Sheffield." She finished her biscuit while continuing to pin him with her unsettling stare.

Harry received her message clearly—not only was Selina not interested in marriage, her sister would defend her in whatever way necessary. He inclined his head and reached for a biscuit, then thought better of it, returning his hand to his side.

Footsteps drew Harry to turn his head toward the doorway. Selina stepped inside, a vision of smart loveliness in a bold yellow walking dress trimmed in black and red.

Harry got to his feet, setting the lemonade back on the tray with no intention to retrieve it. "Good afternoon, Lady Gresham."

"Mr. Sheffield, what a surprise to see you here." She came farther into the room and glanced toward her sister, who rose from her seat.

"He came to invite us to Spring Hollow," Miss Whitford said. "I'll leave you to settle the details." She gave Harry a charming smile that was completely at odds with the brusque young woman he'd just glimpsed. So much so that he wondered if he'd imagined her earlier coolness.

After she was gone, Selina moved toward the window. She turned to face him. "Spring Hollow? This is a purely social invitation?" She sounded a bit surprised—and perhaps flattered.

Harry told her the truth. "Not purely, but I need to pay a visit to Spring Hollow. Since you've offered to help with my investigation regarding the Vicar, I thought you would want to come along," he said.

She took a step toward him. "Why do you need to go there?"

"An informer has asked to meet me there. He has information about the fire."

"Indeed? That's wonderful."

He could see her enthusiasm and suppressed a smile. "Don't feel too encouraged. Most information I receive is useless, but I shall hope this will be one time it is not."

She clasped her hands in front of her. "How can I help?"

"I'm not sure. If nothing else, I just thought it would be nice to escort you—and Miss Whitford. I've heard it's the nicest garden in Clerkenwell, that it's been recently refurbished. There's a new building with supper boxes and an orchestra. Fireworks too."

"It sounds lovely. Thank you for the invitation."

"Your sister suggested I invite Rachel and her husband to come along with us. For appearances."

She gave him an arch look. "Do you have something planned?"

Harry walked slowly toward her. A dark heat sparked in her eyes that fueled his sudden desire. "Nothing specific. Perhaps we can strategize my investigation into the fire. I plan to conduct some interviews with witnesses and neighbors." He stopped before he touched her, but only barely.

"That seems an excellent notion. Your commitment to solving this is commendable," she added softly.

Was she pressing him or was his conscience doing so? He'd studied the law and moved to become a constable because he believed in truth and justice. And perhaps he had been blinded by emotion four years ago—and ever since.

"I lost someone in that fire," he whispered.

Surprised flickered in the depths of her eyes. "Did you?" A moment passed before she said, "You won't find them now."

The frustration from earlier with Madame Sybila mixed with the old sensation of loss and anger. He *had* been a hermit. "I'm not looking for her."

Harry's body thrummed with the need to touch her. He lifted his hand to caress her cheek, but she tipped her head to the side, a spark flashing in her eyes.

"What *are* you looking for, Mr. Sheffield?"

"You."

She took his hand—the one that remained at his side—entwining her fingers through his. Straightening, she closed the bare distance between them and pressed her lips to his.

He put his hand on her then, cupping her neck as he claimed her mouth. He *was* looking for her. He wanted her. Desperately. As the bloody fortune-teller's words echoed in his mind, he clasped Selina to him and pushed the barriers around him away.

Selina's hand curled around his neck, her fingers digging into his nape, as she kissed him back. Or he kissed her back—she'd started this.

Had she? He didn't know. There didn't seem to be a beginning. There would, however, be an end.

Harry pulled away, his breath coming fast.

"I'd be delighted to assist you in your investigation, Mr. Sheffield," she said somewhat huskily. "My 'associate' skills are at your disposal."

He stepped back. "I'm pleased to hear it. I'll fetch you tomorrow evening to go to Spring Hollow."

"I'll look forward to it."

He began to pivot toward the door, but stopped. Turning his head, he said, "Call me Harry. At least when we're alone."

"Harry?" His name from her lips was an aphrodisiac. He was sorely tempted to take her in his arms again.

"Yes?"

"I wonder if I might trouble you with something. The flue—" She glanced toward the fireplace. "It's stuck, and we can't light a fire."

"Allow me." He removed his coat and laid it over the back of the settee. Her gaze moved over him appreciatively. He strove to ignore it lest he decide to kiss her again.

He went to the fireplace and knelt on the hearth.

"It's on the right," she said helpfully.

He reached in and found the lever. Gripping the mechanism, he pulled hard, but it didn't budge. Exhaling, he redoubled his efforts, and at last, it moved. Soot and ash fell, coating his hand and arm. "Got it." He leaned back and stood.

"Thank you." She looked at his blackened hand. "Goodness, you're covered in soot."

"To be expected."

"Let me get you something to clean up." She departed the sitting room, but came back rather quickly. "I should have sent for water and toweling before. My apologies."

"It's fine, Selina." He laughed softly at her fussing. "You must have been a very good wife."

Pink stained her cheeks, and she abruptly turned and left, making him wonder if he'd said something wrong. Perhaps she still missed her husband.

She returned a few minutes later with a cloth and a bowl of water. She handed him the former and set down the latter on the table near the window. He joined her there and dipped his hand into the water.

"Thank you." He glanced over at her as he cleaned the soot away. "Did I say something wrong?"

"Not at all."

"It's all right if you miss your husband."

She shook her head. "That's not it. I—I don't really know. This is rather domestic." The pink returned to her cheeks, but lighter this time.

He could see what she meant. He could easily envision him performing this sort of task for her if they shared a home. If they were married.

And he didn't dislike the notion at all. He suddenly understood her discomfort. This was not what they wanted—according to both of them. Despite that, they were both affected.

Harry dried his hand and did his best to wipe the soot from his sleeve. He set the towel in the basin when he finished. "Thank you."

She gave him a soft smile. "Thank *you*."

"I'm happy to perform any task you require." He fixed his gaze on her. "*Any* task."

"That is good to know."

Heat and longing seemed to gather between them. If he stayed another moment, he wasn't sure what might happen. Best to hasten his departure. "I'll see you tomorrow."

Harry picked up his hat and gloves on his way out. It was time to banish the hermit.

CHAPTER 10

*Y*ou *must have been a very good wife.*

Harry's words rang in her ears long after he departed. Just as his kiss was still imprinted on her lips.

Harry. She could hardly think of him as Mr. Sheffield after the way they'd kissed.

She went to pick up the basin and towel. Looking at the objects he'd used to clean up and thinking of his assistance eliminated an invisible barrier—or so it seemed to her. She brought the towel and brought it to her face, inhaling the barest fragrance of his masculine scent.

"What are you doing?"

Dropping the towel into the basin, Selina spun around to see Beatrix standing just inside the doorway. "Tidying up after Mr. Sheffield. He unstuck the flue."

Beatrix went to the fireplace. "Wonderful! How helpful of him."

Indeed. The entire episode had shown Selina a future she couldn't quite comprehend: a happy domesticity that didn't seem at all right for a woman who'd once been a thief in London's East End. And who continued to commit criminal acts, even if she had begun to completely loathe them.

"Yes, he was pleased to provide assistance," Selina said.

"Is that all he provided?"

"I'm not sure what you're hinting at, but yes. Would you do me a favor and take this to the kitchen?" Selina handed her the basin with the towel and hoped Beatrix would forget about whatever she was hoping to discover.

"Certainly." Beatrix took the items and left the sitting room.

Selina exhaled with relief. She couldn't tell her about the kiss, not when it had been incredibly foolish considering how committed Harry was to uncovering the truth about Madame Sybila's activities. His visit to the perfumery earlier had shown her just how much. It seemed all the tension—his irritation with the fortune-teller and her frustration at being trapped in a cage of her own making—that had built during their interview in Madame Sybila's closet could no longer be contained. Or perhaps that was only how it felt to her. Most likely, since he had no idea she was Madame Sybila.

His appearance at The Ardent Rose had surprised her, at least a little. She'd expected him to return at some point, but not this soon. His anger and frustration with her—with Madame Sybila—had been palpable. He hated that he'd been foiled or that his assumptions had been wrong.

Only they weren't. She was every bit the fraud he thought her to be. There was no charity. And she'd stacked those three bloody cards before he'd come in, with the intention of drawing them in just that way if the conversation had turned contentious.

And it had.

Though it could be so much worse. He'd asked to

see her without the veil. She nearly cracked a smile in the mirror. But it wasn't amusing. If he ever found out she was Madame Sybila, she wasn't sure what he would do.

The agitation she felt intensified. Because he *would* find out. He would continue his investigation until he saw beneath the veil. He was still focused on a four-year-old fire, for heaven's sake!

The revelation that he'd lost someone—a woman —had surprised her completely. That explained his inability to let it go, his determination to bring the Vicar, whom he had been certain was guilty, to justice, and maybe it also explained his solitary life. She'd hit a nerve with the Hermit card, more than she'd anticipated.

She needed a new plan. She couldn't continue as Madame Sybila, not with Harry's methods of investigation. He'd probably visit Finch Lane tomorrow, if he hadn't already, and while Selina had taken precautions, she couldn't afford to pay everyone to do her bidding. Plus, Harry was damned good at what he did.

Furthermore, she *hated* lying to him.

She had to find another way to earn money so they could make it through the Season.

Beatrix swept back into the sitting room. "You haven't moved an inch. What's the matter?"

"Just thinking." Selina waved her hand and went to sit on the settee.

Beatrix joined her there. "Dinner smells atrocious."

Selina winced. "I'm sure it won't be that bad."

"You're an expert liar, but even you can't believe that," Beatrix said on a laugh. "Can't we afford someone better?"

"It isn't that," Selina said. "We need people we can

trust, and Mrs. Vining and Martha are friends of Mrs. Kinnon. Also, no, we can't."

Beatrix frowned at the fireplace. "We don't need a ladies' maid. We've been taking care of each other for years. Forever, really."

"I know, but we pay them very little, and their presence gives us credibility. Besides, not everything is inedible."

Beatrix narrowed her eyes. "Mrs. Vining doesn't make the cheese."

Selina laughed. She was shocked that she had that in her at this particular moment. Beatrix smiled in return.

Turning so she could look at Beatrix, Selina took a deep breath. "What is the plan when you reveal yourself to your father?"

"He'll be overjoyed to have me back in his life, of course, and will provide me with an allowance, upon which we can comfortably live." They both knew that might not happen. "If he doesn't acknowledge me, even privately, I'll rob him blind," Beatrix said, addressing the unspoken. "Either way, we'll be secure."

Selina nearly laughed again. "I've no doubt you could do exactly that." Standing, she smoothed the gauze overlay of her gown. "We need a new plan. I can't continue as Madame Sybila much longer. Harry —Sheffield—is relentless."

Understanding bloomed in Beatrix's face. "'Harry'? You kissed him, didn't you? That's why you're acting funny."

"That hardly matters." Selina wasn't entirely sure why she didn't just confirm what Beatrix had guessed, but surmised it was because of the unsettling emotions she felt toward him. She was normally quite good at keeping such things buried. That she couldn't seem to do that with Harry was beyond troublesome.

Selina continued. "As I was saying, I can't continue as Madame Sybila. I could go back to the East End and change my disguise and name, but we won't earn enough to support your Season."

Beatrix fixed her with a steady stare. "We have other options. If you'll let me."

"Trix, if you get caught—"

"I won't."

"You were once."

Beatrix scowled. "And it worked out fine. Someday, you'll stop bringing that up. I hope." She relaxed her features. "I won't get caught. Will you let me do this? It's my bloody Season anyway. I should pay for it."

Selina wanted to say no. She wanted them to stop all of it entirely. Unfortunately, that was impossible. "Stick to jewelry only. That's easiest to fence and garners the most money."

"What about actual money?"

Selina half smiled. "I will never say no to that. That's the simplest to make use of."

"I can start tonight," Beatrix, said, referring to the rout they planned to attend.

"Don't take any unnecessary risks." Selina hated asking her to take any risk at all, particularly since she hoped to make a life in London.

"Meaning, don't pick pockets. Don't worry, I'll steal from the house." Beatrix gave her a reassuring nod. "Now, what about Harry?"

"Don't pester me about him." Selina scrunched up her forehead. "There's nothing between us. I'm merely keeping him close."

"I meant, what are you going to do to keep him at bay. I should have been more specific."

Selina resisted the urge to roll her eyes at Beatrix's droll tone. "At Lady Aylesbury's next meeting with Madame Sybila, the countess will suggest a visit to the Home for Wayward Children. Madame Sybila will agree, and hopefully, that will be the end of Sheffield's investigation. If it is not, then Madame Sybila will be called away to care for a sick family member." This was the manner in which Selina's various fortune-teller identities left their situations.

"That sounds reasonable," Beatrix said. "You still want me to move forward with our alternative plan tonight?"

An uneasiness crept over Selina, but she shrugged it away. "I think we must."

A familiar gleam sparked in Beatrix's eyes. She couldn't help stealing things, so when she was able to do so on purpose, she felt...right. Selina hated asking her to do it. Surely it was better if she didn't, and not just because of the risk.

She was being foolish. This was how they'd survived the last twelve years—swindling and stealing, doing whatever was required to ensure their safety and independence. That Selina had grown to find it distasteful didn't change the necessity of it. She shook off the sensation of feeling trapped.

"You could indulge," Beatrix said cautiously. "You deserve something—someone—diverting."

In Selina's estimation, people rarely got what they deserved.

~

*A*fter fetching Selina and her sister the following evening, Harry had been forced to ride to Spring Hollow on top of the coach with the coachman due to space. Harry jumped down upon their arrival and paid the entrance fee to the gardens for their entire party. When he finished, everyone had already departed the coach.

"Well, it's not Vauxhall, but it's still exciting," Miss

Whitford said with a smile as they approached the gate.

"Consider it a prelude to Vauxhall," Rachel said. She had been delighted to come along this evening. Nathaniel seemed less enthused, but then this wasn't the type of entertainment he typically enjoyed. He preferred a healthy debate over a good port. Nevertheless, he would do anything to please his wife, whom he adored.

All of Harry's sisters had married well, finding love and even partnership. In some ways, that contributed to Harry's reluctance to wed. He wouldn't settle for less than that. Of course, his family would argue that he never gave anyone a chance to see if such a union was even possible. But maybe that would change. His gaze fell on Selina.

Her golden-brown hair was styled impeccably, with saucy curls framing her face. The elegant line of her jaw and high cheekbones seemed even more pronounced tonight, setting her apart from every other woman he'd known. Dressed in a light-blue evening gown trimmed in black with a silvery gauze overskirt, she looked almost ethereal, like something from a dream that he couldn't actually touch. But he *could* touch her. He had touched her. And he intended to touch her again.

Harry moved to offer her and Miss Whitford his arms. "May I escort you both inside?"

"Yes, please," Miss Whitford answered, sliding her hand around his arm.

Selina didn't respond, but her eyes met his, and he saw an intensity that must surely be a reflection of what he was feeling. And what was that? Anticipation. Excitement. Desire.

They entered through the wide gate and followed the path to the main area were people milled about. The newly constructed supper boxes were on the left side and stood two stories. On the opposite side of the large open cobbled space was the covered orchestra. Music filled the air, and the dance floor—a clearly marked space near the orchestra—was more than half full.

Gaslights illuminated the entire area, but a handful of pathways led away from the main space into the gardens. Nathaniel instantly saw someone he knew and struck up a conversation. After exchanging pleasantries and introducing everyone, Rachel turned her attention to Miss Whitford. "Shall we investigate the refreshment area?" She tossed a glance toward Harry and then to Selina, making her intention clear. She had one goal this evening: to further the connection between Harry and Selina.

For once, Harry couldn't fault her. He wanted the same thing, though not the same end result Rachel probably hoped for.

Miss Whitford's face lit with enthusiasm. "Yes, let's." She linked arms with Rachel, and they left.

Harry turned his head to Selina. "Shall we promenade?"

"That seems to be what everyone wants." She flashed him a smile. "More importantly, however, where are you to meet your informer?"

"I'm not entirely sure. He said to meet him at the bridge at nine o'clock." Harry checked his pocket watch. "Let us find that."

He asked a footman for directions, and they took the indicated path past ponds fed by the spring. The lighting was less here, providing a darker, seductive atmosphere.

"I apologize for my sister's managing behavior," he said. "As you know by now, it is my family's fondest wish that I wed."

"It's quite nice that you have a family who wants the best for you."

"Is marriage really the best, however? I thought our opinions on the matter were aligned."

"They are, but I can still understand why they are trying to see you wed. They think it will bring you happiness because it has for them." She gave him a sympathetic look. "I can also understand how frustrating it must be for you sometimes."

"You said it seemed to be what everyone wants. Does that include your sister?" Because Harry had the distinct impression that unlike his family, Miss Whitford actually supported her sister's wishes.

"My sister is very supportive of what I want. She is also supportive of indulgence." She cast him a sidelong glance, her lids dipping seductively. When she looked at him like that, he nearly forgot his name and his purpose.

Harry's pulse picked up speed as they reached the bridge. "I think perhaps our families see something between us."

"What is that?" she asked when they crossed to the other side.

He steered her toward the edge of the path. "An attraction. That is what I feel. What do you feel?"

So far, the path was empty. Her hand moved on his arm, a caress. "The same."

Clasping her hand, he faced her. He could make out her features in the dim light filtering from the main area—the lush bow shape of her lips, the dramatic sweep of her brows, the gentle, alluring slope of her nose. All of it had become so familiar to him. *She* had become familiar to him. He liked that more than he could say. "Yes, our intentions are aligned—neither of us is looking for marriage. But I wonder if we may be even more aligned in our desires." He edged closer until they almost touched, his lips hovering a few inches from hers. "Would you consider having an affair with me?"

Her lips parted, but the only sound he heard was a loud shriek coming from the main area. She whipped her head around toward the noise, and he looked past her, hesitating only a moment before he gripped her hand more securely and dashed back over the bridge, back the way they'd come.

She went along with him wordlessly, and a few moments later, they arrived in the well-lit central square. A small crowd was gathered, indicating where the trouble had originated.

Harry let go of Selina's hand and gave her a quick look. She nodded, and he broke through the crowd. "I work for Bow Street. What's happened?"

People parted to make way for him until he reached a woman sobbing. "It's gone."

"What's gone?" Harry asked gently.

A man stood at her side, his brow furrowed. "Her bracelet. I told her not to wear it."

Harry frowned at the man. While the advice was good, now was not the time to remind the woman of a poor decision. Turning to the woman, Harry spoke in a soothing tone. "Perhaps it fell off while you were dancing?"

She shook her head. "I wasn't dancing. I was just standing here talking with people while we waited for the fireworks to begin." She indicated another couple standing near the man, who was probably her husband.

"What does it look like?" Harry asked.

"It's gold with rubies. My husband just gave it to me to celebrate the fifth year of our marriage." She looked at the man beside her. "I'm so sorry."

He patted her on the back. "It's all right, dear."

Harry addressed the crowd, speaking loudly. "Everyone back up. We're looking for a bracelet. Please step out of the way."

Selina came up behind him. "What are we looking

for?"

He gave her the description, and they began to scour the cobblestones. While they looked, the fireworks started, flashing overhead and providing added illumination for their search. It didn't matter, however, because after several fruitless minutes, he and Selina—and others who'd joined to help, including Nathaniel—had found nothing.

Harry went back to the woman and took her name and where she lived. "I will file a report about the theft. I'll speak to the management here and will conduct a full search of the area in the daylight tomorrow morning."

"Thank you," her husband responded. "I doubt you'll find it, but I appreciate you trying."

The woman began to cry again in earnest, and Harry left her husband to comfort her. He turned to Selina.

"What do you think happened?" Selina asked.

"I suspect she was the victim of a very accomplished pickpocket. Places like this are rife with them. Her husband is unfortunately correct in that she should not have worn such a thing here." Harry glanced around. "I wonder where the thief got off to. I am not aware of other entrances besides the front gate, and a wall surrounds the entire garden."

"Excuse me. I wonder if I may be of assistance?"

Harry pivoted to see a rather tall gentleman. He was impeccably dressed, a Society gentleman to be sure, but Harry didn't know him.

The man offered his hand. "Allow me to introduce myself. I'm Raphael Bowles, the owner of these gardens."

Taking his hand, Harry inclined his head. "Then, yes, you can help."

The owner turned his head to look at Selina. Harry opened his mouth to introduce her, but she spoke before he could. "Mr. Sheffield, allow me to present my brother."

Surprise sparked through Harry as he looked from her back to Bowles and then back again. He saw a slight resemblance, and it wasn't just their height—both were unusually tall. There was something in the angle of their cheekbones and the shape of their eyes, though it was difficult to see Bowles's very well given the brim of his hat.

A firework flashed overhead, and then Harry could see the man's vivid blue eyes, which were very similar in color to Selina's. He recalled her mentioning that her brother had taught her to shoot, but she'd never said another word about him, certainly not that he lived here in London. Harry was annoyed with himself for not asking. He realized there were many things he didn't know about her.

He wanted to know her better, but perhaps she didn't feel the same about him. Would she accept his proposal?

"Come, let us repair to my supper box to discuss the situation," Bowles suggested. "Give me a moment to speak with the woman." He moved to the victim and her husband.

"Your brother lives in London?" Harry worked to keep any hint of hurt from his tone.

Selina nodded serenely. "Yes."

Harry found her one-word answer frustrating, but then he knew her to be enigmatic, particularly about her family and her past. "You didn't mention that, or the fact that he owns these gardens."

"I didn't know about Spring Hollow. We aren't particularly close." Regret flashed across her features, and Harry felt contrite. She didn't talk about her family or her past because there seemed to be pain.

"That's too bad."

She looked him in the eye. "It is indeed."

CHAPTER 11

Selina's mind swirled as she watched Rafe talk to the woman whose bracelet Beatrix had stolen. There was no question that was what had happened. Beatrix and Rachel approached her as Harry joined the conversation between Rafe and the couple.

The fireworks continued overhead as if the theft and ensuing drama hadn't happened. Most people had transferred their attention to the sky.

"I'm glad I'm wearing nothing of value," Rachel said.

Beatrix's gaze met Selina's and revealed nothing. It didn't matter because Selina knew, and they'd discuss it later. This was a risk Beatrix never should have taken, not while she was in the presence of Harry's sister—and when Harry himself was just a short distance away!

Selina kept her face impassive so as not to expose her inner frustration. Beatrix knew her well enough to probably realize Selina was furious. But there were more important things to address at present.

"I introduced our brother to Mr. Sheffield," she said to Beatrix, who again was careful to guard her expression.

She simply nodded.

"Apparently, he owns these gardens," Selina continued.

"Does he?" Rachel asked, glancing around. "You didn't know?"

Selina shook her head. "We aren't particularly close."

"And why is that?" Rachel looked between Selina and Beatrix.

"We haven't seen each other much since we were children. Beatrix and I were sent to a ladies' seminary." That was all Selina intended to say. Thankfully, Rachel's husband arrived and distracted her.

Beatrix moved closer to Selina and murmured, "Sorry."

Selina looked toward her in displeasure but said nothing. Harry and Rafe came toward them. Taking a deep breath, Selina prepared herself for what would come next. There was always a part to play. She glanced at Beatrix and silently communicated that it was time to focus.

"Good evening, Rafe," Beatrix said. "Selina just told me you own these gardens. How extraordinary."

"I purchased them only last year."

"The renovations are excellent," Harry noted.

"How is the lady whose bracelet was stolen?" Rachel asked.

"Much better, particularly since Mr. Bowles said he would ensure the area was thoroughly searched tomorrow, and if the bracelet isn't found, he offered to replace the value." Harry looked at Rafe with a contemplative expression that made Selina a bit unsettled. "I must tell you, Bowles, while noble, that's a terrible idea. What if the woman is lying and there never was a bracelet?"

"What a cynical suggestion," Rafe said, cocking his head to the side.

"It's my line of work, I'm afraid."

"That would be an awfully elaborate plan," Rafe went on. "One that relies entirely on my offering to replace a nonexistent bracelet, which I have never done."

"Is this the first theft to happen here?" Harry asked.

"To my knowledge," Rafe replied. "Though I have to think it isn't, despite the fact that I've gone to great lengths to ensure the gardens are very secure."

Harry nodded. "The wall and the single entrance."

"It seems to be working."

"Until tonight." Harry straightened his coat. "I would still recommend you not reimburse the woman. If that gets out, you will certainly be targeted as softhearted."

"I somehow doubt that will become a problem," Rafe said with the dazzling smile Selina remembered from their youth. She had to stop herself from laughing. Softhearted was not a description anyone would have used for him. Except for her. With her, his heart had actually existed. She had the sense, however, that it had long since broken and disintegrated.

Like hers.

She suddenly thought of Harry's proposal. Not that her heart—or lack of one—had to have anything to do with it. He'd suggested an affair. There'd been no mention of love. It was the best Selina could hope for. She was incredibly tempted.

Rafe looked around the group with a bright expression. "Shall we adjourn to my box for refreshments?"

"Yes, please," Selina said.

"Allow me to present my sister and her husband," Harry said before conducting the introductions.

Rafe looked toward Selina as if he were going to offer to escort her to the box, but Harry beat him to it. Instead, Rafe offered his arm to Beatrix. Selina looked at them and could maybe believe they were related. They both had blond hair, anyway.

"How shocking to learn your brother owns these gardens," Harry observed as they followed Rafe to his box.

"Yes. I've only seen him once since arriving in London a couple of months ago," Selina said, sticking as close to the truth as possible, as she preferred to do.

"Aside from that, I take it you haven't seen him in some while."

"Eighteen years." Again, she adhered to honesty.

Harry turned his head, his eyes widening briefly. "That's quite a long time."

"Beatrix and I were sent to a ladies' seminary."

"And after, you didn't return to your family? Or had your brother left by then?"

Selina's mind stalled. She'd left the school at seventeen to take a position as a governess. It had been such a wonderful opportunity for someone like her— the best she could have hoped for. How wrong she'd been. A familiar tremor shot through her, and she cursed inwardly.

"My apologies," Harry said softly. "I didn't mean to upset you."

He'd felt her quiver, dammit. "You didn't. I did not return to my family." Thankfully, she didn't have to say anything more, because they'd arrived at the box, but she knew he'd ask. If not tonight, then some other time. She couldn't continue to evade him. He worked too hard to unpeel the layers of her protection. He saw too much.

And she was too drawn to him. She *wanted* him to see. To understand. To comfort.

The urge to tell him everything was nearly overwhelming. She fought to take a breath as her heart began to race.

She couldn't afford such vulnerability. Which meant she had to decline his proposal. Even though she wanted to accept more than anything.

They arrived at Rafe's box, a larger one situated at one end of the ground floor. A rectangular table was surrounded on three sides by chairs, leaving the side closest to the main square open to provide an unimpeded view of the dancing and, perhaps more importantly, the people milling about for all at the table. Rafe went to speak with one of the footmen.

Rachel's husband pulled out a chair for his wife, saying, "What an exciting evening so far!"

Smiling, Rachel glanced up at her husband as she sat. "Yes, and I'm so looking forward to hearing about how Mr. Bowles acquired the gardens." She looked toward Selina and Beatrix, who were still standing. "As well as how it is we didn't know you had a brother, Lady Gresham and Miss Whitford."

Beatrix lifted her hand to her temple. "Actually, I think the fireworks have given me a headache." She looked to Selina. "Would you mind if we went home?"

Thank goodness, Selina thought. "Not at all." She looked to Harry. "I don't want to disturb your evening. We can get a hack."

"Nonsense." Rafe had returned, drawing everyone's attention. "I'll see you both home." He turned to a footman and spoke in low tones. The liveried man departed, and Rafe addressed everyone once more. "My coach is being brought round."

"Thank you," Beatrix said with a faint smile.

Rafe inclined his head toward Rachel, Nathaniel, and Harry. "Please enjoy the rest of your evening. You'll be well taken care of."

Selina let go of Harry's arm. "I'll see you soon," she murmured.

He regarded her with a mix of disappointment and regret. "Yes, soon, I hope."

After everyone said good night, Rafe gestured for Selina and Beatrix to precede him from the box. They walked in silence from the gardens.

When they were outside awaiting the coach, Selina finally relaxed. She turned to Beatrix. "Thank you."

"It seemed as though we should organize our story before we had to share it. Sheffield's sister is as curious as they come." Beatrix rolled her eyes.

"You're quite adept at diverting the conversation, however," Selina said with a measure of pride. Beatrix was a master of changing topics and delighting people with witty observations instead of answering intrusive questions. It was both a skill and a defense employed to keep people from getting too close.

"Thank you," Beatrix said as a coach stopped in front of them.

Large and obviously new, with cobalt lacquer and a pair of gorgeously matched bays, the vehicle had clearly cost a great sum. Rafe told the coachman where they were going.

"You own these gardens and this coach?" Beatrix asked without a hint of subtlety. "Selina, your brother's bloody rich."

"So it would seem," Selina murmured.

Rafe helped them both up into the coach. "Take the forward-facing seat." He then climbed in after them and situated himself on the rear-facing seat, taking his hat off and setting it down beside him.

The coach began to move, and Selina settled herself back against the soft leather of the squab. Rafe's wealth enveloped her, but she felt no bitterness. She couldn't imagine what he'd had to do to earn this much. Considering the path he'd been on when he'd sent her from London, it couldn't have been good.

Rafe fixed on Beatrix. "Why did you steal the bracelet?"

"You saw that?" Beatrix asked, a smile teasing her lips. "I must be losing my touch."

"You aren't," Selina said. "Rafe just never misses anything. And he's probably the only person who can pick a pocket better than you."

"Is that pride I hear?" Rafe asked with a chuckle. "Back when we were children, I recall your fingers being as adept as mine—and much smaller, so you were able to filch things I couldn't."

"Selina taught me everything I know." Beatrix briefly patted Selina's hand.

"Beatrix was not born into this life as we were," Selina explained.

Rafe's brow creased for a fleeting moment. "We weren't born into it either."

Selina didn't remember anything else, but Rafe recalled snippets of their life before their "uncle" had brought them to London. He remembered their parents, their cheerful father, who had started teaching Rafe to ride, and their kind mother, with her bright blonde hair and love of reading, which Rafe had inherited. He'd made sure to teach Selina, which had set her apart from all the other children they'd grown up with.

"We may as well have been," Selina murmured. "She stole the bracelet because she likes pretty things."

Rafe transferred his gaze to Beatrix. "It's only a matter of time before you're caught."

Beatrix shrugged, her shoulder brushing Selina's. "That won't happen."

"Have you tried to pass yourself off as a Society miss before?" Rafe asked, arching a brow.

"On occasion, yes."

"But not in London. People will watch you more closely here."

"Not at a pleasure garden," Beatrix said defensively.

"Ah, well, if that's the only place you're doing it…" His tone clearly said he didn't believe that.

Selina sat up straighter. "Enough. You officially pass the sibling test." She frowned at Rafe, then cast Beatrix a quelling look. "On that note, I said we haven't seen you in eighteen years, Rafe, and just once before since we returned to London two months ago."

"You kept to the truth. As I said earlier, you always were very smart."

She didn't want to feel pleased by his compliment, but she did nonetheless. Pleasing him had been her chief objective before he'd sent her away. "I also told them Beatrix and I were sent to boarding school. And in the past, I've told Harry—Sheffield—that I am an orphan and was raised by family. A poor one at that." Rafe studied her closely. She added, "I didn't specify what sort of family."

"You seem quite close with Sheffield," Rafe said slowly.

"I said that I planned to keep him close. He's reinvestigating the fire on Saffron Hill. That's progress, isn't it?"

Rafe crossed his arms over his chest. "It is indeed. I'd hoped to make further progress with him tonight, but Beatrix ruined the plan with her pickpocketing."

Beatrix scowled at him, and Selina gave her another sharp look before turning her gaze to Rafe. "What was your plan?"

"One of my men was going to share information

I've learned with your Runner. The denizens of Saffron Hill were told to say the Vicar set that fire."

"By whom?"

"That I don't know yet, but someone who frightens them. If your Runner goes digging, I doubt he'll strike treasure."

Selina gave him a level stare. "He's not *my* Runner."

"If you say so." Rafe unfolded his arms, and the movement made him seem larger than his already imposing presence. He commanded the interior of the coach. If he'd been anyone else, Selina might feel threatened. Perhaps. Long ago, she'd vowed not to let men intimidate her.

"How will you get the information to him now?" Selina asked.

"I spoke to one of my men before we left. He'll ensure the message is delivered before Sheffield leaves the gardens."

Selina thought of when Rafe had gone to talk to one of the footmen. "You—and the Vicar—have a loyal following."

"You remember how important that is. Without it, life expectancy is cut at least in half."

A shiver ran down Selina's spine. Perhaps she'd been luckier to escape London than she ever realized. Developing relationships with people was not her strength. She shared loyalty with one person—Beatrix—and wasn't sure she could handle more than that. Which made her sad. She'd expected her reunion with Rafe to come with the love and trust they'd once shared.

Rafe seemed to know what he'd provoked—the realization that he and Selina were practically strangers. "I'm incredibly sorry we lost touch."

"I am too," she said softly. Then she hastened to direct the conversation away from the past. Harry will undoubtedly search for the person who told everyone to lie." She glanced out the window and saw they were close to Queen Anne Street. "You should continue to investigate. The sooner you clear the Vicar's name, the better. Though I still think you should just kill him. The Vicar, I mean."

"I will. Eventually." Rafe glanced between Selina and Beatrix. "Which one of you will fence the bracelet?"

"I will." Selina smoothed her hand over her skirt.

"Take it to The Golden Lion on Shoe Lane. They'll give you a good price."

Selina arched a brow at him. "Is that yours?"

He lifted a shoulder. "Does it matter?"

She didn't want to take his money. But this wasn't a direct transaction, and in this instance, she would accept his...assistance. Finding a fair receiver shop was often difficult, especially in London. "I've been going to a few places over in Whitechapel."

"This will be more profitable. There are several others around Shoe Lane, if you prefer. All will be better than Whitechapel."

Selina inclined her head as the coach pulled onto Queen Anne Street. "Thank you."

Rafe unfolded his arms and leaned forward. "I could just give you the money now. Whatever you need."

Selina paused, but only for a moment. She'd had to rely on herself the past twelve years. After the disaster of trusting someone else—her employer—when she'd worked as a governess, she'd vowed never to do so again. Rafe might be her brother, but she didn't really know him, and hadn't for a long time. "No, thank you."

The coach drew to a stop in front of their house. Rafe reached for the door but didn't move further. "I won't offer again, but you need only ask."

He opened the door and climbed down from the coach. Holding up his hand, he helped her descend, then Beatrix. Selina turned to him. "You should expect an invitation to...something from Lord and Lady Aylesbury."

"Sheffield's parents."

Selina nodded. "Mrs. Hayes—Rachel—will surely want to further interrogate you."

Amusement crossed Rafe's features. "I'll look forward to it. And we'll speak soon."

Selina turned and went into the house with Beatrix. As soon as the door closed, Beatrix spoke. "Why won't you take his money? He clearly has plenty to spare."

"You know why," Selina said tersely. "Give me the bracelet."

Beatrix fished it from her reticule and dropped it into Selina's hand. "Sorry."

"Don't do that again. We have a plan. Stick to it, please."

Guilt flashed in Beatrix's eyes. "Yes."

Selina knew Beatrix couldn't help herself. Exhaling, she briefly clasped Beatrix's hand. "I know it's hard," she said softly. "Don't dwell on it. I'll take care of the bracelet."

"Will you take it to Rafe's receiver shop? Though he didn't confirm it, I assume The Golden Lion is his."

"As do I." Selina would go and see it at least.

They made their way upstairs, but before they retreated to their chambers, Beatrix touched Selina's arm. "What happened with Sheffield?"

"Nothing."

Beatrix stared at her in disbelief. "He took you for a promenade. The path seemed rather dark." The implication was clear.

Selina returned her stare. "Someone shrieked."

Beatrix exhaled. "Good night."

They separated and went to their chambers. Selina closed her hand around the bracelet as she stepped into her room. Walking to the dressing table, she opened her fingers and looked down at the rubies and gold glinting in the candlelight. She dropped the piece onto the table, then removed her gloves.

What would have happened if the shriek hadn't interrupted her and Harry? A kiss, certainly. But would there have been more? Would she have allowed it?

Could she?

Selina closed her eyes, but didn't let the twelve-year-old nightmare rise in her mind. Instead, she thought of Harry. Of his caring, his intelligence, his kisses.

An affair.

She should say no—every part of her screamed a warning at allowing him too close. But some of those same parts also told her she deserved something. It would be so nice to have a joyful memory amidst all the bad ones.

Weariness swept over her. When would it be time to finally let down her guard?

She feared the answer was never.

CHAPTER 12

Selina's presence in Harry's dreams the past two nights coupled with her absence since he'd proposed an affair was driving him to distraction. As he went about his duties, he couldn't stop thinking of her, wondering if he'd overstepped. But no, she'd admitted she was as attracted to him as he was to her.

That didn't mean, however, that she wanted to engage in a liaison.

And yet, she'd said she would see him soon. Soon, he realized, was frustratingly relative. He'd never been particularly patient, especially with something he really wanted.

Perhaps he could initiate a reason to see her. While he'd never taught someone to ride, he could teach her. If she was amenable.

Taking a deep breath, he told himself to focus on the matter at hand as he approached Finch Lane. It took him a quarter hour and several interviews to learn that a fortune-teller had lived at number eight, a rooming house. Harry knocked on the door and waited for the proprietor to answer.

A man in his sixties with a crop of bright white

hair and deep-set blue eyes opened the door. He surveyed Harry from head to foot. "How can I help ye?"

"My name is Sheffield, and I work for Bow Street. I would like to ask you about a fortune-teller." Harry pulled his small notebook from his pocket along with his pencil.

"Not interested in a room, then?" he asked, squinting one eye. "Pity, as I've one available."

"No, thank you. I'd like to know about a woman who let a room recently, a fortune-teller."

The man nodded. "Madame Sybila. Didn't like what she was doin'. I never would've given her the room if I'd known."

"How did you determine she was telling fortunes?"

"She started seeing people in her room, more than just the two women who came to care for her."

Harry scratched a note and looked at the man with interest. "Was she ill?"

"Not that I could see, but I don't think anyone ever got a good look at the fortune-teller. Those women were around a great deal."

"Did they live here?"

"They didn't pay rent, which was another reason I told her to go."

"So they were staying here?" Harry asked eagerly.

"Couldn't ever say for sure, but it seemed like they might be."

"Do you know their names?"

The man frowned. "Blackwell, maybe? Or Blakewell? Blakely? Something like that."

"Can you describe them?"

Scrunching his face, the man thought for a moment. "I think one of them was tall? Or maybe one was just short. I can't rightly recall."

Harry wrote down the man's murky recollections.

"Did Madame Sybila leave anything behind after she left?"

"Not that I could find. She was quite tidy, actually. If not for the heathenish behavior, she was a good tenant. Can't abide that ungodly rubbish, though."

"Did she by chance tell you where she moved to?"

"No, and I didn't ask. Good riddance."

After closing his notebook, Harry stuck it and the pencil back into his coat. "Thank you for your time."

Harry turned from the boardinghouse and looked around the street. He could make other inquiries. Surely someone would have seen the women who'd been visiting—or staying with—Madame Sybila.

Unfortunately, he didn't have time at present. He needed to get to Saffron Hill to pursue the information he'd received at Spring Hollow the other night. Though his rendezvous had been interrupted by the theft of the woman's bracelet, the informer had found Harry later. He'd asked a footman to tell Harry to meet him.

Middle-aged, with a nervous demeanor, the informer had refused to give Harry his name. He'd said the fire in Saffron Hill hadn't been started by the Vicar, but that everyone had been told to say that it was. When Harry had questioned him for more information, the man had been frustratingly ignorant. He didn't know who had told everyone to say it was the Vicar, nor could he say who *had* started the fire. He also couldn't provide a description of the Vicar. And of course, he wouldn't say how he knew this information or why he'd chosen to give it to Harry. The entire encounter had left Harry feeling annoyed and more than a bit skeptical.

Nevertheless, he was on his way to Saffron Hill to see what he could learn. He caught a hack and had it drop him near the location of the fire four years ago.

There was a new building there now. A clothing merchant occupied the ground floor.

Harry briefly closed his eyes and saw the charred remains of the flash house where the feared leader of the gang who'd controlled this neighborhood and his right-hand man had perished along with several children and young women. Blinking, he took in the bustling street around him. There were women shopping, men going into a tavern, and children—so many children. Too many, in fact. Harry had to assume a good portion of them were orphans or perhaps had a single parent who couldn't provide for them. Some were begging, while others carried a haughty air of defiance as they stood in small clusters.

As Harry walked, he considered what the informer had told him—that someone had instructed the residents of Saffron Hill to say that the Vicar had started the fire. Who had the power to convince them all to go along with that story? Would they still? There was only one way to find out.

Harry went into a cobbler's shop situated across and down a few buildings from where the flash house had been. The proprietor had been one of the witnesses who'd reported seeing the Vicar leave the flash house.

The shop was small but tidy. As Harry walked toward the counter, a man with close-cropped dark hair eyed him warily. Though four years had passed, Harry immediately recognized him as the cobbler he'd interviewed.

"Good afternoon, Mr. Gregson," Harry said with a smile.

The cobbler squinted at him. "Do I know ye?"

"We spoke several years ago—after the fire across the street." Harry had reviewed his notes that morning, so he recalled precisely what Gregson had told him. "I was a constable at Hatton Garden. Now I work for Bow Street."

The man's gaze remained guarded. "How can I help ye?"

"I'm here to ask about the fire again. Back then, you told me a man called the Vicar started it. I've some new information that requires me to reinvestigate the crime. At the time, you were confident the Vicar was responsible. However, your description of him doesn't match anyone else's. In fact, everyone seemed to have a slightly different recollection of what the man looked like." Harry cocked his head to the side. "Did someone tell you to say it was the Vicar?"

Gregson paled. His throat worked, but he hesitated to speak. Harry waited patiently, allowing the uncomfortable silence to prod the cobbler to spill the truth. At length, he croaked, "No."

Harry clucked his tongue with a shake of his head. "That's not what I hear. As a man of the law, I remind you of the importance of giving honest testimony, Mr. Gregson."

"Everyone said it was the Vicar." The man seemed to shrug, but the movement ended up looking more like a flinch, as if he were physically trying to keep himself from talking.

"You were just going along?" Harry asked. "I can understand doing that. It's difficult to be the one person who says something different."

The man's eyes widened and stayed that way, making him look incredibly frightened.

Harry continued. "Would it help you to know that I've already spoken to someone who said he was told to say it was the Vicar?"

Gregson exhaled, but the apprehension didn't completely leave his expression. "Who told you that?"

"Ah now, that wouldn't be fair to him, would it?"

Harry leaned over the counter. "The fire was so long ago. Surely whoever cared about it then doesn't anymore."

"Please don't ask me anything more." There was a desperate plea in the man's voice.

"Then direct me to someone else who *will* tell me something. Otherwise, I may bring you to Bow Street for interrogation."

The stark fear returned to Gregson's eyes. "It wasn't the Vicar. I don't even know who he is."

"Who's in charge of this area now?" Harry asked.

"Frost." Gregson cowered, as if uttering the name would bring physical harm down upon him.

"Where can I find Frost?"

Gregson shook his head. "That's all I know. Please, sir," he begged. Though he didn't say what he wanted, it was clear to Harry: he wanted Harry to go away and never return to his shop.

"I'll go in a moment," Harry said benignly. "Who else can I talk to?" Hopefully, his meaning was also clear: *give me a name and I'll leave you alone.*

"Maggie. She weaves baskets down the street a bit." Gregson used his thumb to gesture to his left.

"Does she remember the fire?"

Gregson nodded. "She was in the building."

"Thank you for your...cooperation." Harry frowned. "I'm sorry you're so frightened." No one should have to live like that. Whoever terrified the people of this neighborhood should be brought to justice, and Harry would do his best to make sure that happened. Perhaps he wouldn't have to look further than Frost.

Harry departed the shop and turned to the left. Walking along the street, he finally saw the weaver sitting near the corner of a shop that sold crockery. She was perhaps fourteen, dressed in a pale, dingy gown of indeterminate color. Her dark hair hung limply to her shoulders as she wove a basket in her lap.

Harry went to her. "How much for a basket?"

She didn't look up at him as her fingers continued to weave. "Thruppence."

Squatting down next to her, Harry produced a shilling. "Can I ask you about the fire that happened over there?" He glanced toward where the flash house had been.

Her hand stilled as her gaze shot to the coin in his hand. "I s'pose."

"I understand you were inside the building." He put the coin in her basket. "What do you remember?"

Plucking up the shilling, she held it up and squinted at the coin. Apparently satisfied, she pressed it into something hidden beneath the neckline of her gown. "I was downstairs trying to wash my brother's face. I smelled smoke, but I was too busy with my brother. When someone yelled fire, I scooped him up and carried him out."

"Do you know where the fire started?"

She shook her head and went back to weaving.

"What about who started it—do you know that?" Harry asked.

"Everyone says 'twas the Vicar."

"So I understand," Harry said wryly. "Did you see him?"

Maggie shook her head again.

"Do you know who the Vicar is?"

She glanced up at Harry. "'E worked for Partridge. We all did."

"What did you do for him?" Harry was fairly certain he knew.

"Usually, I pretended my brother was sick—I made 'im look really dirty, and people took pity."

"They gave you money." Likely, she had a minimum amount she was to earn every day to appease

Partridge's requirements. At her nod, Harry went on. "Were you glad when Partridge died?"

She looked at Harry, an edge of fear in her gaze.

"It's all right," Harry soothed with an encouraging nod. "Do you work for Frost now?"

She shook her head a third time but much more vigorously. "My brother does, though."

"Where can I find your brother?"

Going back to weaving, she shrugged. "'E's around."

"One last question, and I'll leave you alone, Maggie. Do you know who told everyone to say the Vicar started the fire?"

The fourth time she shook her head was the least convincing because she hesitated the barest moment. Harry wouldn't press her. "Thank you, Maggie. I work at Bow Street. If you ever want to come and talk to me, I'd be honored. About anything. Mayhap I could even help you." He thought of Winter's home and how an environment like that could transform Maggie's life. Hell, had Winter and Madame Sybila won him over?

No. Selina had. She believed in the Home for Wayward Children, and he was starting to as well.

Harry gave Maggie another shilling before standing and checking his pocket watch. He needed to get back to Bow Street for a meeting. He walked all the way to Holborn before catching a hack to Bow Street.

When he got out at the Magistrates' Court, he ran into Remy, who was also just arriving. "Afternoon, Sheff," he said in greeting. "Where were you about today?"

"Just came from Saffron Hill," Harry said as they walked inside.

"Learn anything?"

Harry stopped and turned to Remy. "What do you know about a man named Frost?"

Remy shrugged. "I've heard the name. Why?"

"Seems like he may be in charge of Partridge's old territory."

"That's not really our concern, as close as it is to Hatton Garden," Remy said, referring to the Magistrates' Court that was closer to Saffron Hill.

"I plan to go and talk to Thorpe." He was one of the constables at Hatton Garden with whom Harry had worked.

"I've got a contact over in Shoe Lane," Remy said. "I'll see what I can learn."

A surge of anticipation rushed through Harry. How he loved the hunt. "Mind if I come along?"

"I don't, but my informer will. He won't talk if I bring someone else."

"Damn." But Harry understood. Some of his informers were the same.

"We better hurry, or we'll be late," Remy said.

As they started toward the stairs, Harry drafted a note to Selina in his head, inquiring as to whether she would like a riding lesson. She could use his mother's old sidesaddle, and he'd borrow a horse from a friend. All he needed was Selina to agree.

To the lesson, but hopefully also to his proposal.

~

*R*afe had been right. Selina went to his receiver shop in Shoe Lane and fenced the bracelet Beatrix had stolen for a very good price. Had the receiver given her more because Rafe had told him to? Probably. But Selina didn't care. To her, it wasn't the same as taking money from him for nothing.

With the money stowed in an interior pocket of her gown and her pistol tucked into her reticule, Selina felt quite secure as she walked to her next destination, which wasn't The Strand. Madame Sybila had met with a few clients earlier, but was now taking the afternoon to complete personal errands. Or so Mrs. Kinnon would tell those who came to inquire.

The day before, Selina had needed to use another excuse—that Madame Sybila wasn't feeling well—so that she could attend a meeting of the Spitfire Society at a new friend's house. A small group of forward-thinking women, the society existed for the purpose of celebrating womanhood and independence, whatever that meant. They also hoped to do something meaningful for women, but that hadn't been explored as the meeting had been cut short due to some sort of fracas involving a kitten.

Selina looked forward to their next meeting with an eye toward starting a charity that would support women. This could be the answer she'd been looking for—a way to sustain herself without having to be Madame Sybila or steal and fence. It also had the added benefit of being a real charity that would help women and perhaps children too. Yes, that was something about which Selina could nurture a drive...a passion.

She'd been driven to find Rafe, and now that she had, she didn't feel the triumph or elation she'd hoped for and expected. The brother she remembered was as good as dead. Eighteen years was a long time. They were adults now, completely different from when they'd last been together. The dream she'd held for so long—that she'd regain the family she'd once had—was also as good as dead.

You have a family. You have Beatrix.

Yes, she had Beatrix, but for how long? Beatrix was well on her way to being the toast of the late Season. Invitations had increased due to Lady Aylesbury's influence, and yesterday, they'd met the Marchioness of Ripley, which could only help Beatrix's cause. It was possible that Beatrix might find herself taken in by her father. He would never officially recognize her as his daughter, of course, bastard that she was, but he could ensure she was well situated.

And give her the approval—and love—she craved.

Where would that leave Selina? Particularly if Beatrix found herself wed to some wealthy gentleman?

It would leave her alone without any dependencies. Selina could do precisely as she wished. Harry's proposal, so present in her thoughts the past few days, rose in her mind. She needed to make a decision.

As if you haven't already.

But did she have the courage to actually do it? Pushing the topic from her mind, as she'd done relentlessly since he'd asked, Selina quickened her pace. The dome of St. Paul's came into view, which meant she was nearly to Ivy Lane.

Cutting through an alley, she made her way to the back entrance of the house they were using for the Home for Wayward Children and rapped on the back door. After several long moments, it finally opened to reveal Theresa. She glared at Selina, her eyes glassy. "Why are you 'ere?"

"You're drunk," Selina said, pushing past her to get inside. "Where's Luther?"

"Upstairs. You're lucky 'e's still 'ere. Was about ta leave."

"Be a dear and fetch him, please." Selina forced a smile. "Remember who's paying you to take a respite from your real occupation."

Theresa wiped her hand over her nose, her eyes narrowing slightly. "Who says I'm takin' a respite?"

Bloody hell. Selina glowered at her. "You better not be servicing clients here."

With a shrug, Theresa ambled toward the front of the house. Selina followed her, moving into the parlor as Theresa went up the stairs.

A few moments later, Luther came in. "Selina, love." He grinned broadly as he came toward her, his nearly ebony eyes twinkling.

She smiled in return, releasing the tension Theresa had caused. "I hope you're keeping a close eye on your 'wife.'"

Luther waved his hand. "Bah, she's harmless."

"She's drunk."

"I let her have gin today. Only the second time since we came here."

Selina doubted that. Theresa had seemed at least a bit muzzy when Selina had visited with Harry. "Well, don't give her any more." Selina took a deep breath and fixed him with a steady stare. "You have one more test to pass, I'm afraid."

"Happy to do it for you," he said, taking her hand. "Tell me." He guided her to the settee and pulled her down to sit beside him.

Selina let go of his hand and angled herself toward him. He edged a bit closer, which she should have expected. He made no effort to disguise his interest in her, which he said hadn't waned in eighteen years. She'd jokingly asked if that meant he'd remained celibate waiting for her. Blushing, he'd apologized because he hadn't. She'd then assured him it wasn't at all necessary, particularly since she'd married, giving him the lie she gave everyone. Except her brother, apparently. Perhaps she did trust Rafe a little.

Focusing on the purpose of her errand, Selina

said, "On Friday afternoon, Madame Sybila will bring a group of society ladies to see the home. You and Theresa, if she's sober, will need to show them the children and discuss your plans for expansion. I suspect one of them may suggest a subscription. We don't want that, so divert the conversation as much as possible."

He put his arm along the back of the settee so his hand was near her shoulder. "'Twill be no problem at all. I am pleased to do whatever I can to help you."

"My hope is that the visit will garner enough donations to put an end to this scheme entirely. You should be back to your regular life within the week." She studied him a moment. "What is your regular life, exactly?"

Luther moved closer, his lips parted in an expression of anticipation. "Why do you want to know? I'm doing well, Lina. Well enough to support a wife." He winked at her.

Oh hell. She didn't want to deal with this, not today. She never should have asked about his life. "Then you should take one. And consider leaving this life behind."

He blinked, his long, dark lashes sweeping over his magnetic eyes. He'd always been handsome. All the girls Selina had known had fancied themselves in love with him. But he'd only ever paid special attention to Selina. She supposed she'd found him attractive, in the way an eleven-year-old girl would find a thirteen-year-old boy attractive. He made her laugh and brought her the occasional pastry he stole from a cart.

Now, however, he was as much a stranger to her as her brother. More so really, because she hadn't spent much time thinking of him at all during the past eighteen years. Unlike her brother, whom she'd missed and hoped to find.

"Like you have left your past behind?" he teased softly.

For years, she'd told herself she'd done exactly that. But how was that really possible when she was still engaged in criminal acts? Disgust rose within her, and she swallowed a sense of panic. She stiffened her spine in an effort to regain control of her emotions. "Forget I said anything." She stood, eager to be on her way.

He also rose, standing close and towering over her. "I'm glad to know you care." He lifted his hand and caressed her cheek.

A vision of a normal life flashed in Selina's mind. It didn't include Luther, but Harry. He worked as a constable while she kept their house and did charity work, helping women and children better themselves through honest means. Not like what she had done. What she continued to do. How much longer could she go on like this? More and more, it seemed there would be a reckoning—and soon.

"Selina?" Luther's brows drew together as he stroked her face.

She wanted to tell him there would be no future between them, but Luther could be volatile, and she needed him through Friday, at least. How she couldn't wait for this entire scheme to be over.

She summoned an appreciative smile. "Thank you for helping me. Truly."

Pivoting, she hurried from the parlor as quickly as she dared, then went out through the front door onto Ivy Lane. Too late, she realized her foolishness. She rarely made mistakes, but when she did, they were often quite large.

This was certainly no exception, for standing across the street staring at her was Harry Sheffield.

CHAPTER 13

*H*arry blinked, wondering if he was seeing correctly. But of course he was. He wouldn't confuse Selina for any other woman. Her face and form were too familiar to him. He saw them even when she wasn't standing across the street from him.

What the hell was she doing there?

He crossed Ivy Lane, and she met him with a smile.

"What a coincidence to meet you here," she said. "I just came to deliver another donation. I'm afraid I couldn't wait until you paid another visit. I was quite moved by their endeavors." She tipped her head to the side. "What are you doing here? I can't believe *you're* making a donation. I'm still not sure you believe they are a legitimate charity."

"I'm not making a donation. I came to keep an eye on things because I was not yet convinced of their legitimacy."

"What do you expect to find?" she asked. "That they've left? I assure you, Mr. Winter is just inside. Would you like to speak with him?"

Harry shook his head. "That won't be necessary. I think you may have changed my mind."

"Have I? You still sound a bit skeptical."

"My mother plans to bring some friends to see it —on Friday, I think she said. She invited me to come along, but I declined. I don't want her knowing I've already been here."

"Because then she'd know you're spying on her activities."

Harry offered her his arm. "Shall we walk?"

"Please." She curled her hand around his sleeve and moved next to him, instantly reminding him of why she'd been ever present in his mind since Saturday evening. And before that, really.

"I'm not spying. I'm investigating. Because I care about her."

"Also because your father asked." When Harry exhaled sharply, she laughed softly. "You're trying to be a good son. That's hard when your parents are at odds. Perhaps you should tell your father to conduct his own investigations. Indeed, perhaps he should accompany your mother on Friday."

"That's not a bad idea." Harry should have thought of it himself. "I'll mention it to him at dinner on Thursday." He looked at her profile, admiring her beauty—and her heart. "What prompted you to take another donation to Mr. Winter today?"

She didn't answer immediately, as if she were choosing her words. "As an orphan, I suppose their plight affects me more deeply than most."

"Surely your situation was different, though." He felt her stiffen.

"I prefer to leave the past where it belongs—in the past." She briefly turned her head and flashed a faint smile. He saw the sadness behind it, however.

Placing his hand over hers as they walked, he said, "Selina, I would like to know everything about you. I hope that someday, you'll tell me about your experience."

"Perhaps I will."

Perhaps. That wasn't a refusal.

Harry decided to change the subject in the hope that she would relax a bit. He could feel the tension running through her. "I learned some things about the fire."

"You have new information?"

"I do. After you left Spring Hollow, I met with the informer. He told me everyone in Saffron Hill was told to say the Vicar had started the fire."

She paused briefly. "That's—that's astounding. Who would be able to get everyone to say the same thing?"

"I had the same question, so I went to Saffron Hill yesterday. I spoke to a cobbler I interviewed four years ago. He was rather skittish, but he gave me a name—the man who's probably head of the gang there now. Frost."

Selina stopped again and turned to face him. "Do you know who this man is?"

Harry shook his head. "No, but I'll find him."

"You think he told everyone to say the Vicar started the fire?"

"It's possible. If he became the leader after Partridge was killed in the fire, he may know something. And he definitely had something to gain from Partridge dying."

"So it seems," she murmured, and he sensed she was thinking. She started walking once more.

"What?" he asked

She sent him a sidelong glance. "May I help with your investigation in any way?"

"I don't know how. My friend, Remington—he's a constable—has a contact in Shoe Lane, so I'm hopeful he can learn something useful."

"Well, if you can think of any way I can help, I'd be happy to. I know this is important to you."

"Thank you, I appreciate that."

She looked about. "Where are we going?"

Harry smiled. "We seem to have a habit of just walking together, which I rather like. Where should we go?" He paused and turned slightly to face her.

"I don't know."

"I'd planned to send you an invitation for a riding lesson, but I'm afraid I can't organize that for this afternoon." He watched for the slightest inkling that would indicate she was interested in doing so. "Would you want to do that?"

"I never thought to ride. Surely it's too late to learn."

"Never. I would consider it my privilege to teach you."

Her gaze softened. "Harry. You are too kind."

He nearly laughed. "I've never been accused of that."

She smiled demurely. "I accept your invitation." Her gaze locked with his. "And your proposal."

Had he heard her correctly? "My proposal. You wish to have an affair?"

She nodded, and the simple motion provoked a rush of yearning within Harry. "We should catch a hack." She pivoted and started walking toward Newgate once more.

Did she mean to begin their liaison now? When they reached Newgate, he hailed a hack. "Where are we going?" His voice cracked slightly as desire sparked inside him.

Her gaze, vividly intense, met his. "To your house. If that's all right."

Harry swallowed, thinking he must have misheard her, but knowing he hadn't. The look she gave him was steady and sure, and it fed his soul. "Of course it's all right." It was bloody spectacular.

He gave the driver his direction and helped Selina

into the hack. Once they were settled inside and they began moving, he spoke.

"The young woman—Mercy—who died in that fire... I'd met her a few months before. She was trying to change her life, and I sought to help." He thought of the basket weaver, Maggie, and realized he wanted to help her in the same way. The way Selina wanted to support the children in Winter's care. "I'd just found a seamstress who'd agreed to take her on as an apprentice."

"Was that all she was to you?" Selina asked. "A charitable endeavor?"

"No, she was much more. Kind, intelligent, beautiful."

"You cared for her, then?"

He nodded. "There wasn't a strong attraction." He pinned her with an aching stare. "Not like with you. But for a long time, I wondered if there might have been. If she hadn't died."

"You were good to help her. Most people ignore young women like her—and children."

"You are incredibly affected by such people and their struggles. You seem to feel their disadvantage keenly. I understand you were an orphan, but you didn't face the same hardships as they did, certainly."

She averted her gaze, turning her head so he could only barely see her profile. "What if I did?" she asked quietly.

What was she saying? That she'd grown up like Mercy or the children at Winter's home? "But you went to school."

"It was a stroke of good fortune and generosity that Beatrix and I were accepted at the ladies' seminary."

He thought she was going to say more, but she didn't. They rode in silence for a few minutes, during which Harry could sense her anxiety. Was she regretting her decision to go to his house?

"Selina, if at any moment you'd prefer to go home, I will take you there instead."

She kept her attention away from him. "Thank you. I will not hesitate to speak my mind." There was a dry quality to her tone that made him smile.

"I can't imagine you would." He leaned closer and whispered, "That's a rather captivating quality."

She swung her head toward him, which brought their lips temptingly close. "Is it? Most men would disagree." Her gaze dipped to his mouth. "But you are not most men."

"No."

"That is why I'm going to your house." Her lashes fluttered as their eyes connected once more just before she pressed her lips to his.

Harry brought his hand up to cup her face, his thumb stroking her cheek as he kissed her back. Thoughts of investigations and the past faded away, leaving just this moment, this delightful sensation.

Selina's orange-honeysuckle scent filled his senses, stirring his desire. She put her hand under his coat and clutched at his side, pulling him closer. Her tongue slid against his as they both deepened the kiss, each of them seeking more.

Harry gave himself to the passion swirling between them. It had been there since the moment she'd tripped into his arms—at least for him. Selina was the most unusual, enigmatic woman he'd ever met. Perhaps that was what had drawn him to her. She was a mystery to be uncovered. Right now, he peeled another layer away. Or was it that she revealed the next one?

As they kissed, she turned on the seat. He slid his other arm behind her and pressed her back into the corner, rising over her. He stroked down her jaw and neck and rested his hand at the base of her throat. He would be able to feel the skin of her neck if he wasn't wearing his bloody gloves. Soon, he hoped, there would be nothing between them. He went completely hard at the thought.

She moved her other hand up to clasp his head, holding him to her as she explored his mouth, taunting him with her lips and tongue. The kiss was fierce and delicious, setting Harry utterly aflame with need.

He ran his thumb along her neck, then moved his lips to follow that path, kissing along her flesh. She arched her back with a soft moan. Harry slid his hand down, caressing her breast. She sucked in a sharp breath as her fingers dug into his nape. He splayed his fingers, lightly clasping her through the annoying layers of her clothing.

She moved beneath him, her body arching and seeking. Harry pressed down against her, his hips meeting hers.

The neckline of her walking dress prevented him from kissing lower than her neck. He dragged his mouth away and looked down at her.

She opened her eyes, and he sat back. Her brows pitched over her eyes. "Why did you stop?"

"We're nearly there."

She sat up, straightening and smoothing her gown over her legs. He noticed then that her hand was shaking. Alarmed, he reached for her, clasping her hand. "What's wrong?"

Her head snapped around just as the coach came to a stop. Silently cursing the interruption, Harry opened the door and jumped from the vehicle. He paid the driver, then helped Selina out.

They stood at the entry to the alley behind the row of terraced houses where his was located. He meant to take her in the back for privacy's sake.

Taking her hand once more, he moved close as the hack rumbled away over the cobblestones. "Have you changed your mind?"

"No. It's just... I haven't done this in a very long time. My husband... We didn't..."

"Oh. Well, that's all right. We'll go very slowly. Or we can wait until you're comfortable."

She looked up at him and gently touched his jaw, her gloved fingertips grazing his skin. "Take me inside. Please."

Harry tucked her hand around his arm and led her to the back of his terrace at number seventeen. He reached for the door, but she stopped him, putting her hand on his. "Wait."

He turned to face her. "I meant what I said. If you've changed your mind—"

"When I left school, it was to take a position as a governess."

She'd gone from governess to wife of a baronet? "Was that your husband?"

She shook her head. "Someone else. I was not anyone of import, certainly not someone who would meet or marry a baronet." She spoke coldly, distastefully, as if she were talking about someone other than herself. Then she began to tremble. "My employer was not a good man. He took advantage of his position and my vulnerability. He...violated me. Physically."

Rage spun through Harry. "Who is he?" Harry didn't care if he was a bloody duke.

"I'm not telling you this to gain your sympathy or your outrage. I'm quite capable of taking care of myself. At least, I am now."

Harry thought of the pistol she said she always carried. Now it made more sense than he could have imagined. His heart ached for her, just as the fury she told him he shouldn't feel anchored in his chest.

"Then why are you telling me? Tell me what you want me to do."

"Just listen." The simplicity of her request quieted the anger inside him.

He cupped her face. "Tell me."

"I was young, just seventeen. After he raped me, I left. I fetched Beatrix from school, and I've taken care of her ever since." The words poured out of her, and emotion clouded her gaze. "My husband, Sir Barnabus, was a kind and understanding man. He was also rather old and had no desire for the marriage bed."

She'd never known a man's touch in a caring manner. Harry was incredibly humbled that she trusted him. "You can still change your mind," he said softly, gently caressing her face with his thumbs.

Her eyes cleared. "I'm not going to. I've waited a very long time for the right moment. The right man. It's now. You're him. Will you take me upstairs?"

"Selina, my darling, I will take you anywhere you want to go." He kissed her sweetly, and then he opened the door.

~

Selina couldn't seem to stop her mouth from uttering secrets she'd long kept buried. No one knew what had happened to her when she'd been a governess except Beatrix. She was torn between feeling regret for having opened herself up to Harry and an overwhelming sense of liberation. Mostly, she just felt *safe*.

The sensible part of her brain told her to go home, to play the role she'd performed the past twelve years. But the part of her that was always pushed to the side, ignored and repressed, longed to be free to pursue her most basic desires: comfort, safety, love.

Not that this was love. That was not an emotion she allowed. Not for anyone except Beatrix, because they only had each other.

Harry took her hand and led her up the backstairs to the first floor. His chamber was at the rear of the small house—smaller even than hers. Decorated in dark, rich tones of burgundy and sable, the room provoked a sense of comfort along with passion. Two things that might have been at odds, but seemed perfect when she thought of him.

He made her feel more relaxed than anyone in a very long time, maybe forever. While at the same time, he kept her on edge, both because of who he was and because of the attraction that smoldered between them. How different would things be if she were not a fraud and he were not a Runner?

He let go of her hand as they entered the bedchamber. Selina removed her gloves and then her hat, glancing around at where to put them. Harry took them from her and set them on a chair near the hearth.

Selina surveyed the room, but mostly focused on the bed against the left wall. Hung with burgundy draperies and covered with opulent bedcoverings, it reminded her of who he was. He might be a Bow Street Runner, but he was also the son of an earl.

That made it hard to forget who she was: a child of the streets with no knowledge of who her parents even were. She was worse than an orphan. If he knew the truth, he would never want her. How could he?

Taking off his hat and gloves, Harry set them on a dresser. Then he removed his coat and laid it over the back of the chair. Seeing him in just his shirtsleeves made him seem even larger—his shoulders more broad, his presence more imposing. Not in an intimidating way, but an alluring one.

Selina stood near the end of the bed where there was a cushioned bench. Harry came and sat. "This is where I put my boots on every morning. And take them off every night." He removed one, then the other, revealing his stocking-clad feet. "I don't know that I've ever removed them in the middle of the afternoon." He pulled off the stockings next and looked up at her with a twinkle in his eye.

She sat beside him and leaned over to unlace her boots. He quickly knelt before her. "Allow me."

Selina sat up and let him take over removing her boots. He did so adroitly, his fingers moving while he kept his eyes locked with hers. The simple task was anything but. She'd rarely had anyone help her dress, even now that she had a maid. This was different, however. Because he was a man. Because he was looking at her with naked desire. Because her entire body thrummed with an answering need.

"How old are you?" he asked softly.

"Nine and twenty."

"I'm just two years older," he said, removing the first boot and moving on to the next.

"But far more experienced, I'd wager." She suddenly felt nervous.

"I possess no rakish tendencies." He chuckled. "I leave that to my brother." He finished with the second boot and set it next to the first. He clasped each of her ankles, his fingers wrapping around her as his thumbs moved across the top of her feet to the front of her shins. "Shall I remove your stockings?"

"Yes." She slowly raised her skirt to her knees and then just above so that the garters were exposed.

Harry slid his hands up, his fingers gently grazing her calves. Then he removed one garter and stocking, sweeping them from her leg as she pointed her toes.

He repeated the action on the other leg—as did she. "Beautiful," he breathed.

He moved between her legs and lifted a hand to her face, his palm caressing her cheek. Then he kissed her, bringing her head down so he could plunder her mouth. It was at once tender and wild, unleashing the passion that had smoldered between them this past fortnight. Selina thrust her hands into his hair, clutching at him lest he decide he didn't want this.

Would he? Of course not. Men didn't change their minds about such things. Yet Selina had schooled herself to always be prepared to be left wanting, alone.

Harry held her firmly, his lips and tongue wreaking a delicious havoc on her senses. Then he plucked at the buttons of her spencer, and they had to work together to get it off, given how tightly it fit around her arms.

"Women's clothing looks lovely, but is truly a pain in the arse," Harry quipped with a half smile.

"The fancier and more expensive it is, the worse it gets." Selina preferred her simpler gowns when she wasn't pretending to be a baronet's widow. She unknotted his cravat. "Men's clothing doesn't seem to change much, with the exception of fabric."

"There are various choices of things to wear on our lower halves. But yes, other than that, it's relatively boring. Which is fine by me."

She stripped his cravat away and dropped it to the floor. Her gaze fixed on the flesh now exposed by the open neck of his shirt. Captivated, she bent her head and pressed her lips to the hollow at the base of his throat. He groaned softly, emboldening her. She flicked her tongue over him, tasting him.

He whispered, "Selina," before capturing her head and kissing her once more.

Everything happened in a haze after that. He lifted her to stand and worked at her clothing, methodically stripping each piece away with a deft ability. Meanwhile, she only managed to unbutton his waistcoat.

When she stood before him in nothing but her chemise, he paused to look at her. Selina couldn't have imagined the expression in his eyes—a mix of admiration and awe. No man had ever gazed at her like that.

The last vestiges of her fear and anxiety melted away. She swept the chemise down over her body and let it pool at her feet.

Harry swallowed. "You take my breath away."

She stepped forward, intent on making him as naked as her. That simple act—both of them being bare—already changed everything she thought she knew about sex. In her experience, and she'd seen plenty before she'd left London, it was a hurried, animalistic, and sometimes brutal deed in which no one removed their clothing.

Tugging his shirt from the waistband of his breeches, Selina maintained eye contact, losing herself in the seductive depths of his tawny gaze. He pulled the garment over his head, revealing the muscular expanse of his chest. Selina sucked in a breath at his stark male beauty. Unable to resist touching him, she ran her fingertips over his collarbone, then dragged them down to his nipple.

His breath hissed from his mouth, and he suddenly swept her up and carried her to the side of the bed. Setting her down on the edge, he moved between her legs. She unbuttoned his fall, but stopped short of pushing his breeches down, probably because he started kissing her again. And touching her, feather-soft caresses along her nape, her back, and then along her side and up her sternum. Finally, his hand closed around her breast as he'd done in the hack, but this was so much better.

Selina gasped into his mouth and clutched at his shoulders. He dragged his thumb over her nipple, and the ensuing sensation was akin to the tension she felt when she took an especially great risk—a coiling of emotion and physical desperation that could explode at any moment.

He kissed along her jaw and down her neck. She cast her head back and closed her eyes, focusing entirely on what he was doing to her and the reaction he coaxed from her body. She quivered with a need she'd never known. How was it possible she'd come this far in her life without feeling this bone-deep desire for another person?

Because it made her vulnerable. And vulnerability was unsafe. Until now. Harry made her feel exposed, but in a way that made her feel honored, as if he would take care of her always.

His fingers squeezed around her nipple, sending a shock of need straight to her sex. She'd seen and heard people enjoying this act, and now perhaps she understood.

Harry's mouth descended, his tongue and lips teasing her flesh as he made his way to her breast. He held her in his hand as his mouth closed over her nipple. Heat flooded her sex, and she whimpered, desperate for him to touch her, to relieve the pressure.

He was, however, quite content to focus on her breasts, his hands and mouth arousing every part of her. She held him, pulling at him to move closer, to end her torment.

One of his hands trailed down over her abdomen, then along her thigh. She tensed even more, anticipation spiraling through her as his fingertip grazed her sex. She dug her fingers into his shoulder and back as she whispered his name. It was an urgent plea to set her free.

"Lie back." He gently pushed her backward. She went, helpless to resist whatever he wished to do. She wanted everything he would give her.

He stroked between her legs, stoking the fire inside her. She gripped the coverlet as her muscles clenched.

"Relax just a bit, love," he coaxed as he focused his touch on the top of her sex, a particular spot that felt absolutely divine.

She tried to do as he bade, forcing her limbs to uncoil. But it didn't last long. Something was building inside her, a tension, a pressure that simply must be released. And she couldn't do it herself. She needed him.

"I can't—" She didn't know what she couldn't do. "I need—" She knew what she needed—or whom. "I need *you*."

His finger moved inside her, stretching her, filling her, giving her precisely what she longed for. Selina arched up, seeking more of him. Then he did the most astonishing, terrifying thing. He put his mouth on her.

She only knew that was what he was doing because she felt the flick of something wet and opened her eyes. Looking down her body, she saw the dark red of his hair, felt the lick of his tongue against her, and let out a pent-up breath.

This was surely wrong and terrible, but she wouldn't stop him. She couldn't. He kissed her there, in much the same way he did her mouth, his tongue exploring and then flattening, his lips gently sucking. Then his finger was inside her again, working in concert with his mouth, pulling her inexorably to a great, unimaginable height. His thrusts grew faster and deeper as his mouth closed over that sensitive part of her.

At last it came—the freedom she'd so desperately been searching for. She let go of the coverlet, her hands splaying against the fabric as her body splintered. Tumbling into a feverish darkness, she arched and moaned, then clasped his head. He filled her and held her, anchoring her through the torrent.

Then he was gone. Still floating, she opened her eyes the barest amount to see him pushing his breeches and small clothes down over his hips. The sight of his cock—thick and rigid—stole her breath.

He rotated her on the bed and climbed on beside her, looking down into her eyes. "Tell me to stop, if that's what you want." The words were ragged, his tone breathless. His eyes were dark and wild.

"That is not what I want." She pulled him over her, spreading her quivering legs. She'd never felt more alive. Bringing her head up, she kissed him, claiming him as hers. At least for now. Now was more than she'd ever had. Now was enough.

"Bring your legs up around me," he said against her mouth. Then he was there—his cock against her sex. Slowly, he slid inside, and she closed her eyes once more.

Yes, this was what she'd craved. She wrapped her legs around him and lay back against the pillows as he surged forward, filling her completely. Long distant memories rose and faded. She wouldn't allow them to intrude. This might look the same mechanically, but there was nothing similar to what had been done to her and what she currently invited.

Harry brushed the curls away from her face as he began to thrust, gently at first. He whispered words of longing and beauty. Their bodies twined together, moving rhythmically and gradually picking up speed. He kissed her ear, her jaw, her lips. Then he kissed her breast again, his lips and teeth tugging at her sensitive nipple, making her cry out as the tension that had just been released a short time before built again.

There was nothing to be feared here, just a growing ecstasy. Selina, eager to fly once more, clasped his back, moving one hand to cup his backside. He increased the speed of his thrusts, creating an almost unbearable friction. Selina cried out over and over as she took flight. She dug her fingernails into his flesh, holding on to him lest she fall alone.

She didn't want to be alone—not now.

He stroked into her hard and fast, pushing her over the edge into helpless oblivion. Casting her head back, her body stiffened as the liberating wave swept over her. There was joy and satisfaction. Selina smiled.

Then he was gone.

Her eyes flew open, and she felt wetness on her abdomen. A sense of dread gripped her. "Why did you stop?" What had she done wrong? The beauty of the moment faded.

Harry rolled to his side and gathered her in his arms. He stroked the curls back from her temple. "Selina, my darling, don't be upset." He kissed her forehead. "I had to remove myself before spilling my seed. It's an unfortunate necessity to prevent a child."

"Oh." She wished she didn't feel so stupid. "You must think I'm incredibly naïve."

"Not at all. I think you're sweet and lovely, and I'm humbled you would share yourself with me in this manner." He kissed her cheek and then her mouth, his lips lingering softly against hers.

He was humbled. She knew good men existed. Men who were kind and generous. Men like Sir Barnabus. She'd just never imagined to find herself having an affair with one. She'd never imagined herself having an affair at all.

Selina cupped his cheek. "You're a good man." She wished with everything she had that she was a good woman, that she was worthy of him.

He kissed her again, and she closed her eyes to dream.

CHAPTER 14

Selina had spent the previous evening in a haze following the afternoon she'd spent in Harry's bed. She still couldn't quite believe it had happened. Maybe that was why she hadn't said anything to Beatrix. Selina had been grateful for the card party they'd attended, as it had provided a wonderful —and necessary—distraction.

Before dropping her off on Queen Anne Street, Harry had said he'd arrange her riding lesson for this morning in the park. They'd start early to avoid being seen by a crowd of people, and they'd go to a less-used area. He fetched her in his gig and drove them to Hyde Park.

She'd felt awkward and shy seeing him after what they'd done. "I'm a bit nervous," she admitted.

He steered them into the park and sent her an encouraging smile. "Don't be. Hyacinth is a very gentle horse, and my father's groom is quite accomplished at working with new riders."

"Your father's groom?" Did his family know about this? She would be surprised if they did.

He chuckled. "I can see what you're thinking. The groom—he's called Trask—is loyal to me and very discreet. You'll be using my mother's old sidesaddle, for she no longer rides."

"I see. And the horse?"

"Belongs to my friend, the Marquess of Ripley."

She turned her head sharply. "The marquess is a friend of yours?"

"Yes. We were in Christ Church together at Oxford. You know him?"

"I do not, but I've met his wife. She was quite lovely." Selina tried not to think about the fact that Harry had attended Oxford. It wasn't surprising, and as a former barrister, he was rather well educated. She felt utterly deficient beside him. A beggar and a fraud. She shifted uncomfortably.

"She is indeed," Harry said. "How did you meet?"

"At a gathering of the Spitfire Society."

He drove them through the park, and Selina saw two grooms with a pair of horses up ahead. "Ah, that group of women—what do they do exactly?"

"I'm not entirely certain, but I hope to find out at our next meeting." As Harry drew the gig to a stop, she asked, "Why are there two grooms?"

"Jakes is here to watch over my gig during your lesson. I was going to do it, but Trask thought I should ride with you."

"Of course you should." Selina didn't think she could have done it if he wasn't with her.

He grinned at her. "It's so nice to be wanted."

"You are." The words slipped from her mouth before she knew she meant to say them. She did want him—and not just as a riding instructor or a lover. He made her feel wanted too. And safe. It was a strange and heady sensation.

Harry hopped out of the gig and came around to help her down. Jakes, a young man with ink-dark hair and round cheeks, took over the management of the vehicle, and Harry thanked him for doing so.

"Good morning," Harry said to Trask as they approached the horses.

"'Morning, Mr. Sheffield." Trask inclined his head, then turned to Selina. He offered her a bow. "My lady."

It had taken some time for Selina to grow used to being called "my lady," and she still wasn't sure she liked it. But then everything felt wrong of late—except Harry. "Good morning, Trask."

The groom pulled the hat tight onto his head as he straightened. In his fifties, he had a grizzled appearance, as if he'd seen a great many things, and not all of them pleasant. He also had a twinkle in his blue eyes and a fan of creases from their edges that indicated he had a sense of humor. Selina relaxed a little.

"Mr. Sheffield says you are new to riding, so I suggested he review the fundamentals, such as whether you've ever talked to a horse."

"Trask thinks that's critically important," Harry said with a touch of humor.

Selina smiled, looking from Trask to Harry. "Yes. I know how to drive."

"I didn't know that." Harry raked her with an appreciative glance.

"What will I be learning today?" Selina asked Harry.

"How to mount. Then we'll take a walk. How does that sound?"

"Like just enough." She let out a high-pitched laugh.

Harry came toward her and lightly touched her back. "Don't be nervous," he whispered. "Come meet Hyacinth."

He walked with her to the horse who bore the sidesaddle. Smaller than Harry's mount, she possessed warm eyes that seemed to reflect her docility.

Selina paid close attention as Harry explained the

saddle and how it differed from a men's saddle. Already, she decided this was another area in which women were given short shrift.

"You're sure it's not a problem that I'm not wearing a riding habit?" She didn't have one, of course. Nor did she have money to have one made, which was just another thing that weighed on her mind. This deception was getting harder and harder to support. And she was frankly losing her will to do so.

Harry gave her a reassuring smile. "It may be a little snug, but it will do. Ready to mount?"

She nodded, and Harry moved his hand to clasp her waist. The connection jolted straight to her core, reminding her of the more intimate ways he'd touched her yesterday. She resisted the urge to press back against him.

"You're going to put your left foot in the stirrup there." He pointed with his free hand. "I'm going to lift you. Then you'll swing your right leg up and bend it around the pommel." He gestured to the round protrusion at the front of the saddle.

"What if Hyacinth moves?"

"She won't, but Trask will be holding the lead. You're quite safe."

Selina exchanged a look with the groom, who had a firm grip on the lead rope. "Thank you," she murmured.

"Put your hands up on the saddle to help lift your body. Ready?" Harry spoke near her ear, and she tried not to think of how close his lips were.

"Yes."

Both of his hands gripped her, one pushing beneath her backside, as he lifted her up. She did as he'd instructed, putting one foot in the stirrup and curling her right knee around the pommel. The fabric of her gown pulled, and she saw right away

why a habit with its voluminous skirts was
necessary.

She looked down at him as she tried to find security in her seat. "Wouldn't it just be easier if I wore
breeches and rode like a man?"

He laughed. "Probably. But unacceptable, which is
too bad." His gaze moved over her with a promising
heat that only fanned the flames of her desire. He
stared a moment too long at her backside, and she
wondered if he was thinking of the way he'd just caressed her. She certainly was.

Harry handed her the reins. "Take these. You'll
need them." He winked at her. "Trask is going to hold
the lead, however, so you won't really need to steer.
Not today."

That implied there would be other days. She
thought of the life she'd envisioned yesterday when
she'd been with Luther. She and Harry together. He
could finish teaching her to ride.

As much as she wanted that, she couldn't see it
happening.

"Now, try not to lean forward," Harry instructed.
"Center your weight on your right thigh. It will take
some getting used to." When she did so, he continued. "This is when talking to your horse comes into
play—you'll tell Hyacinth to 'walk,' and she will
follow your command."

"It's really that simple?"

"For now, yes. Things will get a touch more complicated when we move faster, but that won't happen
today."

She narrowed her eyes at him dubiously. "What,
exactly, is a touch?"

"Well, it's not a specific form of measurement," he
said, grinning. "Knowing you as I do, I feel confident
in saying it will not be beyond your ability. Will that
suffice?"

Knowing her as he did. She did think they'd come to know each other rather well and was pleased to hear he thought so too. "Yes. I trust you."

The realization that she did made her breath catch. She never trusted anyone. And he would never trust her, not if he knew the truth.

Don't think about that just now. Enjoy this moment.

"Ready to walk?" Harry asked, interrupting her thoughts, for which she was most grateful.

"Yes." She watched as he went and leapt effortlessly atop his horse.

Harry steered his mount next to hers. "You know what to do next."

Gripping the reins more tightly than was probably necessary, Selina made herself relax. "Walk."

Hyacinth stepped forward, moving sedately as Trask held the lead rope. The sidesaddle was not particularly comfortable, nor was her position. She could see how this would take *plenty* of getting used to. As Hyacinth moved, Selina felt every shift of the animal's muscles and seemingly every pebble on the ground.

"How on earth is it possible to canter like this?" she asked Harry, who walked beside her.

He laughed. "Carefully. And not until you have more skill. You'll get there, however, even if it doesn't feel like it."

"How long did it take you to learn to canter?"

Harry grimaced. "About five minutes, much to the groom's horror."

"I'm sorry I missed that," Trask said. "I've heard the story of course. Mr. Sheffield managed to stay on the pony and wasn't scared for a moment."

Laughing, Harry said, "That's not exactly true. I recall being frightened for a split second."

Selina shook her head, grinning. "You do not."

He gave her a sly glance filled with humor. "No, I

don't. I'd watched my father ride enough that I knew exactly what to do to make the pony run and I did it."

"He always was too smart for his own good, as long as I've known him," Trask noted, chuckling.

Yet Selina had been able to deceive him and continued to do so. A wave of shame crashed over her, and she nearly blurted the truth to him right there.

But she couldn't. Not with all that was at stake for her future—and for Beatrix's.

She grew angry. Couldn't she just enjoy herself for one morning without thinking of how to survive?

Yes, she could, and she meant to do just that.

"Well, don't tell me how to make Hyacinth canter, thank you."

"Not until you're ready," Harry said. "You're doing very well. See, I told you Hyacinth was gentle as a newborn fawn."

"I don't recall you saying *that*," Selina said with a laugh. "But yes, she's quite lovely." Selina patted the horse's neck. "Aren't you, girl?"

Hyacinth twitched her mane in response, and Selina closed her eyes for a brief moment as she felt the animal move beneath her. She could get used to this...

Suddenly, Hyacinth whinnied and began to move faster. Selina's eyes flew open in panic. "What's going on?"

"Damn rabbit," Trask swore. He pulled on the lead and talked to Hyacinth, urging her to walk again. Thankfully, she did.

Selina had leaned forward to throw her arms around Hyacinth's neck. She breathed hard as she worked to calm herself now that she knew she was safe.

"Sit back and center yourself," Harry said softly. "Are you all right?"

"Yes. I was just surprised. I'd closed my eyes for just a moment."

"I saw that," he said. "You seemed to be enjoying yourself."

"I am." Her eyes met his, and she saw the same sentiment reflected back at her—happiness. Joy. This was perhaps the best moment she'd ever experienced.

They completed their walk, and Harry helped her dismount. Selina's legs felt a bit shaky as she patted Hyacinth's neck and thanked her for the ride.

"Thank you, Trask," Harry said. "I'll let you know when we'll do this again. Mayhap after Lady Gresham procures a riding habit."

"That would be advisable." Trask bowed to Selina. "My lady, it's been a pleasure."

"The pleasure was entirely mine," she said warmly. "Thank you."

Selina's chest tightened. How she wished she could do this again.

Harry escorted her back to the gig, and Jakes went to help Trask. Once Selina was situated in her seat, Harry climbed in beside her.

"What did you really think?" he asked. "I know you were spooked for a moment."

"It was wonderful. Thank you." She wanted to touch him, to kiss him, to show him how much she appreciated his thoughtfulness.

"There's no one here, save the grooms who are behind us and occupied with their task," he said huskily, his body pitching toward hers. "Do you mind if I kiss you?"

"Please do." She put her hand on his shoulder and leaned into him as his mouth claimed hers. The kiss was sweet and electric. It further suffused her with that foreign sensation of happiness and joy—of rightness.

Reluctantly, he pulled back. "I suppose I must drive you home."

"I suppose you must."

He picked up the reins and shifted in his seat. She couldn't help but look over to see if he was aroused as she was. "It's too bad you can't come upstairs when you take me home."

His nostrils flared. "You're a vixen to tempt me. Unfortunately, I need to work. But perhaps I may stop by later this evening."

She leaned toward him as he started to drive. "Come to the rear of the house, and toss a pebble at the window of the sitting room—I'll be waiting."

Selina meant to hold on to this happiness as long as she could.

~

 $\mathcal{F}$ or the first time in, well, ever, Harry was eager to get through the weekly dinner at his parents' house because he had somewhere else to go. More importantly, he had *someone* to see.

After visiting Selina last night, they'd arranged for him to come again tonight. He wanted to see her every day, and damn if that wasn't terrifying. What was happening to him?

He took special care to cloak his buoyancy. His family would pounce on it—on him—like starving wolves.

"Good evening, Mr. Sheffield," Tallent said, taking Harry's hat and gloves. "Your father has asked that you join him in his study again."

Harry had expected that. "Is Jeremy by chance here?" Harry had sent him a note pleading with him to come tonight. When they were here together, it was easier to keep the wolves at bay.

Tallent gave him an apologetic look. "I'm afraid not."

Harry exhaled in disappointment. "Thank you, Tallent."

Making his way to his father's study, Harry reviewed in his mind what he intended to say. And braced himself for his father's anger.

"Harry, pour yourself a glass of brandy and join me," Father said from his chair by the hearth. The day had been cool, so there was a low fire burning.

Harry fetched his brandy and took the open chair situated across from his father. "I was hoping Jeremy might be here."

Father grunted in response before sipping his brandy. He looked over at Harry, one eye narrowing. "Your mother is going to that Home for Wayward Children tomorrow with the charlatan. I thought you were working to prove the woman is a fraud."

"I told you the charity looks to be real. As for the rest, as I said before, is it really so terrible if Mother visits the woman?" Harry thought of his last visit to Madame Sybila. Her reading of his cards had been unsettling—because there'd been a note of truth. But not anymore. No one could call him lonely or a hermit now. Had the fortune-teller somehow pushed Harry to start a liaison with Selina? And if so, should he thank her? The notion stalled his mind for a moment.

"Harry? What say you?"

Harry blinked, realizing he'd missed whatever his father had said first. "Sorry, I was lost in thought. What did you say?"

"I said it *is* terrible. The woman fills your mother's head with ridiculous notions about the family increasing, you and Jeremy marrying, and a pile of other nonsense."

"Does any of it cause harm?" Harry asked.

"It does to me, because I have to listen to it." He sounded incredibly disgruntled over something that didn't matter. "And it's a waste of money! Why can't she do as other women and buy fripperies?"

Harry was fairly certain his mother did that too. But it wasn't as if his father couldn't afford any of this. "If the fortune-teller isn't stealing money from her, there's nothing to be done. It's not a crime for her to sell the services she advertises."

"What about those tonics?" Father asked. "Didn't you say she sold tonics that are likely fraudulent?"

Had Harry mentioned that to him? He couldn't recall. He still hadn't obtained one to see what it was.

"I'm still looking into the tonics. For now, I think you must accept that this is something Mother will continue to do. Think of it as a hobby."

Father snorted before tossing back the rest of his brandy.

"Perhaps you should go to the Home for Wayward Children with Mother tomorrow."

Scowling, Father waved his hand. "I am busy tomorrow. Besides, Rachel's going with her and will report back. At least she still thinks this entire affair is deplorable."

"What's deplorable?" Jeremy walked in and went straight to the brandy, pouring himself a glass.

Father snorted. "This business with the fortune-teller."

Jeremy turned, brandy in hand. "I thought Harry was taking care of that."

Harry stood. "I am. However, so far, I haven't found evidence of a crime. Just an annoying waste of money—according to Father."

Sipping his brandy, Jeremy nodded. "When I heard Father mention an affair, I thought he was referring to something Harry was doing." He arched a brow and quirked the barest smile at Harry.

What the hell? Harry stared at him. How could he possibly know about him and Selina? That had just happened the day before yesterday, and he'd been very careful taking her into his house and then seeing her home.

Father turned to look at Harry. "What are you doing?"

"Nothing." Harry gritted his teeth, then sent a hot, brief glare at his brother. The last thing he needed was his family knowing about his affair with Selina. Their relentless matchmaking would reach an unbearable pitch.

"Ah, well, that's unfortunate. You could probably use some sort of romantic liaison, according to your mother and sisters." He stood from the chair and went to put his empty glass on the sideboard. "Let's join them in the library."

Father departed the study, and Jeremy came toward Harry. "I was only teasing, but clearly, I hit a nerve. Is there something you want to share, brother?"

Harry scowled at him. "No, and if you mention a goddamned thing to anyone else, I will tell everyone whom you're shagging."

Jeremy's jaw twitched. "I would ask how you know, but you're the best bloody constable in London, so I would do well to remember you know everything."

No, not everything. He still didn't know who was behind saying the Vicar had caused the fire and why they'd sought to pin the crime on him. He also didn't know if Madame Sybila's tonics were legitimate. He did, however, know how Selina felt and tasted, and the delightful sounds she made when she came apart in his embrace.

"I pay attention to what my brother is doing,"

Harry said with a shrug. "We have to stand together against them." He gestured toward the library.

"Yes, we do." Jeremy clapped him on the shoulder, and they walked to the library together.

Mother greeted them with a sigh of relief. "I was afraid you'd both left." She smiled. "I'm glad to see you didn't."

Harry and his brother went to either side of her and bussed her cheeks, causing her to smile even wider.

"Oh, how I love my boys," she said. "Alas, we are still not quite complete, as Delia and Edward aren't here. Delia isn't feeling well. I do hope she'll be able to join us tomorrow for our excursion to the Home for Wayward Children. Madame Sybila and I have put together quite a group." Mother's eyes sparkled with anticipation.

Harry looked to Rachel. "I understand you're going too?"

"I am. Someone has to play the skeptic."

Their mother sent her a sharp glare. "No, they don't. If you're just going to be critical, you don't need to come."

"I won't criticize," Rachel said. "I promise." She sent a wink toward their father who hid a smile then looked at Harry as if to say, "See, your sister's being helpful."

"Everyone listen to me." Mother's voice rose above the room in the stern way that never failed to make her children stop whatever misbehavior they were about. "I enjoy Madame Sybila's company very much, and if I choose to spend my pin money on visiting her, I will do so. She actually helped me find my emerald necklace, which I'd misplaced for a few days after our soiree. Furthermore, she is supporting an excellent cause, which, after I see it for myself, I am inclined to also support rather strenuously." She

looked around at everyone assembled, her gaze settling on her husband, daring him to speak.

His eyes narrowed and his jaw clenched, but he
said nothing.

Imogen looked up at their mother from the settee
where she sat with her husband. "Will Lady Gresham
be joining us?" She darted a look toward Harry,
which told him they'd continued their matchmaking
efforts—at least among themselves.

"Unfortunately not. She is otherwise engaged."

"Pity," Rachel said. "We shall have to find another
event to invite her to. We do like her, Harry."

"Mrs. Mapleton-Lowther told Mother she saw
you at a perfumery. Were you perchance buying
something for a lady?" Imogen waggled her brows
at him.

Harry looked from Imogen to Rachel to his
mother and then at all three of them. "Please just
stop. All of you, stop. Lady Gresham is a lovely
woman, but neither of us is interested in a match.
That's the end of it. If you persist in trying to force us
together, I'll stop coming to dinner for the rest of the
Season."

"Promise?" Jeremy quipped.

"As if you're here every week," Rachel said sar-
donically. "Our apologies, Harry. We thought there
might be something between you and Lady Gresham.
Honestly, she seems the perfect match for you—she's
mature, intelligent, and she doesn't shy away from us
at all."

Add that to all the other ways in which they fit together, and it did seem she was…perfect. Harry finished his brandy, and Tallent thankfully arrived to
announce dinner.

As they moved toward the dining room, Harry
and Jeremy lagged behind once more. Jeremy set his
empty glass down and moved to Harry's side. "Lady

Gresham, eh?"

Harry glowered at him. "Don't."

"Your secret is as safe with me as mine is with you. Shall we go in to dinner?"

After dinner, Harry drank port with his father and brother, then took the opportunity of Jeremy's departure to leave himself. He stole into the small garden behind Selina's house and crouched behind a shrubbery as he peered into the sitting room.

Selina sat in a chair, while her sister reclined on the settee reading a book. He moved closer and saw that Selina also had a book open on her lap. She looked so lovely, her profile illuminated by a candle flickering on the table beside her chair.

Harry waited until Miss Whitford stood up from the settee and left the sitting room. Before he could toss a pebble, however, Selina rose and left the room. He frowned as he waited for her to return.

The sound of the exterior door opening startled him.

"I know you're out there, Harry."

Standing, he took a few steps toward the door, where she stood just outside. "How? I hadn't yet tossed the pebble."

"I was expecting you, so I was looking. I must say, for a Bow Street Runner, you're not very discreet."

He laughed. "I usually am. However, you've quite upended my typical skills."

She sauntered toward him, her eyes narrowing slightly in a thoroughly provocative manner. "Have I? Your...skills seemed quite adept last night. But perhaps I should reconsider my invitation." She stopped in front of him and slid her palms up his chest to curl her hands around his neck.

He kissed her, reveling in the soft, delicious touch of her lips against his. "I'd be happy to exhibit any of my abilities—for your consideration." He angled his mouth over hers and pulled her flush against him as he clasped her waist.

"I think that would be best. For the basis of settling on the truth of your capability." She took a step back. "Come upstairs."

He arched his brow at her. "If you insist."

"I do." Her lips curved into a seductive smile, and Harry couldn't refuse. Nor did he want to.

She took his hand and led him into the house. No, he wasn't a hermit any longer. He just hoped it would last.

CHAPTER 15

*P*ortraying Madame Sybila outside the confines of her small closet where she could reside in shadow and mostly sit made Selina anxious. To reduce the opportunity for mishap, she'd arranged to meet Lady Aylesbury and her friends at the Home for Wayward Children. That had allowed her to get into her costume at the home and then await their arrival.

She'd augmented her usual disguise by applying heavy cosmetics under the veil, including the addition of a larger nose. Over the years, she and Beatrix had accumulated a variety of implements to change their appearance. Her veil wasn't quite as thick as usual—she needed to see where she was going—but she also wore a hat with a wide brim to further shadow her face. Finally, she'd added a walking stick, which Luther had procured for her, both to help with navigation and to complete the disguise.

"I can't even tell if you're a woman beneath that," Luther remarked as Selina emerged from one of the upstairs chambers in her full disguise.

She tapped her walking stick. "Good, that's entirely the point."

"That I should think you're a man?" He grinned.

Selina flipped up the veil so she could find her way down the stairs—and so she could ask him about what Harry had told her. Because Luther's real last name was Frost.

"Luther, what business do you have in Saffron Hill?"

His smile faded. "If you want to lecture me about changing my life again, don't bother."

"Did you take over Partridge's interests?" She couldn't quite bring herself to ask if he'd started the fire, knowing it had killed innocent people.

"Not entirely, no." He moved toward her, his features dark. "We all do what we must to survive, Lina. You know that."

Yes, she did. Just as she knew she was struggling with that more than ever.

"Come on, you need to get downstairs." Surprisingly, he didn't offer her his arm. Good, because she didn't want his help. After his flirtation the other day and now this...tension, she felt awkward being around him.

Adding to the apprehension caused by both her disguise and Luther was the fact that Beatrix was probably even now pilfering something from Mrs. Mapleton-Lowther's house. Since the woman was about to arrive here, Beatrix had convinced Selina that it would be a good time to sneak into her home and remove the very spectacular brooch she'd told Madame Sybila about during their last meeting.

It was a risky endeavor, but opportunity didn't always provide for the most lucrative results. This brooch would earn a hefty price that would bring them much closer to their goal so that they wouldn't have to worry about how to fund the rest of Beatrix's Season.

Selina descended the stairs, and as she reached the entry, she heard voices outside. She quickly brought the veil down over her face. Turning, she asked Luther if he was ready.

"I am, and so is everyone else."

Except Theresa. She'd been drunk again today, and Selina had made Luther take her somewhere else lest she ruin the entire enterprise.

There was a rap on the door, and Luther answered it promptly. "Good afternoon. Welcome to the Home for Wayward Children." He held the door wide as more than a half dozen women filed in.

Selina couldn't really make anyone out, but she knew the attendees included Harry's mother and sisters—though how many or which ones, she didn't know—Lady Balcombe, and Mrs. Mapleton-Lowther. At least she hoped Mrs. Mapleton-Lowther was there. If she'd stayed home, it would likely wreak merry hell on Beatrix's plan.

"Madame Sybila, you're here," Lady Aylesbury said. She came close enough that Selina was certain it was her. "Do you need assistance?" She seemed to glance at Selina's walking stick.

"No, thank you," Selina said in her French accent. She hunched her shoulders slightly to change her stature.

"Welcome to the Home for Wayward Children," Luther said again, this time more loudly. "Let us gather in the parlor." He motioned for everyone to move into the front room that looked out to Ivy Lane.

Selina took up a position near the door, moving as little as possible, and listened to Luther deliver his address.

"My wife and I started this home by accident." He smiled self-deprecatingly, or so Selina imagined. She could picture his expression in her mind. With his good looks and charm, he would win these ladies over without much effort.

"Unfortunately, Mrs. Winter is not here at the moment. She's on an errand for one of the children, who is sick." He paused for a moment. "Mrs. Winter and I were not blessed with children of our own, so it just made sense that we take in children who no longer have parents."

"Are all the children here orphans, then?" someone asked. Mrs. Mapelton-Lowther, Selina thought.

"Most of them," Luther answered. "There are a few who have a parent who is no longer caring for them. These are children who need love and guidance. As well as food and clothing."

Selina heard the smile in his voice. He wanted them to know they were in need, hence the women should donate money. He was really very good at this.

"Would you like to meet some of the children?" he asked.

"Yes, please," Lady Aylesbury said.

"I'll be just a moment." Luther left.

Almost immediately, Selina heard Rachel speaking quietly to Lady Aylesbury—they stood nearby.

"Mama, how can you be sure Mr. Winter will use the money you donate for the children? Perhaps he will take the money and gamble or drink it away."

"I am reserving my opinion, Rachel, and I am not inclined to think the worst. Unlike you."

Selina heard the irritation and disappointment in the countess's voice and almost felt sorry for Harry's sister.

A moment later, Luther returned with several of the children. Over the next few minutes, the women asked questions of the children, who responded as if what they were saying were true. That they were lucky to be here, that they were well cared for, that they felt like they were finally part of a family, that they had hope for the future.

Their comments pulled at Selina's heartstrings. What she wouldn't give to have felt that way, both when she'd lived in London with Rafe and after, when she'd gone to school. That these children were playing a part also tugged at her emotions—and not in a good way. She shoved the sensation away.

"Mr. Winter, what sorts of things do you need?"

"Clothing, books, money for food, and the other items I mentioned. Also for medicine. Mrs. Winter is now fetching a tonic, which is an extra expense."

"And you manage all this yourself, all these children—how many are there again?" Rachel asked.

"Fourteen today," Luther said. "The number varies. Some children don't stay. They don't believe they will be cared for here." His tone was sad and appropriately heart wrenching.

"So they leave?" someone asked, sounding aghast. "How can we stop that?"

"I'm not sure." Luther gave the woman a bright smile. "We do our best. Any funds you donate go entirely to the children. I work as a blacksmith. However, it's becoming more difficult to maintain that work while I help Mrs. Winter care for the children. And we do hope to train them for domestic service."

"You can't keep working at the smithy," Lady Aylesbury said. "We must start a subscription so you will have a steady income. Then you can focus your efforts entirely on the children. I wonder if we might take a tour of the home to see what we could do to improve your situation?"

"Yes, of course. I can answer any of your questions, as can Millie." Luther gestured to the girl next to him. She was one of the oldest, maybe twelve.

Selina had said they didn't want to accept a subscription—because this wasn't real. But what if it was? What if she truly started a home for wayward children? The idea seeded in her mind.

Luther left the parlor, and most of the women filed out after him before the loud slam of a door crashed from the back of the house.

Selina hoped that was just one of the children. "Would you like me to check on that, Mr. Winter?"

"Yes, please," he called from halfway up the stairs. The women following him continued on their way. However, the two that had not—Harry's sisters, Rachel and Imogen—stayed behind with Selina.

"You go on ahead," Selina urged. "I've seen the home before."

"Are you sure you don't need assistance?" Imogen asked.

"No, thank—"

Selina was interrupted by the arrival of Theresa, who'd swept in from the back of the house. Her dark hair was partially up, but lank strands hung around her face and neck. She looked pale except for the dark purple circles under her bloodshot eyes. "I forgot 'tis fancy lady day!"

She was still drunk. Blast it all! Selina rushed toward her, making sure to use the walking stick and maintain her slight hunch. "Mrs. Winter, my goodness, you look as if you've become ill yourself. Likely from tending to the sick child. Let me help you upstairs."

"We can help her," Rachel offered, coming toward them.

Theresa turned on Selina. "I don't want your 'elp. Luther's always going on 'bout you. 'Ow smart you are, 'ow pretty you are, 'ow—"

Selina took her walking stick and moved it atop Theresa's foot, pressing gently—for now. "Mrs. Winter, you sound as if you're feverish. Best to be quiet and go get some rest."

Theresa glared at Selina. "I'm feverish, awright." She lunged toward Selina, reaching for the veil.

Horrified, Selina reacted quickly—too quickly. She jerked back to avoid having the veil torn from her face, and in so doing, lost her balance. Rather than try to remain upright, she used her stick to take Theresa down with her.

Rolling so she was closer to Theresa, Selina whispered, "If you ruin this, you get nothing. Just go upstairs to your room and stay out of sight."

Theresa's eyes widened briefly. Then Imogen helped her up while Rachel crouched down beside Selina.

"Are you all right, Madame Sybila?" Rachel asked with concern.

"Oh, yes, I'm fine. Poor Mrs. Winter needs to lie down, I'm afraid. We should see her upstairs."

"I can do that," Imogen said.

As Rachel helped Selina to stand, Selina's hat teetered. She felt her veil begin to shift. Moving more adroitly than she probably should have, Selina righted herself, then readjusted her hat to keep herself covered lest Rachel see beneath the veil. Though Selina wore cosmetics, she worried Rachel would still recognize her.

Rachel retrieved the walking stick and handed it to Selina. "You're sure you're all right? That was quite a fall."

Selina had landed on her hip, and it did hurt. She prayed Harry's sister hadn't seen anything that would lead her to the truth. God, this was becoming completely untenable. "I'm fine, thank you." She *would* be fine as soon as this bloody excursion was over. If she hadn't already decided Madame Sybila needed to go, she would have done now.

Hopefully, Beatrix would find success today, and they would be that much closer to having what they needed. Selina would do one more week as Madame Sybila and then be finished.

The rest of the visit transpired without further incident, and by the time the ladies left, Selina was in desperate need of a glass of whatever wine or alcohol Luther had in the house. "All I have is gin," he said when she asked.

"Then gin it is." Selina dashed upstairs to change out of her costume. When she returned to the sitting room at the back of the house, her disguise stashed in a portmanteau save the walking stick, which she'd left upstairs, Luther was there with two glasses of gin as well as the bottle.

He handed a glass to Selina as she set down the portmanteau and her bonnet, then tapped it with his. "To a successful afternoon."

Selina let out a sharp laugh before taking a fortifying drink. She winced slightly, for she hadn't drunk gin in some time. "I hope it was successful. Theresa almost bloody ruined everything."

"I heard the commotion. What happened?"

"She came in drunk and blathering. She called you Luther and went on about—" Selina stopped herself. She didn't want to tell him what Theresa had said and invite any discussion about how Luther might feel about her.

"I had to knock her down to shut her up."

Luther chuckled. "Just as terrifying as you were when we were children." His eyes glowed with admiration, making Selina uncomfortable. Yes, she'd had to exert her physical prowess in the past—she'd been taller than all the other girls, and it had helped—but she didn't do that anymore. She hadn't in a very long time.

"I'm not really," Selina said, taking another sip of gin and then setting the glass down. She picked up her hat and veil from the chair where she'd placed them.

Luther touched her forearm. "I don't care who you are—a fortune-teller, a Society lady, or the girl I've known nearly my whole life. I know *you.*"

Selina jerked away from him. "You don't know me at all. It's been eighteen years since you saw me last. You know nothing, and don't pretend you do."

He dropped his hand to his side, his eyes darkening. "Maybe I don't. But I made you a promise that I would take care of you. I still take that seriously."

Selina's chest constricted, but she forced herself to breathe. "I release you from that promise. The only person I expect to take care of me is me." Except the idea of Harry caring for her stole into her mind along with a flash of joy. She put on her bonnet and picked up the portmanteau before departing through the back door and making her way to Newgate, where she caught a hack.

She didn't need anybody. She hadn't needed anybody for a very long time. For the first time—with Harry—she *wanted* somebody. For the first time, she glimpsed a future of happiness, *if* she could find the courage to tell him the truth.

Her breath caught. She'd never considered exposing her secrets before. She'd already revealed more to Harry than to anyone else. Could she fully open herself to him? Would he accept her? More importantly, would he forgive her?

CHAPTER 16

"You look rather pleased with yourself," Remy noted as Harry joined him and Dearborn at a table at the Brown Bear on Monday afternoon.

"Do I?" Harry didn't bother suppressing his smile. He couldn't seem to stop his joy from leaking out.

Twice more, he and Selina had stolen away since he'd gone to her house on Thursday evening. He'd gone to her house again on Friday night, and then she'd come to his on Saturday afternoon. He could hardly wait to see her again, especially since they hadn't seen each other yesterday. Perhaps tonight...

"Why is that?" Dearborn asked before taking a long drink of ale.

The serving maid brought a tankard for Harry, but didn't linger.

"No particular reason," Harry lied. He had no intention of sharing his affair with anyone, least of all Remy and Dearborn. It was bad enough that he'd all but told Jeremy. But then, who else would Harry tell? "When I came in, it looked like you two were deep in discussion," Harry said, diverting the conversation. "Working on something?"

"Yes, actually," Dearborn said with a gleam of an-

ticipation in his eyes. "There's been a string of robberies in Mayfair. Prominent households. I was just
assigned the case."

Harry could see the young man's eagerness and
recalled when he'd started as a constable four years
before. "I haven't heard about these thefts."

Remy snorted. "You think you should have because you come from a prominent family?"

Harry gave him a sardonic smile. He was used to
being teased about his station. "Perhaps. Perhaps not.
You know I'm not one for gossip. Who are the
victims?"

Dearborn pulled out a small notebook and read
from it. "Mapleton-Lowther, Whitney, Tilden,
Balcombe."

All those names were familiar to Harry. They
were friends of his parents. "What's gone missing?"

"Jewelry." Dearborn returned the notebook to his
pocket.

Harry thought of the bracelet theft at Spring Hollow. To his knowledge, it had never been found. He
wondered if Bowles had given the victim its replace-
ment cost.

Dearborn continued, "It looks like nearly all the
robberies are happening while events are going on at
the victims' houses—during a rout or a ball."

"An excellent time to steal something—when
everyone is occupied." Harry took a drink of ale. "But
you said nearly all?"

"One was in the middle of the day," Dearborn
said. "Last Friday."

"A guest could be the culprit," Remy said, cocking
his head to the side in contemplation. "Though that
would be strange. Presumably, any guest to an event
like that wouldn't need to steal things."

"Perhaps need isn't part of it." A few years back,
Harry had caught a young woman stealing in a shop.

She'd tucked a pair of gloves into her reticule. When Harry had taken her aside, she'd been surprised because she hadn't even realized she'd taken them. Her genuine puzzlement—and alarm—had quite convinced Harry that she hadn't been lying. He'd let her go on the promise she'd pay more attention and never to do it again.

"Greed, then," Remy said with a slight sneer. "That wouldn't surprise me." He inclined his head toward Harry. "No offense to you and your kind."

Harry clenched his teeth before taking a drink of ale. He might be used to taunts, but that didn't mean they didn't irritate him from time to time.

"Any news of the Vicar?" Dearborn asked.

Remy swallowed a drink of ale. "I heard a rumor he's no longer going to lend money."

Harry frowned into his tankard before setting it down. "I suppose he'll fade away again, and we'll never catch him."

Remy blew out a breath as he tapped his fingertips on the table briefly. "That happens sometimes."

"It's still wrong," Harry said. "He should pay for his crimes."

Dearborn looked between Harry and Remy. "But we don't really know if he's responsible for that fire. Wasn't there another man you were looking into?"

Harry nodded as he leaned back, one hand curled around the base of his tankard. "Frost. I spoke with Thorpe at Hatton Garden, and he confirmed Frost is in charge in Saffron Hill."

"I did the same," Remy said with a short laugh. "But not with Thorpe. It seems Frost is less of a menace than Partridge was. He doesn't own any flash houses, just receiver shops. And he doesn't press children into his gang. Though he makes it enticing to work for him. He's quite magnanimous, from what I hear."

"Still a criminal," Harry said brusquely.

"Definitely."

"Do you think he's the one who started the fire?" Dearborn asked. "Instead of the Vicar, I mean."

Harry exhaled. "It's possible. I want to talk to him. He should be easier to find than the Vicar, eh?"

"One would think," Remy agreed. "I'll try to find him too. One of us will run him to ground."

Harry picked up his tankard. "Bring him to Bow Street."

"Will do," Remy said, clacking his ale against Harry's.

Dearborn rushed to add his to the toast, then they all drank.

Harry dropped his mug to the table. "How are Alice and the children, Remy?"

"Loud." Remy chuckled. "How is your family? Any new women they're hoping to match you with?" He sniggered.

"Yes, but I think I've set them straight. Again."

Dearborn ran a hand through his hair. "My mother does the same thing. Lately, she keeps trying to pair me off with the girl down the lane." He shook his head. "It's so bad, I don't want to go round there!"

"Harry's a glutton," Remy said. "He still goes to his parents' for dinner every week."

"Not quite *every* week."

"Who's the young lady this time?" Remy asked. "Another chit whose father is too high in the instep to see her wed to a Runner, even if he is the son of an earl?"

Harry pulled out his pocket watch in an effort to avoid this conversation. "I need to be going."

Remy grinned as he leaned over and stage-whispered to Dearborn, "That's Harry's blatant attempt to avoid discussing it. Which tells me the chit is maybe worth a second look." He winked at Harry.

Finishing his ale, Harry stood. "See you later, lads." He shook his head, smiling before dropping coins on the table and taking himself off.

Selina was worth a second, third, and fourth look. And he'd be damned if he was going to discuss her with Remy and Dearborn. Or with his family. What they shared was special.

It was also tenuous. They'd made no promises, no assurances, and there were no expectations—at least on his part. He'd wager she had none either.

For now, that was perfect. But would it remain that way?

~

*A*fter dinner, Rafe sent a coach to fetch Selina to his new house on Upper Brook Street. An imposing structure with a grand Palladian façade, it was beyond anything Selina could have imagined.

Inside, she followed Rafe's butler into the ground floor sitting room. The size and grandeur were awe-inspiring. She couldn't believe this was his.

The sitting room boasted a large fireplace, windows that looked out to the substantial garden behind the house, and two seating areas—one clustered in the center of the room and another near the windows that included a round table. Several paintings stood against the walls, clearly waiting to be hung.

She felt small and strange.

"Lady Gresham, welcome," Rafe said as he strode into the sitting room.

Selina snorted into a laugh. "This is excessive, isn't it?"

"Is it?" He surveyed the room, then looked back to her. "Wait until you see the drawing room upstairs— it's not finished yet. Nothing is, really. But we're working on it."

She wanted to know how he could possibly afford all this, but also didn't want to ask for specifics. Not yet. Maybe they would get to a point where they were open with each other.

Maybe they wouldn't.

Instead, she focused on the reason for her visit. "I've been trying to see you."

"I know. I got your note. As you can see, I've been busy." He'd finally sent her a message that afternoon, inviting her to come here to his new house.

"Are you going to host a ball?"

He frowned. "Do you think I should?"

Selina threw up her hands. "How should I know? I infiltrated Society for one purpose—to promote Beatrix. Once that is finished, I'll be done, thank goodness."

"You don't like London?" he asked. "Society, I mean. London is far more than just this." He gestured to the large room.

"Society is rather superficial."

"Haven't you met anyone you like?"

She had, actually. The Spitfire Society ladies. Harry's family.

Harry.

Selina ignored Rafe's question. "You could host a ball for Beatrix since she's your sister. In fact, you probably should."

"You raise a valid point. However, I have not been properly introduced. I'll need to establish some contacts in Society first."

"You haven't been invited to the Earl of Aylesbury's house?" Selina had been certain that Rachel would encourage her parents to do so.

"Not as of yet."

"I'll see what I can do to make certain that happens."

"Thank you. I have other...connections I can exploit."

His choice of words made her flinch inwardly, which was also strange. This was the life they led—they sought opportunity and then made the most of it. If they didn't, they starved.

Well, Rafe was clearly not in danger of that any longer. But it seemed he had other ambitions. She looked at him intently. "What do you hope to accomplish?"

"Simply to establish a solid footing here in Society."

There had to be more to it than that, but maybe there wasn't. As children, they'd dreamed of a comfortable life. Specifically, he'd longed for a library, one of the things he remembered most about their home before their parents had died. And a horse. Unlike Selina, he'd learned to ride before they'd been orphaned.

"Does this house have a library?" she asked.

A slow smile crept across his lips. "You know it does. I'll show you when it's finished—I've a great many books to buy." He really was incredibly wealthy. Books were very dear.

Selina pushed those thoughts from her mind to refocus on why she'd come. "I wanted to talk to you about Luther. Could he have started the fire in Saffron Hill?"

Rafe went to the hearth and leaned his elbow on the mantelpiece. "It's possible. He was there, of course. He knew I planned to kill Partridge."

Selina walked around the settee towards Rafe. "Maybe he started the fire to cover what you did. He loved you like a brother."

"Yes, but don't for a moment believe that Luther won't look after himself first. You don't know him as I do," Rafe said darkly.

"Perhaps you should have told me that when I returned to London instead of pretending you were dead." She didn't bother keeping the irritation from her tone. "Instead, you let me rely on him to make my Madame Sybila scheme believable."

"Has he ruined things?"

"No, but the woman he's using as his 'wife' is drunk most of the time and nearly did." She decided not to mention Luther's behavior toward her. Rafe might try to protect her, and she could take care of herself.

Rafe exhaled. "Luther sometimes makes decisions with too much emotion. I'd wager he was trying to help the woman."

Too much emotion. As opposed to Rafe. "Not like you," she said. "You've always had a calm demeanor."

"Mostly." His eyes bored into her for a moment. "What about you? How much does emotion play into your actions, particularly with Sheffield?"

Selina's pulse picked up. "What do you mean?"

"You're having an affair. Don't bother denying it." He lifted a shoulder. "Do what makes you happy. Lord knows we've not had enough of that in this life, have we, Lina?"

She hadn't. Apparently, he hadn't either. "Would you please stop watching me?"

"No. I care about you. I'm sorry I lost track of you when you left the school." His voice lowered to an almost inaudible whisper. "I regret that."

"Don't. I managed." She vowed again to never tell him what had happened to her. He'd blame himself, and it wasn't his fault. "You did me a great favor sending me away." She sought to lighten the mood. "Now look at you. Obviously, you're good at making money."

"Good enough." He nearly cracked a smile, but instantly sobered. "You, however, have struggled. I was going to send you a note tonight. It's come to my attention that Bow Street is investigating a series of robberies in Mayfair. Is that our 'sister'?"

Damn. Of course it was. "Jewelry?" At his nod, she blew out a curse. "This is how we make our money—that and Madame Sybila. We had just one more theft planned, then we would be finished."

"You can't do it."

"I know." Frustration curdled inside her, but there was also a surprising relief. She would shut Madame Sybila down immediately. "Thank you for telling me."

"Of course."

She expected him to offer her assistance again, but he'd indicated he wouldn't. Evidently, he'd meant it, for he said nothing.

"What of Luther?" she asked. "I can't believe he would set that fire and kill innocent people. People like…us."

"I struggle with that too, but if there was a benefit to him, he may have done it. Or, he may have set the fire to protect me, as you suggested."

"I'll speak to him. I need to close down the Home for Wayward Children anyway."

Rafe stretched his hand along the mantel, his fingers resting atop the marble. "That's smart. I hope you have what you need." There was a question buried in his tone, but Selina ignored it.

"We'll be fine." She turned to go.

"Perhaps you and Beatrix would like to come for dinner some night? We should ensure our stories are the same, since we are to be a family."

Pivoting, Selina saw that he'd moved away from the hearth. "That would be wise. Just send word when you're ready."

"I will." His blue eyes, vivid in their intensity, were so familiar and yet so unknown, like the rest of his face. Especially that scar. Selina was torn between staying to ask how he'd gotten it and leaving. In the end, she left.

A short while later, Selina entered the sitting room on Queen Anne Street and found Beatrix frowning over a piece of embroidery. "You look frustrated," Selina said, crossing to the decanter and pouring two glasses of Madeira.

"You know how I am with needlework."

"Hopeless, but I do appreciate your tenacity." Selina picked up the wine and went to where Beatrix sat.

Blowing out a grunt, Beatrix thrust the gloves into a basket beside her chair and accepted the glass. "Thank you."

"You won't be thanking me after you hear what I have to say, and I fear your frustration will only grow to anger." Selina sipped her Madeira before sitting on the settee. She leaned back and briefly closed her eyes.

"Well, after that prologue, I am in utter dread."

Cracking her eyes open, Selina sat up straighter and took another drink. "I've just come from Rafe's. His house is..." She widened her eyes and let that speak for whatever adjective Beatrix deemed appropriate.

Beatrix gave her an arch look. "You said it was on Upper Brook Street. What were you expecting?"

Selina narrowed her eyes at Beatrix. "Have *you* been to a house there?"

Beatrix laughed. "That obnoxious, eh?"

"I felt like a slug."

"You don't look like one. I am sure you appeared right at home. You are not the girl who left Mrs. Goodwin's seminary."

No, she wasn't. "Rafe told me Bow Street is investigating the theft of jewelry in Mayfair."

Beatrix had just taken a drink of Madeira and

coughed. When she recovered her breath, she blinked at Selina. "Is Sheffield looking into it?"

"I don't know. It doesn't matter. All of it stops. No more stealing, no more Madame Sybila. I'm going to clean out the room at The Ardent Rose tomorrow and then shut down the Home for Wayward Children."

Beatrix sat forward in her chair, her eyes wide. "But we weren't finished. We don't have enough money."

"We received a good amount of donations at the tour last Friday. It will be enough." Selina hoped it was. She'd just cut some expenses. They could walk to balls, couldn't they?

"I wouldn't get caught," Beatrix grumbled, sitting back in her chair.

"We can't take the risk." Especially if Harry was on the case. He was already too close. "It's best if Madame Sybila leaves town, and you must stop stealing. I mean it." Selina pinned her with a severe stare. "Please don't risk everything we've worked for—the future *you* deserve."

Beatrix said nothing as she lifted her glass and took a long drink of the wine.

"Beatrix," Selina hissed. "Tell me you understand. It all ends now."

"I understand." Beatrix shot her a disgruntled glower. Then she took a breath and nodded. "I do understand. We're done."

Exhaling with relief, Selina's mind churned as she considered what she had to do tomorrow. And then what? Then she had another six or eight weeks of this interminable Season. Unless Beatrix achieved her goal of winning her father's approval and support before then.

She would also have six or eight weeks of Harry. The past week—the times she'd shared with

Harry—had been a dream. But it couldn't continue, as much as she wanted it to. She wanted more riding lessons. She wanted to read his treatise about the trial of Sir Thomas Overbury. She wanted to spend time with his oversized, boisterous family and feel as though she were a part of something more than herself. But none of that was to be.

As soon as the Season was over, she would leave London. She had to. She couldn't afford to stay. Part of her screamed to end things now, that it was wrong to continue. No, that it was wrong to have started. She owed him the truth, but telling him would expose Beatrix and ruin her hopes. If it was just Selina, she'd tell him.

Finishing her wine, she stood and bade Beatrix good night before going up to her chamber. The moment she opened the door, she knew something was amiss.

Harry stepped out from behind the curtain hanging around the window. "Oh good, it's you."

A line of cold sweat beaded along the back of her neck. Had he overheard her and Beatrix's discussion? "Good heavens, Harry. I see you're better at stealing into places than you are at spying in gardens."

He came toward her, his lips curving into a smile. "I was particularly motivated this evening. I couldn't wait to toss a pebble at the window."

Relief coursed through her. No, he couldn't have heard anything. He kissed her, a now-familiar touch of his lips followed by the sweep of his tongue and the answering sway of her body as she melted into him. Suppressed emotion swelled inside her: sadness, anticipation, regret…desire. Shame.

She pulled back. "Harry, I need—" The words stalled in her throat. She wanted to tell him who she really was, who she pretended to be—who she longed to become.

"What do you need?"

"You. I need you." Eager to lose herself, she pushed his coat off and steered him toward the bed.

Grinning, he began to pluck the pins from her hair. "Did you lock the door?"

"Damn," she breathed before going to set the lock.

She removed her shoes with haste and strode toward him.

"In a hurry?" Harry asked with a smile.

"Don't talk." She cupped his face and kissed him with ardent need, as if *he* were what she needed to survive. Not whatever she had planned for tomorrow or next week. Just him. Now. This.

He finished pulling her hair down, letting the pins fall to the floor. Stroking his hands through her locks, he kissed her again and again, their lips parting and meeting between sighs and darker sounds of need.

She pulled his cravat away and hurriedly unbuttoned his waistcoat. Grasping the hem of his shirt, she pushed it up, exposing the hard plane of his abdomen and chest. He tossed the garment to the floor as she put her mouth on him, her lips and tongue moving over his nipples and up to the hollow of his throat.

He clasped her head, moaning as she stroked her hand over the ridge of his cock straining against his breeches. He abruptly turned her and furiously unlaced her gown, pushing it down over her hips as soon as it was loose enough. Her petticoat followed, then he attacked the laces of her corset. That garment joined the others at her feet, leaving her clad in just her chemise and stockings.

His hands moved over hips, pulling her back against him so that she felt his erection against the top of her backside and the small of her back. He skimmed his palms up her front and cupped her breasts through the chemise.

"No talking?" he whispered against her ear before kissing along her neck.

Sensation and need throttled her. "I can't," she managed between gasps.

"Then let me. What do you want, Selina? My hands here?" He tugged on her nipples. It wasn't enough. She pulled the chemise up, and he helped take it over her head before throwing it away.

He put his hands on her again, cupping and squeezing, then pinching. "Better?"

She cast her head back into the crook of his shoulder, closing her eyes. One of his hands moved down over her belly, then pressed over her mound. Arching into his palm, she moaned softly, her legs parting.

He slipped a finger into her folds. "Better still? Do you want to come like this?" He speared into her, filling her so she cried out. She pumped her hips forward, desperate for more.

But no, she didn't want to come like this. He'd told her she could be on top of him. She wanted that.

Turning, she kissed him, using her teeth to tug on his lower lip before she spoke. "On the bed. Show me how to be in control."

He smiled against her mouth. "Everything about this will be yours to manage."

He stripped away the rest of his clothing, then climbed onto the bed. Sprawling atop the coverlet, he looked up at her. "Straddle me."

She looked at the nest of dark reddish-brown curls between his legs from which his cock stood, thick and rigid. Reaching for him, she knew she'd find moisture at the tip. She leaned over the bed and touched him. Without thinking, she put her mouth over him, tasting his salt.

His hand twined in her hair. "God, Selina." He guided her to move. "Like that. Use your tongue."

She curled her tongue around him as she glided her mouth down then back up.

"And your hand." He sounded as if he couldn't breathe.

He curled his hand around hers, showing her where to clasp him at the base. "Go as fast—or slow—as you like. But I do prefer fast. At least right *now*." The last word came out on a guttural groan because she'd started to move more quickly, sliding her mouth up and down, taking him deeper each time.

He clasped her shoulders and pulled her up. "Stop. Please. Or I'm going to come straight down your gorgeous throat."

His words enflamed her. She looked up at him, saw the anguished need in his gaze and in the lines of his face and felt a power she'd never imagined. It wasn't a power over him, but over herself and her choices. She wanted this. She wanted him.

"Straddle me," he repeated.

This time, she followed his command, climbing onto the bed and throwing a leg over his thighs. She splayed one hand on his chest and curled the other around his cock. His hand met hers there as he moved her over him and guided himself to her sex.

His gaze was locked on where they would join. "Lower yourself. Gently." He swept his tip against her folds, then began to pierce her as she moved her hips down.

"God, this is the most erotic thing I've ever seen. You are so beautiful."

She'd said no talking, but his words were as arousing as his body and his touch. He clasped her hips as he filled her completely. Just the position of him inside her nearly made her climax.

"Move, Selina."

Putting her hands on his chest, she braced herself as she began to move over him, rising and falling, slowly at first. Then she remembered what he said about liking fast. Plus, the friction she was creating wasn't enough. She needed more. Her body demanded more.

He cupped her breasts, drawing on her nipples and crafting an intense pleasure. She began to pitch forward, her hips and legs pumping over him as she chased her release. He put his mouth on her breast, and she cried out, squeezing her eyes shut.

Then she felt his touch on her clitoris, and she broke apart. Spasms racked her body as her muscles clenched around him. She was having a hard time maintaining her rhythm. "I can't," she repeated, but for an entirely different reason.

Suddenly, Harry flipped her, his body barely leaving her as he pressed her back into the bed. and he drove into her once more. He picked up where she'd left off, thrusting between her quivering legs as she wrapped her body around his. Wave after wave of pleasure swept over her. She reached the peak and fell, her desperation quieting. Then he was gone from her, to spill his seed where it couldn't take root.

After a few moments, he came back to her, settling between her legs once more as he gathered her in his arms. "My apologies for taking over."

"It was fine," she murmured. "No, it was brilliant." It was just what she needed. *He* was just what she needed.

He kissed her temple, her cheek, her lips. Selina held him close, wishing for the courage to tell him what she must. She would. She had to.

And she prayed his heart wouldn't be broken like hers.

$\mathcal{K}$nowing Madame Sybila would not be seeing clients since it was Thursday, Harry stole into the back of The Ardent Rose. He crept along the corridor leading to the fortune-teller's small closet, listening for anyone who might approach. He heard murmured conversation from the perfume shop just before he quickly opened the door and ducked inside, intent on investigating her tonics —and whatever else he could find.

His breath stalled as he stared at the empty room. Not entirely empty, because the table, chairs, and dresser were still there, but everything else was gone. There was no tablecloth, no incense, no cards.

Maybe she put those things away before she left each day. Harry went to the dresser and began opening the drawers. Most were empty, and the one that wasn't contained just empty perfume bottles.

Swearing under his breath, Harry looked around the room, his mind spinning. His eye caught the faint outline of a door in the back corner. How had he not noticed that before? He thought back and realized there'd been a drape hanging in that corner, likely to hide the door.

Harry went and opened it, revealing a narrow—

empty—closet. What had she kept in here? He stuck his head inside and caught a faint scent that was all too familiar: orange and honeysuckle. That bloody woman had worn Selina's scent.

The door behind him opened, drawing Harry to turn.

Mrs. Kinnon gasped, her brows shooting up as she lifted her hand to her chest. "My goodness, Mr. Sheffield! I thought I heard something in here."

"Where is Madame Sybila?"

"She's gone to take care of a sick family member away from London. I don't know when, or if, she'll be back," the shopkeeper said sadly.

She'd run. Because she was a fraud.

Pushing past Mrs. Kinnon, Harry cut through the shop and stepped out onto the pavement. He stalked along The Strand until he hailed a hack—he was in far too much of a hurry to walk to Cheapside.

His blood thrummed as the hack carried him toward St. Paul's, moving far too slowly. He hoped he was wrong and that Madame Sybila truly had left town to care for someone. But instinct told him he was not.

At last, the hack arrived at Ivy Lane. Harry paid the driver and turned to look at the Home for Wayward Children. The misspelled sign was gone from the window.

With leaden feet, Harry went to the door and knocked loudly. He was surprised when someone answered. It wasn't Mr. or Mrs. Winter or a child. Instead, an older man with a balding pate and a substantial girth greeted him.

"May I help you?" he asked pleasantly.

"This was a Home for Wayward Children last week. Where are the Winters?"

"Oh, they moved on. Said they had too many children for my house."

"Where did they go?" Harry asked, anger curdling in his gut.

The man shrugged. "I didn't ask. Not my concern, though I am sorry to lose their rent."

Harry felt as though he might explode. "You must know that this home they were running for children was a fraud."

The man blinked and acted as though he was surprised to hear it, but Harry knew better. "Was it?"

"I work for Bow Street. Perhaps you would like to come to the Magistrates' Court to answer questions." Seeing the man blanch, Harry pressed his advantage. "Or you could answer my questions here."

"I swear I didn't know it was a fraud," the man said, his voice climbing. "A friend asked me to do a favor."

Harry clenched his jaw. "What friend?"

"Josie—we go way back."

"Where can I find Josie?"

The man shook his head. "I don't know. She used to live in Whitechapel, but she doesn't anymore. Not for a long time."

Dammit! "If you think of where she might be or where the Winters might have gone, you will come to Bow Street and tell me."

"Please, sir, I've told you all I know."

"They preyed on innocent people, lying to them and stealing their money." That they'd used the plight of children to run their scam made Harry sick.

The man looked stricken. "I swear I didn't know. I thought they were helping those children in earnest. Were they not?"

There was no way the fortune-teller had left town and the Winters had decided to move on at the same time. Harry didn't believe in such coincidence.

He pulled his small notebook from his coat. "Tell

me your name and everything else you know about the Winters and your friend Josie."

A short time later, Harry climbed into another hack, his anger mounting. Innes, the man who owned the house on Ivy Lane, hadn't given him much to go on. He could only remember Josie's name from when they were young—before she was married. Since he didn't know where she currently resided, Harry had little hope of finding her.

He'd probably have better luck finding the Winters. Maybe. He considered asking his friend, the Marquess of Ripley, to draw their portraits from Harry's descriptions. But Ripley was a newlywed, and Harry wouldn't trouble him.

The hack let him out on the corner of Queen Anne Street. It was a short walk to Selina's house where he knocked on the door. He expected to see the housekeeper and was surprised when Selina herself answered.

"Harry," she said, her eyes instantly lighting with pleasure. It was that look, along with the subtle curve of her mouth, that drove him forward.

He stepped inside and closed the door behind him, then took Selina in his arms and kissed her. The anger and frustration poured out of him into the kiss. She put her hands on his head, holding him as she kissed him back, meeting the desperate stroke of his tongue with her own.

He pulled back. "Where's your housekeeper?"

"Out."

He briefly claimed her mouth again. "Your sister?"

"Upstairs."

"Good." He tossed his hat onto a table near the door, then stripped his gloves away before sailing them toward the table and missing.

He put his hands on her again, clasping her waist and drawing her against him. Selina cupped his head again, pressing her fingers into his scalp. "What's wrong?"

"Just—" He couldn't form the words. "I need you." He kissed her again and began steering her backward.

She stepped back and took his hand, then led him into the sitting room, where she closed the door. Her bright blue gaze was dark and steady. "What do you need?"

Harry stroked his fingertips down her face, then brushed his thumb across her lower lip. "You."

Her tongue darted out and licked his thumb. He pressed the digit into her mouth, and she sucked. Harry's cock hardened completely. "Selina," he breathed, closing his eyes briefly.

Her hands came between them and unbuttoned his fall. Then she reached into his smallclothes, her fingers wrapping around his cock. He sucked in a breath, need raging through him.

She gently pushed him backward, as he'd done with her in the entry, until the backs of his legs hit the settee. She pressed him down, and he sat. Lifting her skirts to her waist, she straddled him, her knees on either side of his hips. He took the slippers from her feet and cupped her soles as he kissed her.

Pressing down, her sex met his, and a rush of desire shook his body. No woman had ever affected him this way. He couldn't get enough of her. The more time he spent with her, the more she gave him, the more he wanted.

Harry scooted forward so he was on the edge of the settee, then curled her legs around his waist. He slipped his hand between them and guided his cock into her warm, wet sheath.

She clasped his shoulder and cupped his head, her lips meeting his again and again as they moved together, slowly, rhythmically at first, their bodies gliding in perfect harmony.

He grasped her waist and back as he held her, his hips moving with hers. She felt like heaven, her muscles gripping his cock while her hands twined through his hair and her fingers stroked his neck and shoulders.

Pleasure built, and he quickened the pace, twitching his hips faster as he thrust into her. Her sex clenched around him as she orgasmed. Harry's balls tightened as his neared. He needed to pull out, but fuck, he didn't want to. He held off as long as he could, relishing the feel of her around him. Her touch was a balm and a joy.

Wrapping his arms around her waist, he pulled her up just before he came. He spent himself as he held her tight, gasping her name.

She brushed her lips against his temple, then pulled her leg over him as she settled beside him. Harry leaned back against the settee, his eyes closed as he took deep breaths to calm his racing heart.

As he came back to himself, his mind returned to coherent thought. "Madame Sybila was a fraud. She's gone. The Home for Wayward Children is gone. She stole from my mother and her friends." He opened his eyes and turned his head to look at her. "And you."

Selina had lowered her skirt and was wiping a hand across her forehead. She didn't say anything, and he couldn't blame her. She'd been defrauded just like the rest of them.

He realized he hadn't come here to tell her they'd been duped—well, he had, but that wasn't the primary reason. In his moment of defeat, he'd sought comfort in Selina's arms.

There was nowhere else he'd rather be.

~

*S*elina hoped Harry couldn't see her hands shaking. Standing, she sought to put distance between them.

What would that accomplish? Was she going to feel less awful across the room? What about two days from now? Of course she wouldn't. The pain and regret, she suspected, would remain for some time, if not forever.

The coldness that had entered her bones the day Rafe had sent her from London and that had never truly left, overtook her body. She went to the window and wrapped her arms around her middle as if that could help restore some warmth. But nothing could. Not even telling him the truth.

She faced the window as he spoke. "The shopkeeper at The Ardent Rose said she left town to take care of family, and the man who owns the house on Ivy Lane said the Winters moved on with their children. I don't believe any of it."

Selina turned to see him staring up at the ceiling. He'd buttoned his fall, putting himself back together, at least externally. Internally was another matter. He sounded angry and almost helpless.

"What am I going to tell my mother?"

Selina's chest tightened. There was nothing she could say. Guilt and shame nearly overwhelmed her. She'd swindled so many people, for good reason, she'd thought, but in this moment, it all felt so horribly wrong. "I'm so sorry, Harry."

He sat up straight and looked at her. "Why should you be sorry?"

She'd imagined stealing away after ending her schemes, just as she'd done every other time before, even with Barney. But this was wholly different. She couldn't just leave. Not without telling Harry the truth.

"I have to tell you something." She licked her lips, which had gone dry as a desert. "There is no good way—" Desperate for air, she sucked in a breath and blew it out. The words were so hard. Not the ones about her crimes, but about where she'd come from. When he learned what she'd been, he would be awash with disgust. She forced herself to speak. "I know you've wondered about my past. The truth is that I was very poor, so poor that I was forced to steal in order to eat. I've had to do things I am not proud of."

Harry stared at her, seemingly frozen. Then he got slowly to his feet. "You stole." It wasn't a question, but she could see the confusion—and emotion—scrambling his features. "My mother's necklace was stolen. It went missing during the soiree. You were there." He looked directly at her. "But she found it. After you came to dinner." He went quiet, and Selina simply couldn't speak. "The woman at Spring Hollow. You and Beatrix were there too."

Watching him put the pieces together tore Selina apart. She should say something. But nothing would come. It was as if the ice had immobilized every part of her.

He paced away from the settee. "Other jewelry has gone missing from Mayfair, stolen from my mother's friends. Like her, they saw Madame Sybila. A brooch was stolen from Mrs. Mapleton-Lowther's house on the afternoon my mother and the others visited the Home for Wayward Children. With Madame Sybila."

He stopped cold and pivoted to face her once more. His gaze slowly raked her. She could see his mind working, calculating all he knew. The facts were all there.

"Harry—"

He cut her off, his voice ragged. "Your scent. Orange-honeysuckle. Madame Sybila smelled like that too, as did her room when I searched it earlier."

Her knees wobbled as she came to a stop in the middle of the room. "I never meant to hurt you. I've done what I must—"

He held up his hand. "Selina, do you think I'm a hermit?"

She lifted her hand to her mouth, tears stinging her eyes.

"You walked beside me," he whispered. "And tripped beside me when I told you about Anne Turner, the *fortune-teller*. You helped me. You shared your body with me."

The truth flayed her as surely as a physical lash. "I lied about who I was, but everything between us, everything we shared was true."

"Don't." He bared his teeth. "Just tell me."

Her heart, which she'd long thought broken, shattered. "I am Madame Sybila."

CHAPTER 18

*I*t was as if the world around him had slowed, like a dream.

Or a nightmare.

Thoughts assaulted his brain: Selina leaving the Home for Wayward Children when he'd gone to check on it. The two young women—one tall and one short—who'd visited Madame Sybila on Finch Lane. His father had sent him a note the other day saying Rachel had witnessed bizarre behavior by Mrs. Winter and the fortune-teller during her visit to the house on Ivy Lane.

The regret in her eyes told him everything he needed to know but never wanted to.

"When I—Madame Sybila—told you I was a lost child, it was the truth. I lived on the streets of East London until my brother sent me away to boarding school. There, I met Beatrix—she isn't really my sister." Selina twisted her hands together. "Not by blood. We had only each other, and ever since then, I've done whatever I had to in order to care for her. Would it help you to know that I actually do give money to charities, particularly those that help children?" The truth, if that was what it was, tumbled from her mouth like an avalanche.

"No." The word came cold and hard, like one of the rocks from the avalanche striking the ground and leaving a crater. "You're a thief and a fraud. You stole from my mother. And her friends." He wanted to rail at her. More than that, he wanted details. "Tell me about the Home for Wayward Children."

"It was a fraud, as you presumed. Winter is an old friend, and his wife... I didn't know her at all. He hired her to help."

Everything had been carefully constructed. She'd done this before. "The children?"

"Also hired. I gave them extra money when I sent them home."

Harry stared at her. "Your ruthlessness knows no bounds."

"It wasn't like that. You don't understand. You couldn't. You're the son of an earl. You've never wanted for anything." Her voice rose in anguish, but he was unmoved.

"That excuses nothing. You're a liar and a thief. Tell me about the jewelry you stole."

She stiffened. "Madame Sybila doesn't earn enough to pay for a successful Season. Beatrix has a —a problem with taking things, which, in times of need, has proven helpful."

"So you take advantage of her problem?" He realized he shouted the question. Taking a breath, he worked to calm his anger. "Where is the jewelry now?"

"Gone. I fenced it all." Her chin quivered, and she blinked.

He swore under his breath. "I want an accounting of where and when. You will hope that I can recover it. Send it to me at Bow Street as soon as possible."

"You should arrest us," she whispered.

Harry wiped his hand over his face. "Yes, I

should." There was so much more he wanted to ask, to say, but he couldn't think past his fury and humiliation. She'd completely deceived him. He was an utter fool. Heart hammering, he pinned her with a dark stare. "Don't run—I'll find you." Anguish cut through him, a knife cleaving his flesh. "Damn you, Selina."

To think, he'd not only believed her, he'd been captivated by her. She was the first woman he'd imagined spending his life with. What did that say about him?

Reeling with self-disgust, he spun on his heel and stalked from the sitting room.

~

*S*elina stood frozen, locked in that ice that had held her hostage for so long, unable to move. The sound of the front door slamming made her twitch. The room closed in around her, making her feel as if she were already in a jail. But hadn't she been for some time? She thought she had control, choice, the ability to forge her own future.

Instead, she was trapped by her past. At least in her mind.

A sob rose in her throat, and her eyes burned. *No, no, no.* After all this time, all this hurt... Now, she would cry?

Selina went back to the settee, where the memory of his hands and mouth on her provoked a profound emptiness. She'd never know that sense of belonging, that bone-deep joy she'd shared with him again. Her knees buckled, and she sank onto the cushion.

Hot tears snaked down her cheeks. She couldn't breathe.

"Selina?"

Beatrix's soft voice somehow broke through Selina's pain. Then Beatrix was beside her on the settee, her hand on Selina's back, gently stroking as she laid her head on Selina's shoulder.

"What happened?"

Selina didn't want to say. No, she *couldn't*. That was different. So she wiped her face and turned her head to look at Beatrix. "Where were you?" She'd told Harry that Beatrix was upstairs, but that, like so many things she'd said to him, was a lie.

Beatrix lifted a shoulder. "Just out."

"Were you spying on your father again?"

Beatrix had taken to stealing into the garden next to her father's house so she could see into his study.

"No."

Selina stared at her in frank disbelief. "You're wearing breeches, and your hair is pinned so that you could hide it beneath a hat."

"Fine, yes. Why are you asking me about that when you're crying? I've never seen you cry. Not once." Beatrix's eyes were wide with deep concern. "Tell me what happened."

Selina stood and walked to the windows. Her body felt as if it were carved of wood. "I told Harry the truth."

"What truth?" Beatrix's question was sharp and apprehensive.

Turning, Selina saw that Beatrix had risen also. "Everything. That I'm Madame Sybila. That we stole the jewelry."

"*I* stole the jewelry," Beatrix said fiercely.

"I fenced it. Harry wants a list of where and when I sold the pieces."

"That's easy."

"I can't do it." She'd sold all of it to the Golden Lion. "Rafe likely owns the shop, and I don't want to involve him."

"You'd rather go to jail?"

"Beatrix, we may go to jail anyway." Selina pressed a hand to her suddenly throbbing temple. "I told him you had a problem with taking things. I'll persuade him not to arrest you."

"Stop trying to protect me." Beatrix pinned her with a dark stare. "I knew what I was doing. As I always remind you, we do this together. We always have. You have always protected me, even when I am foolish and unable to control my impulses. *Especially* at those times."

Love for Beatrix swelled in Selina's heart. "I'll go to the Golden Lion first thing tomorrow and retrieve the items."

"They'll charge you more than what you sold them for."

"I know. But it has to be done." Selina actually felt a weight lifting from her. She hated that she'd stolen from the women who'd trusted her. Particularly Harry's mother. "I have to return the donations too."

"We'll have nothing," Beatrix said, sounding defeated.

"Close to, yes. I'm sorry."

Beatrix came toward her. "It doesn't matter. I don't care about the Season, not compared to what you've lost." She fell silent a moment, and Selina feared her throat would crack under the pressure of unshed tears. "Will he forgive you?"

A near-hysterical laugh bubbled in Selina's chest, but she didn't let it out. "Why should he? I betrayed him horribly."

"Do you love him?" Beatrix asked.

Love. Selina barely knew what that felt like, and that was only sibling love. Romantic love? She'd never experienced it. She'd never expected it. But she knew pain, and she absolutely felt that. Not for herself, but for the hurt she'd caused Harry. How she wished she could take it all away, to make it so that she'd never deceived him.

Selina swallowed, wishing the ball of emotion clogging her throat would go away. "It doesn't matter. There is no hope. There never was any."

Beatrix put a hand on her hip. "Why not? You are free to choose what you do, and a life with Harry would be comfortable and, dare I say, happy. Especially since he loves you too."

Scrubbing her hand across her forehead, Selina pressed her lips together. "He doesn't. He's likely going to arrest me."

"He would have done so already." Beatrix smiled. "Ergo, he loves you."

"How can he?" Selina raised her voice, which she almost never did. "I stole from his mother. I lied to her and to him. We—" She couldn't bear to say what they'd done together. The moments they'd shared in each other's arms were the happiest she'd ever known. And now the guilt that accompanied them nearly drove her to her knees.

Gasping, Selina clapped her hand over her mouth. But it was useless. The tears came again, streaming down her face unchecked. Beatrix wrapped her arms around her and held her tight. Though Selina was much taller, she leaned her head against her sister's—for she was her sister in every way that mattered—and let the emotion flow out of her.

After some time, Selina finally took a step back. She wiped her hands over her face, but she really needed a handkerchief. "Who knew I could be such a watering pot?" She tried to smile, but the attempt failed.

"It's lovely, actually," Beatrix said, sounding far more positive than anyone ought. "You need a bath and some tea with brandy. Perhaps not in that order.

Then you'll sleep. We'll return the money, get the jewels back, and make things right with Harry."

Selina nodded, though she knew the last was not possible. Nothing would ever be right with Harry, nor should it be. She'd glimpsed joy for the first time, and now she knew her suspicions were true: happiness was not for her.

~

The last five days blurred together in Harry's mind. He still couldn't quite believe the woman he'd fallen in love with—for surely he had—had lied to him so thoroughly and easily.

When he'd gone into the Magistrates' Court the day after he'd learned the truth, he'd been shocked to find a package had been delivered to him containing nearly all the jewelry that had been stolen, along with a note saying the last piece would arrive soon.

"Soon" had ended up meaning three days, since the bracelet Beatrix had stolen from the woman at Spring Hollow had just been delivered yesterday. Harry had returned it to the victim, who'd been most grateful.

He should have arrested Beatrix and Selina by now. Why hadn't he? Though the stolen items had been returned, the sisters—no, they weren't even sisters—had still committed crimes.

Because you can't bring yourself to do it.

Which made him a terrible constable. Contributing to that was the fact he hadn't been able to find Frost. Harry had come to Saffron Hill nearly every day in an effort to find the man. So far, he'd proved as elusive as the bloody Vicar.

Despite that, Harry would continue his search. He strode into a court off Saffron Hill and began asking after Frost. Some people knew of him while others didn't. Those who did could only offer suggestions of places that Harry and Remy had already checked— and were keeping watch over.

Harry walked into a small tavern, the Lantern, and instantly recognized it was a flash house. Several women noted his entry and exchanged looks. Harry watched as they silently communicated who would claim him as their quarry.

Then he recognized one of them. Crossing the common room, Harry stopped in front of a dark-haired woman with familiar dark eyes. "If it isn't Mrs. Winter," he said. "You're a long way from Ivy Lane."

Her lips parted, and panic flashed in her gaze.

Harry took her arm. "Come and sit with me." He guided her to a table and put her in a chair. He sat down beside her. Another woman appeared at the table. She wore an apron, and Harry assumed she was a serving maid. "Two ales, please," Harry said. "Though I suspect Mrs. Winter here may prefer gin." He could smell it on her.

"Who's Mrs. Winter?" the maid asked. "That's Theresa."

"Yes, who is Mrs. Winter?" Harry mused. He looked toward Theresa, who seemed to shrink beneath his attention.

The maid took herself off, and Harry said nothing more as he waited for Theresa to speak.

"What do you want?" she finally asked.

"Who are you, and why were you pretending to run a charity for children?"

"You know who—or wot—I am," she said, her voice coarser than he recalled from the Home for Wayward Children. But then, she'd been playing a part.

"You aren't a Mrs. at all, are you?" Harry asked, perhaps unnecessarily. "Who is Mr. Winter?"

"Luther's a friend. 'E paid me to pretend to be 'is wife."

"*He* paid you?" How was he involved with Madame Sybila? Rather, Selina. Harry stiffened as the nearly ever-present sense of betrayal swept through him. "Not a fortune-teller?"

Theresa sniffed. "That fortune-teller's a right bitch."

Despite Harry's anger toward Selina, this woman's insult raised his hackles. He pushed that aside to do his bloody job. This woman knew Madame Sybila or Selina or, probably, both. "Why?"

"She used poor Luther. The sot's in love with 'er. 'E paid me to do the job, but I don't even think she paid 'im."

"What of the children?" Harry was particularly concerned about them and where they were now. Some of them had been quite small.

"Those wot 'ad parents are back with them. I s'pose she paid 'em, or so Luther said. 'E'd also say the sun shone out of 'er arse."

"And the children without parents?" Harry asked.

Theresa shrugged. "Don't know."

The serving maid dropped two tankards on the table, sloshing ale over the sides in her haste.

Hefting her mug, Theresa took a long drink. "Actually, one of the girls lives a few doors over. She lodges with a friend or somethin'."

"You said Luther—Mr. Winter—is in love with the fortune-teller?" Did Selina love him in return? Had everything between her and Harry been a lie? He had to assume so. Perhaps she was with this other man even now. Why would she pay him if she planned to share her earnings?

"Known each other since they were children, 'e said. 'E's always loved her, but she doesn't love 'im

back as far as I can tell. Like I said, she used 'im."
Theresa curled her lip before drinking more ale.

"Where can I find Mr. Winter now?"

Theresa smacked the tankard back on the table
with a laugh. She wiped the back of her hand over
her mouth. "Mr. 'Winter.'" She sniggered. "That's not
even 'is name. You 'ave to look for Luther Frost."

Winter… Frost… It was as if the names caused ice
to form in Harry's veins. Could he be the same Frost
that Harry was looking for?

Harry leaned slightly toward her. "Where can I
find Frost? He lives in this neighborhood, yes?"

"Sometimes. 'E comes in 'ere from time to time.
That's 'ow we met a few years back. 'Aven't seen him
since we finished the job."

"And when was that?"

Theresa scrunched her features. "I'm not good
with days. Wot's today?"

"Tuesday," Harry said patiently. "A week ago,
maybe?"

"Sounds about right."

It was just over a week ago that Harry had heard
about Bow Street investigating the robberies in Mayfair. Had Selina known about the investigation and
decided to abandon her criminal enterprises?

The reminder that she'd done all of it right under
his very nose turned his stomach. Apparently, she'd
never been concerned he'd discover the truth. Why
would she? He'd been thoroughly smitten, completely under her spell. Perhaps her role as a mystical
woman was not entirely false.

No, Harry didn't believe that. He was a fool, but
she was just a woman. A woman who'd intrigued and
manipulated him from the very start. He thought
back to how they'd met. Had she even tripped into
him by accident? Then the next time he'd seen her,
she'd been walking on Mount Street near his parents'

house. Another coincidence he didn't believe. Everything she'd said and done had been a lie.

And yet, he also thought of the small things she'd revealed, both as herself and as Madame Sybila. She'd been a lost child, an orphan, a victim of a horrible act perpetrated by her employer when she'd worked as a governess. He'd considered whether all those were lies, but somehow, he didn't think they were. Perhaps that made him even more of a fool.

"You need anythin' else?" Theresa asked. She scooted her chair closer to his. "We could go upstairs." Her ale-and-gin-soaked breath wafted toward him.

"No, thank you." He gave her a few coins. "If you see Frost or know where I can find him, send word to Bow Street. I'll pay you more if your information leads me to find him."

She quickly pocketed the coins. "Ask the fortune-teller. She'd probably know where to find him."

Yes, she probably would. As much as Harry didn't want to see Selina again, he would have to.

He stood and stalked from the tavern. Outside in the court, he took in the animals and people—adults and children—along with the dirt and disrepair. Was this how Selina had grown up? The thought of her in a place like this tightened his chest. He'd always believed that criminals weren't born as criminals. Circumstance played a large part in what people chose to do—what they *had* to do.

He wanted to know what had driven Selina to become who she was today. Because whether he liked it or not, he'd fallen in love with her, and it seemed he couldn't just shut that emotion off.

Striding from the court, Harry made his way down Saffron Hill. Was she still in her house on Queen Anne Street or had she, like Madame Sybila, fled London? The latter seemed most likely, and he realized that by not arresting her, he'd given her the chance to do so. Perhaps because he'd hoped she would.

But now he'd changed his mind. He wasn't quite finished with her yet.

CHAPTER 19

Selina and Beatrix had feigned illness to avoid the engagements they'd committed to since Selina had told Harry the truth. Until today. Tired of waiting to see what Harry might do, they'd gone to a Spitfire Society meeting, which had turned out to be beneficial. They'd made a new friend, Lady Satterfield, who would be a useful ally to Beatrix in her quest to impress her father.

If that could even happen. Selina was still worried that Harry would arrest her and Beatrix, though Beatrix continued to insist that he would have done so already if that was his intent.

The Spitfire Society meeting had also opened up another avenue of opportunity. The ladies had discussed charities they could support, and Selina had brought up the Magdalen Hospital. Lady Satterfield had been so interested that she'd suggested they take a tour. Selina didn't have a farthing to give them, but perhaps she could help in other ways. For the first time, she thought of a different future. There was no brother to be reunited with, no sister to see secure—if Beatrix's father welcomed and took care of her. She could do something that would maybe, hopefully, *finally* bring her peace.

Selina had gone to her room after returning home, as had Beatrix. A gentle knock on the door drew her from her reverie.

Standing from her small dressing table, Selina answered the summons. Mrs. Vining stood over the threshold, her mouth dipped in a rather extreme frown.

"Mr. Sheffield is here."

Selina's heart hammered as a tremor ran through her. With a nod, she moved past the housekeeper and went downstairs. She paused halfway down. Harry stood in the entry.

Though it had been only five days since she'd seen him, it felt like much, much longer. He held his hat so she had a clear view of his beautiful tawny eyes with their long lashes and dark auburn brows. He was impeccably dressed in his well-cut but entirely serviceable constable costume—dark gray coat, light gray waistcoat, and black breeches. He'd told her once that he dressed to blend in so his clothing was always either gray, black, or brown. Except for the times she'd seen him at his parents' house. Then, he'd worn a brighter waistcoat.

She realized she was staring. Blinking, she swallowed as she finished descending the stairs.

"Good afternoon," she said cautiously. "Do you want to come to the sitting room, or should I get my hat and gloves?"

"The sitting room," he said tersely.

He waited for her to precede him. She went to the other side of the room so there could be as much distance between them as Harry could want. Turning to face him, she asked if he wanted to sit.

"I do not. I came here with a proposition. It's come to my attention that you know and have worked closely with Luther Frost. I won't arrest you or Miss Whitford if you tell me how I can find him."

"I rather preferred your previous proposal," she said without thinking, as if they could still flirt with one another.

His gaze locked with hers, provoking a longing she knew would never be satisfied. At length, he said, "Where can I find Luther Frost?"

Selina straightened, eager to provide what help she could. "He moves around a bit, but I visited him on Peter Street near Saffron Hill."

"He hasn't been there in some time." Harry's voice was cold. "Where else?"

"Somewhere in Cheapside, maybe?"

"We looked for him there too, and we have people watching over these places. He's disappeared, and I need to speak with him."

"Why, if you don't plan to arrest me?"

"This has nothing to do with you. Unless you were somehow involved with the fire on Saffron Hill four years ago. Perhaps that's yet another truth you kept from me."

Of course. Selina felt foolish for not putting that together. "I had nothing to do with the fire. I wasn't even in London. I haven't been here since I was eleven."

"But you knew I was looking for Frost, and you didn't tell me you had a relationship with him."

She could lie again and say she hadn't realized it was the same Frost, but she couldn't bring herself to say one more thing that wasn't true. "How could I without divulging who I really was?"

"Of course. It always comes back to you and your lies. Are you lying still?" He took a step toward her. "I need to find Frost."

"I'm not lying—I don't know where he is."

"It's my understanding that he's in love with you. You don't love him in return?"

"No." Her chest felt as if it were covered in bricks.

"I love you." The revelation didn't make her feel any lighter.

Harry seemed frozen, his gaze glued to hers, his hands tensely gripping the brim of his hat.

Selina closed the distance between them. "I didn't realize that until it was too late," she said softly. "And I had to have help. I don't know what love feels like."

His jaw twitched. "I've tried to understand how you could be so deceptive. I don't know what to believe. You've given me nothing to trust." His tone was even, without a hint of emotion.

It would be easier if he were anguished or angry. Selina could deal with that. But this was terrifying. She'd caused him to feel…utterly bereft. "I'm not sure I trust myself. Ever since my employer…" She looked away from him. "I told you what he did. I was changed. I wasn't me anymore. Not until I met you."

The gentle touch of his fingertips beneath her chin drew her to face him once more. He abruptly dropped his hand, as if her flesh had burned him.

"I can't imagine the life you've led," he whispered. "Or maybe I can, and it's too harrowing to contemplate."

"The day we met, I pretended to fall. I did that so you wouldn't go after the child who'd stolen something. I saw myself twenty years ago."

"I wondered if that had been a lie too."

Selina flinched. "Not everything between us was false. Everything I felt for you, and I hope what you felt for me, was real."

He blinked, his lashes dipping slowly before he looked at her in disbelief. "You can't think there could be a future for us?"

"No." She swallowed. "But maybe if you understood my past, you could forgive yourself for trusting me."

"Forgive myself, but not you?"

She shook her head. "I don't want you to forgive me. I don't deserve that."

"Tell me who you were."

"Our parents—Rafe's and mine—died when I was very small. A man who claimed to be our uncle, but who later confessed he was not, brought us to London. He used us. He would say I was sick, and people gave him money. Then he sold us to Partridge to work as pickpockets." Selina swallowed. She'd never told anyone the next part, not even Beatrix. "When I was eleven, one of the men who worked for Partridge tried to take me for himself. He was drunk, and I fought him. He fell out the window and died. After that, Rafe sent me away to school. He said it wasn't safe for me in London."

"He was right." Now there was the barest thread of anguish in his voice.

"Because of Rafe, I had the opportunity to be something other than a prostitute. When I had the chance to become a governess, I was so happy, so relieved. It was more than I'd ever dreamed." She clutched her hands together, her muscles tensing. "But then my employer did what the other man couldn't. He made me a whore."

"No." Harry's eyes turned fierce, his brows pitching down his forehead. "He did not."

"I ran away and fetched Beatrix from the school—she was incredibly unhappy there and had nowhere else to go. We had no means, no family. I'd lost touch with Rafe, and I was too afraid to come back here." It had taken her years of building her confidence and regaining her self-worth before she could return. "We lived the only way I knew how, and I thank God for that, because without my ability to steal and scheme, we would have starved. Or worse—we would have been at the mercy of men." She straightened her shoulders. "I swore I would never depend on anyone ever again."

"I take it you were never actually married."

She hated that he had to—rightfully—question everything she'd ever told him. "No."

He stared at her, but she couldn't read him. She wanted so badly to touch him, to heal him.

"I'll try to find Luther," she said. "But he may be trying to avoid me. I kept refusing his advances."

"Please don't put yourself in any danger. Promise me?"

She would promise him anything. "Yes. Luther wouldn't hurt me."

"Because he loves you."

She hated his dispassion. "But I don't love him."

"Let me know what you find out."

Selina couldn't stop herself from edging closer to him. "I will. There are people I can talk to. From...the past."

He nodded. She reached up and barely grazed her fingertips against his jaw. "I'm so sorry, Harry. I wish things were different, but I don't know how they could be." She stood on her toes and brushed her lips over his. Then she stepped back.

Harry seemed completely detached. Good. He was better off that way.

Without a word, Harry turned and left. Selina stared after him while her knees melted to water. After she heard the front door close, she wobbled to the nearest chair and wilted onto it.

"Why did you let him leave like that?" Beatrix strode into the sitting room and stood with her hands on her hips.

Selina looked up at her while her body fought to calm itself. "Were you eavesdropping?"

"Yes. Why did you let him leave?"

"Why would he stay?"

"Because you love him, and he loves you." Beatrix looked at Selina as if she were mad. "You belong together."

"He does *not* love me."

Beatrix let out a breath of pure exasperation. "Of course he does. Weren't you listening?"

"Yes, and I was standing right in front of him as he stared at me with the coldest expression you can imagine." Selina shivered.

Beatrix rolled her eyes and dropped her hands from her hips. "It was obvious to me, and I was just listening outside."

"How can you possibly tell?"

"He is clearly jealous of Luther. And when he stopped you from saying what Boyer did—" Beatrix clamped her lips together. "Sorry. I didn't mean to say his name." They'd agreed long ago to never say it again. Beatrix came forward and squatted down in front of Selina. "Harry cares for you. I can tell. You forget that for a time—a time I remember quite clearly—I had two parents who loved each other. Even if they weren't married," she added. "Unlike you, I know what that looks and sounds like."

Yes, Selina did forget that sometimes. Beatrix had memories Selina couldn't imagine. She was so bloody deficient in every way! "How could Harry possibly care for me? Or want me? Or love me?"

"Why does there have to be a reason? You're an amazing woman who would captivate any sane, in- telligent man."

Selina shook her head. "That's not me."

Beatrix stood and threw her hands up. "It *is* you. Or it should be anyway. You are the strongest person I know, and yet you so often fail to truly believe in yourself. You don't even think you can love, but you can. You *do*."

She did. She loved Harry so much. Shouldn't that

make her feel good? It sure as hell shouldn't make her feel weak or defeated.

Selina pushed herself out of the chair. "I should fight for him." It came out sounding a bit like a question.

"Yes, you should," Beatrix said firmly. "You have never shied away from risk. It's time for you to take the biggest one."

Beatrix was right. Selina wanted him. She wanted a future with him. First, she had to tell him everything, every horrid detail of her background.

She should also tell him that her brother and the Vicar were one and the same, but she didn't want to endanger her brother's plans. Not after everything they'd been through since their parents had died.

Selina had known fear before, but not like this. She'd experienced joy and hope—and love—which would make the loss of it that much harder to bear.

~

*H*arry threw himself into a chair in one of the offices at the Magistrates' Court. It had been a grueling day, during which he'd gone to a wedding in Mayfair and arrested the bloody groom for extortion. Yesterday, a friend of a friend, the Viscount Colton, had come to report the extortion.

The tale had been rather involved, but it included the Vicar, who'd loaned money to the viscount. The groom, Chamberlain, whom they'd arrested, was the one who'd put the viscount in touch with the Vicar. Unfortunately, the groom could only say the Vicar lent money from St. Dunstan-in-the-West, which was of no use to Harry since he already knew that.

Furthermore, Selina hadn't sent any word about Frost. Harry had to accept she'd probably lied to him again. Except he knew she was still in London. He'd checked last night, standing across the street from her house like some sort of prowler.

He might be a fool, but he believed everything she'd told him the other day. Every horrible, heartbreaking detail.

A clerk knocked on the door before opening it. "Mr. Sheffield? There's a...girl here to see you."

Weary, Harry waved his hand. "Have her come in." He straightened in the chair.

The girl walked slowly into the office, her head turning this way and that as she surveyed her surroundings. She shifted her weight nervously before looking at Harry.

He recognized the basket weaver from Saffron Hill immediately. "Maggie, it's good to see you."

She tucked an errant strand of dark hair behind her ear. She ought to have a bonnet. Harry would see to that.

He stood and went to stand near her, then offered an encouraging smile. "How can I help you?"

"You said I should come see you if I needed anything. I need my brother to stop being a thief. 'E's going to get caught and end up on a convict ship."

That was all too possible, unfortunately. "What would you like me to do?"

"You wanted information about the man who started the fire. If I tell you, will you 'elp 'im?"

"I will do my very best." Harry knew that would only happen if the boy wanted to be helped. "I could also help you find an apprenticeship. Would you like to learn to make hats?"

She shrugged. "I already know how to make baskets."

"Hats may not be so different." He lowered his voice conspiratorially. "Sometimes I think women's hats could be used as baskets."

This elicited a smile from Maggie. It was gone too

soon, however. "The man who told us to say the Vicar started the fire—'e was like you."

"What do you mean?"

"A gentleman."

Harry wondered if it could have been Frost. The man had demonstrated his ability to play a role. "Was it Frost?"

A look of consternation crossed her face. "I don't think so, but I can't say for sure."

"Your brother would know if it was Frost, wouldn't he?"

She nodded.

"And where can I find your brother?" She'd been vague when Harry had spoken to her before, but he believed her story would change. She was motivated now.

"You can find 'im at the Lantern—it's in a court off Saffron Hill—most nights."

Harry knew precisely where that was of course. He realized he hadn't asked Maggie about Frost's whereabouts. "Do you know where I can find Frost? I understand he has lodgings on Peter Street, but he hasn't been seen there of late."

"'E and the boys—like my brother—'ave a place they 'ide. An alley off Chick Lane."

Brilliant. Harry would go there straightaway. "Thank you, Maggie. Would you like me to see you home?"

She hesitated, but eventually nodded shyly.

Harry smiled at her again. "Wonderful." He picked up his hat and went to open the office door. "What's your brother's name?" Harry would do what he could to help the boy. If he wanted it.

"Elias Dwight," she said as Harry gestured for her to precede him.

Downstairs, he was intercepted by another clerk, who said he needed to take care of some paperwork regarding Chamberlain—the man he'd arrested earlier.

"Damn." Harry ran his hand through his hair.

Remy approached him, a line running across his forehead with concern. "What's the trouble?"

"I was just about to leave. I need to see this young woman back to Saffron Hill." Harry looked around for Maggie, but didn't see her. Where had she gone?

"Mr. Sheffield?" the clerk prodded.

"I got a lead on Frost," Harry said to Remy. "He may be hiding out on Chick Lane. I was going to go now, but I have some urgent paperwork."

"Want me to go for you?" Remy offered.

"Would you?" Harry was disappointed he couldn't go, but it was more important to make some bloody progress.

"Not a problem. You mentioned a young woman?"

"Yes, I was going to see her home—she lives in Saffron Hill. But she seems to have disappeared. You go on."

Remy clapped him on the shoulder. "I'll find you later. Hopefully, with news."

Anticipation surged in Harry. He turned to the clerk and followed him to fetch the paperwork.

The clerk who'd showed Maggie upstairs approached Harry again. "Mr. Sheffield?"

Harry was glad to see him. "Have you seen the girl you showed upstairs?"

Shaking his head, the clerk held out a missive. "No, but a message was just delivered for you."

Opening the parchment, Harry caught his breath as he recognized Selina's handwriting. She knew where to find Frost—Chick Lane—and said she'd meet Harry there this evening. Harry checked his pocket watch. She'd be there soon.

Dammit! Harry frowned at the clerk. "Does this need to be done right now?"

"Yes, sir." Scowling, Harry took the paperwork from the clerk, intent on finishing it as quickly as possible so he could follow Remy.

So he could get to Selina.

She hadn't lied to him. Still, he wasn't sure he could ever trust her. Her confessions from the other day had weighed heavily on him. Maybe she'd been right that he couldn't forgive himself for trusting her, for allowing himself to be a fool.

A fool blinded by love. Was he still?

No, he knew what she was. He also knew why. What he didn't know was if he could accept her. But, oh, how he wanted to.

CHAPTER 20

*C*hick Lane was incredibly narrow, with wood-and-brick buildings three stories tall that made the street feel even more close. The Fleet Ditch ran nearby, providing a permeating stench of offal and damp.

Selina couldn't imagine Luther living here. Actually, she could. What she couldn't imagine was living here herself. Which surely would have happened—or somewhere similar—if she hadn't left London.

Or perhaps Rafe would have been able to protect her. He'd certainly come out all right. Better than she could have dreamed. But what had it cost him? She wasn't sure and didn't know if he'd ever reveal the truth to her.

He had, however, helped her find Luther, and she was most grateful. It was a small thing to do this for Harry, but she was glad for the chance. She knew nothing could ever erase her betrayal. Hopefully, this would help him. That was all she wanted.

Rafe, who'd tracked down Luther's hiding spot, had offered to come with her this evening, but she'd said Harry would meet her. Besides, if Rafe came, it was likely that Harry would find out he was the Vicar. Since Rafe had decided to permanently retire his other identity, they'd agreed it was best he stayed in Mayfair as Raphael Bowles.

The Duck and Swan backed up to the Fleet Ditch. A covered porch jutted into the street, making the space in front of it even narrower than the rest of the lane. Prostitutes loitered outside. One had just snagged a customer and drew him inside with a leer.

Selina felt the familiar weight of her pistol in her reticule and took a deep breath. She wasn't afraid, just a bit nervous. Though she'd dressed in plain, serviceable clothes—the black she wore as Madame Sybila—she still felt as though she stuck out.

She walked inside, where lanterns illuminated the busy common room. It was barely dusk, but it would have been quite dark in here without them. The ceiling was low, and there were no windows. There were also a great many people. Some sat in groups laughing or arguing. Others stood together, tankards dangling from their fingertips.

Selina moved to the side so she could survey the room to see if Luther was present. It was likely he was upstairs somewhere if he was trying to remain out of sight. Which it seemed he was, since Harry hadn't been able to find him. Did Luther know Bow Street was looking for him?

"What are you doing here?"

Turning sharply, Selina saw Luther frowning at her, his dark brows forming a vicious V on his wide forehead. He'd come from a doorway that was just behind him.

"Looking for you," she said.

He grinned at her. "That's the best thing I've heard all day. Still, you shouldn't be here. It's not the safest of places. Let us get out of the main room." He put his arm around her waist and led her to the door he'd come from. "Do you need another favor?"

She extricated herself from his embrace and

moved into the room. "No. What I need is to under-stand what happened four years ago, when my brother supposedly died."

Luther grimaced as he joined her inside. "Rafe made me promise not to tell you."

"So he said." She didn't hide her irritation. "Did you start the fire?"

Glancing furtively into the common room, Luther pulled her farther into the small private dining chamber, to the other side of the table. Like the common room, it was windowless but also lit with lanterns, two to be precise. "Careful what you say around here, Lina."

She took her hand from his. "Please don't call me that." She was Selina now. Or Lady Gresham, and only because she had to be if Beatrix were to achieve her goal. Lina and Madame Sybila were dead.

"Your wish is my command." He held out a chair at the rectangular table.

She didn't want to sit. Moreover, she didn't want to give the indication she was staying. Where the devil was Harry?

She clasped her hands together, her reticule hanging from her wrist against her thigh. "Tell me about the fire."

Luther exhaled, and he let go of the chair. "Yes, I started the fire. Partridge was a menace—Rafe wasn't the only one who wanted him dead."

"But you knew Rafe was going to kill him."

He slowly nodded. "I had a chance to improve my lot, and I took it. A gentleman of influence asked me to kill Partridge by starting a fire."

Selina took a step toward the table and put one hand on the back of a chair. "If you knew Partridge was going to be dead already, why start a fire that would kill innocents?" The boy she'd known would never have willingly hurt innocent people—children. But maybe he wasn't the boy she'd known. None of them were the same, and why would they be?

His eyes hardened. "The Runner paid me a hefty sum to burn it down."

"Why?"

"Because he wanted me to take over Partridge's territory. Partridge refused to pay him a protection fee, and I had no problem doing so. The fire also covered Rafe's act, which was an added bonus—one I would think you would appreciate."

She gripped the chair, the wood biting into her palm. "How can I be grateful for that when children died?"

He stared at her coldly. "Children die every day, and we were always grateful it wasn't us, weren't we? You've forgotten what it's like to live here." He sneered. "What it takes to survive."

Maybe she had. What he'd said a moment ago finally sunk into her brain. "Did you say a Runner paid you to start the fire?"

"Did he?"

The answer came from behind Selina. She turned to see a man standing just inside the room as he pulled the door shut.

"We don't have a meeting," Luther said, his eyes narrowing.

"No, we don't. Nevertheless, I'm here for a payment. And to inform you that one of my comrades is keen to find you. You need to better your hiding place." The man inclined his head toward Selina. "Who's the trollop?"

Luther snarled. "Watch your mouth, Remington."

Remington? Selina had heard that name... Her stomach clenched. He was a Runner. He was also Harry's friend. This was the man who'd paid Luther? And now he was collecting payments from Luther.

He was utterly corrupt. "It was you," was all Selina could manage to say.

But Remington ignored her as he kept his eyes fixed on Luther. "I think you're the one who needs to watch his mouth." Remington tsked. "You can't be telling people about me. Or about the fire. The Vicar started it, if you recall."

Luther scoffed. "Only because you said so. What difference does it make now?"

"It makes every difference if you're going to say I paid you to do it. Now we have to kill this poor chit." Remington moved around the table toward Selina.

She opened her reticule, but Luther grabbed her arm and shoved her behind him. He faced Remington. "She won't tell anyone about you. You have my word."

"Unless you plan to cut out her tongue, I can't believe that won't happen—your word or not." His tone was mild as if he threatened people every day. "Stand aside, Frost."

"You won't touch her." Luther pulled a pistol from his waistband, but before he could raise it, the Runner launched forward, knocking him backward into Selina. They all crashed to the floor.

It took Selina a moment to regain her breath and her wits. She rolled to the side as the men fought. A loud gasp filled the room, and the commotion stopped.

"Dammit." The Runner rose, his chest heaving. He scowled down at Luther's body. Blood pooled beneath him. "I really didn't want to kill him. He was a good soldier." He swiveled his attention to Selina who scrambled to her feet. "Until you." He advanced on her. "You're a pretty thing. Did Luther already pay you? I don't mind paying again, though there's no point when you won't see morning."

At last, she managed to pull her pistol from her

reticule. Shaking, she held it up. "Harry will be here at any moment."

Remington stopped barely a foot from her. "Harry? You know Harry?"

Selina nodded.

There was a beat of silence, and then Remington began to laugh. His eyes crinkled, but that didn't do a thing to banish the hostility from his gaze. "Harry isn't coming, dear. He sent me in his stead. How sad for you." He knocked the gun from her hand before she could fire, sending it skidding across the table. "But happy for me as I will get to have my fun after all. Now be a good girl and stay quiet."

He stepped toward her, and all Selina could see was the face of the man who'd said almost the exact same thing to her twelve years earlier.

～

*H*arry took the stairs two at a time up to his office so he could complete the damned paperwork. He stopped short at the landing as Maggie stepped in front of him.

"There you are," he said. "I thought you'd gone."

She shook her head, and he saw fear in her eyes. "That man you were talking to. I recognized him."

Harry frowned. "The clerk?"

"The tall man with the dark hair."

The clerk was a shorter fellow with bright blond hair. She had to mean Remy. "Where do you recognize him from?" Likely, she'd seen him around Saffron Hill, particularly since he'd been helping Harry look for Frost. Harry tried to remain patient because she looked scared. But he was anxious to get the paperwork done so he could get to Selina.

"He's the man who told us to say the Vicar started the fire. My brother says he visits Mr. Frost."

A buzzing sound filled Harry's ears, and his blood went cold. Remy had gone to talk to Frost. And so had Selina.

Harry started down the stairs then abruptly stopped. Turning, he looked up at Maggie. "I need to get to Chick Lane right away. I'm sorry." He flew down the stairs and found the nearest clerk. "I'll have to take care of this later. Put that girl in my office. And give her tea and some biscuits." He thrust the paperwork into the clerk's arms.

Then he fled the building and broke off at a run toward Saffron Hill, which was over a mile away.

By the time Harry arrived at the Duck and Swan in Chick Lane, he was overheated and filled with dread. He rushed into the dim interior of the tavern and looked around wildly. No one looked familiar— he didn't see Selina or Frost or Remy.

A woman with rouged cheeks and red lips came toward him, swaying her hips. "Evening, sir. Care for an ale? We can share one." She put her hand on his chest.

"I'm looking for Luther Frost or a woman who might be with him. She's tall, with golden-brown hair. Beautiful." Harry saw a flicker of something in her eyes and quickly pressed a coin into her hand.

The prostitute pouted. "She came in a little while ago. There." She inclined her head toward a door tucked into the front corner of the common room.

"Thank you." Harry barely finished speaking before he turned and rushed to the door.

He flung it open and stepped inside to see Remy towering over Selina, his hand clutching her arm. "Remy?"

Remy looked at Harry over Selina's head. "Harry, what are you doing here?"

"I came to meet her."

She turned and jerked her arm from Remy's

grasp. "Harry, he killed Luther." She glanced toward the floor.

Harry followed her gaze and saw Frost's prone form. He also saw blood. Returning his attention to his friend, Harry took a cautious step toward them. "What happened, Remy?"

Selina answered. "He paid Luther to start the fire."

Remy struck Selina, and she fell against the wall with a soft groan.

Harry pulled his pistol from his coat, but Remy dove under the table. He wrapped his arms around Harry's legs before Harry could reposition himself and knocked Harry off-balance.

Falling to the floor, Harry kept ahold of his gun, but he couldn't get a good shot. Remy reached for it, his hand closing around Harry's as he struggled to wrest the weapon away.

"Get off him!" Selina cried.

Harry looked up to see her standing a few feet away holding a pistol. Likely hers. Thank God she carried one. Still, he wanted her far away from here. "Selina, go. I can take care of this."

His distraction was all Remy needed. He managed to knock Harry's pistol away, sending it sliding across the floor.

Harry pushed at Remy, but when he didn't fight back, Harry chilled.

"He has a knife!" Selina's warning came as the blade flashed in the lantern light.

Harry grabbed Remy's wrist just before the knife came down. The blade was still precariously close to his chest.

Something moved over the back of Remy's head, followed by a crash. Remy let out a low sound, then slumped over Harry. Thankfully, Remy's hand went limp, otherwise, the knife might have pierced Harry's breast.

Harry shoved him to the side, breathing heavily. He stared up at Selina. "What did you do?"

"I hit him with a pitcher."

Pieces of pottery littered the floor. Remy groaned.

Harry scrambled to his feet. "Can you go out and find some rope? I need to bind his hands."

She nodded and hurried from the room.

Working quickly, Harry found Remy's pistol and checked him for any other weapons besides the knife. He took both and set them in the middle of the table. He caught sight of Luther on the floor, his face ashen and still in death.

Selina returned with a length of rope. "Will this do?"

Harry took it from her with a nod, then knelt to bind Remy's hands behind his back. He tied them tightly with the best knot he knew.

"I was afraid to shoot him. I didn't want you to get hurt."

Harry looked up at Selina and saw the fear in her eyes. He rose and went to her. A red mark from Remy's hand had begun to brighten her cheek. Harry wanted to kill him. "Are you all right?"

She nodded, but a tear leaked from her eye. He caressed her face. "You're safe now."

He went to the doorway, keeping his focus on Remy, and called out, "I need someone to run to Bow Street. Fast. Ten shillings."

A boy dashed to the doorway. "I can do it, sir."

Harry gave him five shillings. "The rest when you return with at least two constables. Tell them Harry Sheffield needs assistance and a cart. And hurry."

The boy nodded and took himself off.

Remy groaned louder, and Harry bent to turn him over. Then Harry dragged him to the wall and propped him up to sit against it.

Harry glanced at Selina. "What happened?"

"I arrived and met Luther in here. He told me a Runner paid him to start the fire. Then Remington showed up and asked for a payment that was due."

Harry fixed a furious stare on his friend—former friend. "What was the payment for?"

Blood trickled down Remy's head from the wound Selina had inflicted with the pottery. "Everything she says is a lie."

Many things, but not everything, Harry had learned. "You'd have me believe that *she* killed Frost?"

Remy winced, then lowered his gaze. He didn't say anything.

"Why were you holding her when I arrived?" Harry asked.

"Because he intended to rape me." Selina wouldn't lie about that. But Harry didn't think she was lying about any of this. Now he *really* wanted to kill Remy.

Harry crouched down and grabbed the top of Remy's hair. He pulled Remy's head back, forcing him to look up. "Don't fucking lie to me, you piece of filth."

Remy sneered. "I did offer to pay her."

"Before you promised to kill me," Selina said.

Harry knocked his head back against the wall, drawing a yelp of pain from Remy. "Speak of her again, and I'll finish what she started." He kept his hand tangled in Remy's hair. "Why did you pay Frost to start the fire?"

Selina answered. "Because Luther agreed to pay Remington a protection fee when he took over Partridge's gang."

Harry stared at the man he thought he knew. "You took money?"

"You shouldn't have cared about the damn fire. About any of it." Remy's lip curled. "But you've such a soft heart. What did it matter that there were a few less whores and thieving brats? That was a good thing. Partridge refused to pay me. Frost didn't. We turn our heads and let them rule over their little kingdoms. They should pay for our ignorance—and our protection."

Harry despised corruption. He tugged on Remy's hair, causing him to flinch as he met Harry's gaze. "Did you really threaten to kill her?"

Remy spit to his right toward Selina and glanced up at her. "Fucking whore."

Fury exploded in Harry, and he hit Remy's head against the wall once more. This time, Remy slumped to the side, unconscious.

"Harry!" Selina came toward him and touched his shoulder.

Standing, Harry swore. "He's fine. For now."

He turned to her. "I want to see you home, but you should go before the constables get here. I don't want to involve you in this."

"But I'm a witness. I can say what happened."

"Then you'll have to explain why you were here. That won't reflect well on Lady Gresham. Or Miss Whitford. I have his knife and can prove he used it to kill Frost. Remember, I used to be a barrister. Remy won't go free."

"You're rather brilliant." She gave him a small smile that made his heart trip. "I can make my way home."

"You have your pistol?"

She went and found it on the other side of the table, freezing for a moment as she looked down at Luther. A sob escaped her lips before she clapped her hand over her mouth.

Harry reached for her without thinking. He pulled her against him and pressed his lips to her temple beneath the brim of her bonnet. "I'm so sorry. I know he was your friend."

She held him tightly as she buried her face in his chest.

He brushed his lips against the edge of her ear. "You need to go. I'll come see you later."

She stood back and looked up at him in surprise. "You will?"

"There are things to say. Aren't there?"

"I've said everything important." She brushed at the wetness on her cheeks. "I love you."

Impossibly, a smile broke over his mouth. "I know."

She smiled back, and his breath hitched.

"*I* have things to say," he clarified. "Go now. I'll see you soon."

She tucked the pistol into her reticule. "You'll take care of Luther?"

"I will." He stepped aside so she could pass.

She had to step over Remy's sprawled legs on her way to the door. Pausing at the threshold, she turned her head. "Thank you."

And then she was gone.

Harry looked down at the man he'd called friend. Nothing was as it seemed. Good people were bad, and bad people were good. Or something. He wiped his hand over his face and contemplated just what things he was going to say to her.

CHAPTER 21

*T*he clock chimed once, prompting Selina to get up again and pace the sitting room.

Beatrix glanced up from her book. "If you keep doing that every quarter hour, you're going to wear a hole in that carpet."

"He should be here by now." A thousand scenarios had run through Selina's mind, and she kept landing on the worst one. "What if Remington escaped his binding and attacked Harry? What if he killed him? I shouldn't have left."

"That's ridiculous."

"I'm going to Bow Street." Selina strode from the sitting room, then stopped short as she heard a knock on the front door.

She raced forward and threw the door open. Harry stood on the doorstep, his handsome features exhausted.

"You're here." Those were the only words she could seem to manage.

"I'm here." He glanced past her. "May I come in?"

Selina shook her head briskly to clear it of her idiocy. "Of course." She held the door as he walked into the hall, then closed it firmly.

Beatrix stepped out of the sitting room. "Good evening, Mr. Sheffield."

"Good evening, Miss Whitford."

"You look as if you need a brandy," Selina said.

He gave her a single nod. "Yes, please."

She preceded him into the sitting room and went straight to pour him a drink. Turning, she saw that he'd come inside, and Beatrix had followed him.

Selina took him the glass and ignored the pull she felt toward him as their fingers brushed. She wanted to take him in her arms and soothe the anguished lines in his face.

"I'm sorry," Beatrix blurted. "About stealing things. I can't help myself, but I do try."

Harry swallowed a drink of brandy, then arched a brow at Beatrix. "You're telling me the only reason you stole that jewelry was because you were compelled to do so?"

His sardonic tone gave Selina a rush of hope.

Beatrix grimaced. "No. We needed the money. Sorry."

"Beatrix, I don't think you're helping," Selina said softly.

"She's not harming matters," Harry said. "You're both thieves. But you've returned the jewelry. And, apparently, the money. My mother sent a note earlier that she'd received a letter from Madame Sybila returning the money she'd donated to the Home for Wayward Children after learning it was a fraud."

Selina wrung her hands. "I considered telling her the full truth, that I'm Madame Sybila, but if I did that…"

Harry finished for her. "If you did that, there would be no possibility of a future between us."

"And this is where I take my leave." Beatrix looked between them. "I know you love each other. I also know this didn't start as it should have. Please make sure it ends that way." She pursed her lips before spinning about and leaving the sitting room, closing the door as she went.

"Your 'sister' is impertinent."

Selina couldn't draw a deep breath. Hope filled her chest, silly as it was. "Exceedingly."

"She's also right. I know you love me." He glanced down at the brandy in his hand. "And, as it happens, I love you too."

Selina slapped her hand over her mouth before a sob escaped. But Harry noticed anyway.

He set his glass down on a table and walked toward her. "Are you all right?"

She nodded. "It's been a terrible week."

"Yes, it has." He pressed his lips together, and she braced herself for whatever he might say next. "I wanted to despise you. And then I despised myself because I couldn't. Nor could I even arrest you as I should have. What kind of constable does that?"

Oh, she'd ruined him. Selina's heart cleaved in two. "I'm so sorry, Harry. Please, arrest me. I should pay for my crimes."

"I think you already have," he said softly, eliminating the space between them and taking her hand. "When I think of your childhood, of the dangers and hardships you've faced, I am torn between a furious anger and a deep despair." He gave her a weak smile. "How you didn't succumb to your circumstances, I don't know. But then I suppose you did. You became what you had to in order to survive."

He understood. Dear God, he understood. Selina started to collapse, but he caught her, putting his arms around her waist. "I've got you, my love."

Harry pulled her against him, and the solid warmth of his chest calmed her like nothing else could.

"What happened with Remington?" she asked.

He stroked her back. "He'll be charged with Frost's murder tomorrow."

She tipped her head to look up at him. "You took care of Luther?"

"I did. Does he have family we should notify?"

"No, but I will tell those who need to know." She sucked in a breath. "Rafe."

"Ah yes, I presume your brother knew him, since you were children together."

Selina pulled back from him. "I should tell you something else—the last revelation. I think." Her life had been so twisted with lies that she wasn't sure she'd uncovered them all, including the ones she told herself.

His eye twitched. "I don't know if I can take anything else."

"It's not about me. My brother—oh dear, you aren't going to like this." She took a deep breath. "Rafe is the Vicar."

Harry's eyes widened and his jaw dropped. "*What?*"

"I didn't know. At least not at first. When I returned to London two months ago, I learned my brother had died—in that fire on Saffron Hill that the Vicar had supposedly started. When I met you, and you were looking for the Vicar, I thought you could help me find him. I'm horrified to admit I wanted revenge." She wiped her hand over her forehead. "I suppose this was about me after all."

His tawny eyes darkened with hurt. "That's why you befriended me?"

She put her hands on his forearms. "Not entirely. I also needed to keep you close—because of your interest in Madame Sybila. But that isn't the entire truth either." She briefly closed her eyes. "I'm learning to be honest with myself as well as everyone else. The truth is that I liked you from the start. And I was attracted to you. From the moment you saved me from falling face-first into the pavement."

He narrowed one eye at her. "Why should I believe you?"

"You shouldn't. Not at all. But I'm hoping and praying you will."

"You are a consummate actress," he said cautiously. "A spectacular fraud. And yet, I can't believe you pretended everything that went on between us."

She stepped closer to him until their chests touched, and put her palm against his cheek. "I didn't. I couldn't. I'd never been with anyone before, not like you. I knew I shouldn't—both because it was dangerous and because it wasn't right. But I couldn't help myself. I was falling irreversibly in love with you."

Harry took her hand from his cheek and pressed a kiss against her palm. "I wish you'd trusted me."

"I don't—didn't—trust anyone except Beatrix. Not even Rafe." She dipped her gaze briefly. "But the day you gave me the riding lesson, I told you I trusted you. I meant it."

Harry frowned. "Speaking of your brother, what of the Vicar?"

"Retired. Rafe is entirely Raphael Bowles, Upper Brook Street's most recent resident. All his business dealings are entirely legitimate." He told her he was transferring the last of his receiver shops next week. "I understand you may still want to arrest him, but I'm asking you not to. We have a great deal of years to make up for, and I hope we will have the chance."

He gave her an arch look. "Upper Brook Street? It seems as though Bowles should have offered to help you."

"He did, but I refused. I don't like to rely on others." She clutched his hand tightly. "I will, however, rely on you."

"How can I deny you the only blood family you

have?" he asked softly. Selina could hardly believe his kindness. "So long as he remains legitimate."

"He will. We *both* will. Beatrix too."

"Well, that's a relief. It would be very embarrassing if my sister-in-law was caught stealing."

Selina froze, her eyes locking with his. "Your what?"

"My sister-in-law. Which Beatrix will be, if you agree to be my wife."

"You can't mean that." Selina tried to back away as she fought to draw air into her suddenly laboring lungs.

He held her fast, drawing her against him. "I'm not letting you go, not unless you really want me to. Yes, I do mean it. Selina, Sybila, Lady Gresham, whoever the hell you are, marry me."

Selina stared into his eyes and saw something she'd never imagined—a future and happiness. The tears she'd shed the other day returned, but these were from joy. "Yes. And I know precisely who I am finally. Who I *want* to be." She smiled up at him. "Yours."

Harry kissed her, infusing her with a strength and wonder that filled her with emotion until it overflowed. She wrapped her arms around his neck and held on to him fiercely.

After several minutes, Harry broke the kiss and rested his forehead against hers. "My family will be unbearable when I tell them."

"They'll be ecstatic."

"Unbearably ecstatic, yes." He kissed her cheek. "Will you promise to protect me from them?"

"I will do anything you ask for the rest of our lives. You've given me a gift I never expected and that I'm still not sure I deserve."

He cupped her face and stared deep into her eyes. "Don't say that. Ever. You deserve this. We deserve each other." He kissed her hard and fast. "Now, if you don't mind, I am exhausted and need to go to bed."

Selina unwound her hands from his neck. "Of course. I'll walk you out."

"Out or up?" He arched an auburn brow at her.

"Oh! You want to stay?"

"I definitely don't want to leave."

"Then stay." She stood on her toes and kissed him, her lips lingering on his. "Forever."

Harry swept her into his arms and carried her upstairs.

*J*ust two days later, Harry escorted his betrothed into the library at his parents' house. He hadn't told them why he'd wanted to have a family dinner, and his mother hadn't pressed. She'd just been delighted to have him come since he'd missed Thursday. Then he'd asked her to make sure *everyone* was there, and she'd become incessant in demanding why.

He still hadn't told her.

And so when he entered the library with Selina on his arm, followed by Rafe and Beatrix, his mother's jaw had promptly dropped to the floor. Then she'd burst into tears.

"Good heavens, pull yourself together," Father said, patting her back.

"Does this mean what I think it means?" Mother managed between sobs.

Rachel went to stand with her and rubbed her arm. She narrowed her eyes at Harry. "It better, or this will be a terrible jest."

"Not even I would do that," Harry said with affront. "That you would think that says more about you than it does me." He waggled his brows at his sister.

Rachel snorted. "That is accurate."

Mother sniffed as Father gave her a handkerchief and she dabbed her eyes. "Please, don't keep me in suspense."

Harry guided Selina to the side and gestured to her siblings. Rather, her sibling and not-sibling, not that anyone would know Beatrix wasn't their sister. Unless her father—the bloody Duke of Ramsgate—identified her as his bastard daughter. In that case, all the secrets would be out. Harry had learned a great deal about his astonishing new family to be in the past two days.

"Father, Mother, everyone, allow me to present Selina's brother, Mr. Raphael Bowles. You already know their half sister, Miss Whitford. And of course, Rachel, you and Nathaniel have already met Mr. Bowles." They decided on making that clear since Rafe's surname was different from Beatrix's. Part of Harry felt uncomfortable participating in their false-hood, but he also knew why it was necessary. They very much wanted to leave their past behind and start anew. In the end, he thought that was the best path, and he'd vowed to support them.

Imogen's gaze flicked from Harry to Selina and back to Harry again. "Did you just call her Selina?"

"I did. It is not uncommon to refer to your be-trothed by her given name."

Mother's sobs started anew, and all three of his sisters gasped in unison. This was followed by Rachel practically shouting, "I knew it!"

Jeremy, late as usual, strolled into the library. "Knew what?"

"Harry is marrying Lady Gresham," Delia said, beaming from the settee.

"Bollocks."

Mother threw a glare at her eldest child. "That is not an appropriate response!"

"It is if I'm to be the only one unwed. Now I shall bear the full brunt of your machinations." He looked over at Harry. "Congratulations. I suppose."

Harry couldn't help but laugh and was glad when Selina did too. Soon, everyone joined in. Except Rafe. He smiled, but he didn't laugh. Though Harry hadn't spent much time with him, he'd already determined that the man had a darkness that went deep into his soul. If you looked too long or too hard into his gaze, you felt the emptiness and had to turn away.

Harry was exceptionally glad Selina had left London when she did. He also understood what had driven them both to do the things they'd done. Neither was proud of their pasts. In fact, they sought to make amends, if they could.

Everyone came forward to hug Harry and Selina, welcoming her and her siblings to the family. After some time, Mother demanded everyone's attention. "When will the banns be read?"

"Tomorrow," Harry answered. "Is that soon enough?"

"Of course. Have you already chosen a day to wed? There is so much to plan. Can we hold the wedding breakfast here? Harry, I'm sorry, but your house is not large enough."

No, it wasn't, and he would need to move soon for it wouldn't support a family either. "Yes, you can host it here if that's acceptable to Selina?" He looked at the woman beside him, love for her expanding his chest.

Selina nodded. "I'd be honored, thank you. My brother would like to host a ball before the end of the Season—to celebrate our marriage and for Beatrix. He's purchased a house on Upper Brook Street."

Harry's father's brows shot up. "Indeed?"

"I'm looking forward to supporting my sisters," Rafe

said evenly, wisely answering the question as if Father was referring to Rafe's intentions and not the fact that he'd purchased a house on bloody Upper Brook Street.

Jeremy handed Rafe a glass of brandy. "Be careful. You will find yourself the toast of your own ball once the young ladies and their mothers set their eyes on you."

"But he doesn't even have a title," Beatrix said.

"He has money and will shortly be related to an earl by marriage," Rachel said wryly. "That will be enough."

It was a buoyant, jubilant evening—some, namely his sisters, might even have called it raucous. By the time Rafe had dropped his sisters and Harry on Queen Anne Street, Harry was yawning.

"Are you sure you want to come in for a nightcap?" Selina asked as they walked to the door.

"Yes." He looked at her intently as Beatrix preceded them into the house. "Unless you think I should go home for once," he whispered. He'd spent the last two nights here, waking up with the sun to rush home.

Her eyes danced with promise. "I think you should never go home."

"Minx." He resisted the urge to carry her into the house and directly up the stairs.

"I'm going up to bed," Beatrix announced as Harry followed Selina inside. "You can go into the sitting room and pretend to have a nightcap before you creep upstairs, or you could just be efficient and go up now." She shrugged. "I won't tell. Good night!" She waved her fingers at them and bounced up the stairs.

Harry chuckled as he drew Selina into his arms. "I don't need a nightcap, do you?"

Selina shook her head. She caught her lip between

her teeth as she unknotted his cravat. "I only need you."

"I wish it was that simple. You saw tonight that with me, you get an entire, extended, obnoxious family. Are you sure that's what you want?"

She held on to the ends of his cravat as she tipped her head back. "I'll admit that when I first met them, I was intimidated. I found them utterly captivating, but also terrifying. I've never had a family, not like that."

"Well, you have one now, and I can't promise they won't continue to be terrifying. I can promise, however, they will love you. Though not as much as I do."

"I still can't believe you do. I may never believe it, just so you know."

"Then I will simply have to tell you over and over and over again. I love you. I love you. I love—"

She put her fingers against his lips. "Stop. It's too much. I am too full."

"I could make a very lewd remark about how that isn't remotely true, but I'll abstain." He stroked his hand along her nape.

Selina leaned up and tugged at his earlobe with her teeth. "Please don't. That, I can never get enough of."

"Skipping the nightcap, then," he said, picking her up.

"Harry, you've carried me upstairs every night."

He started up the stairs. "And I may carry you tomorrow night and the night after. And the night after that. This is what you're agreeing to. If you want to change your mind, you better do so before church tomorrow." He made a face. "But then you'll have to deal with my mother and sisters."

She shuddered in his arms. "I'd rather not. Marriage it is, I suppose." She sounded resigned.

"Damn, but you are still far too good at pretending." He went to her chamber, and she pushed open the door. "I can't tell if you're jesting."

She slid down his front, keeping her arms around his neck. "Then I shall just have to show you. Surrender to me, Mr. Sheffield, and I will show you the truth of my undying love."

He put his lips to hers. "I am yours."

Don't miss A SCANDALOUS BARGAIN, when Beatrix sees something she shouldn't and finds herself making a deal to help Lord Rockbourne after the shocking death of his wife. Can a woman who can't stop stealing and a widower in need of redemption find love, or will their secrets destroy them both?

THANK YOU!

Thank you so much for reading A Secret Surrender! It's the first book in The Pretenders trilogy. I hope you enjoyed it!

Would you like to know when my next book is available and to hear about sales and deals? Sign up for my VIP newsletter at https://www.darcyburke.com/readergroup, follow me on social media:

Facebook: https://facebook.com/DarcyBurkeFans
Twitter at @darcyburke
Instagram at darcyburkeauthor
Pinterest at darcyburkewrite

And follow me on Bookbub to receive updates on pre-orders, new releases, and deals!

Need more Regency romance? Check out my other historical series:

The Untouchables - Swoon over twelve of Society's most eligible and elusive bachelor peers and the bluestockings, wallflowers, and outcasts who bring them to their knees!

The Untouchables: The Spitfire Society - Meet the smart, independent women who've decided they don't need Society's rules, their families' expectations, or, most importantly, a husband. But just because they don't need a man doesn't mean they might not *want* one…

Wicked Dukes Club - six books written by me and my BFF, NYT Bestselling Author Erica Ridley. Meet the unforgettable men of London's most notorious tavern, The Wicked Duke. Seductively handsome, with charm and wit to spare, one night with these rakes and rogues will never be enough…

Love is All Around - heartwarming Regency-set retellings of classic Christmas stories (written after the Regency!) featuring a cozy village, three siblings, and the best gift of all: love.

Secrets and Scandals - six epic stories set in London's glittering ballrooms and England's lush countryside, and the first one, Her Wicked Ways, is free!

Legendary Rogues - Four intrepid heroines and adventurous heroes embark on exciting quests across Regency England and Wales!

If you like contemporary romance, I hope you'll check out my **Ribbon Ridge** series available from Avon Impulse, and the continuation of Ribbon Ridge in **So Hot**.

I hope you'll consider leaving a review at your favorite online vendor or networking site!

I appreciate my readers so much. Thank you, thank you, *thank you.*

AUTHOR'S NOTE

I love the research involved with writing historical fiction. One of my go-to references is the 1817 map of London by W. Darton. This is where I look for neighborhoods and specific streets in London during this time. This map shows a Queen Ann Street intersecting with Portland Street (which is now Great Portland Street). When you compare that 1817 map to a modern map of London, the area looks vastly different! It's amazing how many streets in London are lost to time. I decided to spell Queen Anne Street with an "e" in this book because the majority of the advance readers (my editor and beta readers) found that the Ann spelling made them stop and wonder if it was spelled correctly, as Queen Anne is the more widely known modern spelling, at least in the US.

Other historical tidbits: the Lambeth Asylum for Orphan Girls was a real place, but is noted by several different names, including Asylum for Female Orphans. I chose one title and went with it. The Brown Bear pub existed at 34 Bow Street across from the magistrates' court at 33. I recently started watching Ripper Street, a BBC show set during the 1890s about the police in Whitechapel at Lambeth Street. There is a Brown Bear pub in the show near the police station, which I found interesting since I knew there was a Brown Bear on Bow Street too. I wonder if the Brown Bear in Whitechapel (which I believe was founded shortly after the one in Covent Garden) took its name from the pub across from the Bow Street Magistrates' Court.

Researching **A SECRET SURRENDER** was great fun! I do hope you'll contact me if you have any questions or further information to share.

ALSO BY DARCY BURKE

Historical Romance

The Untouchables

The Forbidden Duke
The Duke of Daring
The Duke of Deception
The Duke of Desire
The Duke of Defiance
The Duke of Danger
The Duke of Ice
The Duke of Ruin
The Duke of Lies
The Duke of Seduction
The Duke of Kisses
The Duke of Distraction

The Untouchables: The Spitfire Society

Never Have I Ever with a Duke
A Duke is Never Enough
A Duke Will Never Do

The Untouchables: The Pretenders

A Secret Surrender
A Scandalous Bargain
A Rogue to Ruin

Love is All Around
(A Regency Holiday Trilogy)

The Red Hot Earl
The Gift of the Marquess
Joy to the Duke

Wicked Dukes Club

One Night for Seduction by Erica Ridley
One Night of Surrender by Darcy Burke
One Night of Passion by Erica Ridley
One Night of Scandal by Darcy Burke
One Night to Remember by Erica Ridley
One Night of Temptation by Darcy Burke

Secrets and Scandals

Her Wicked Ways
His Wicked Heart
To Seduce a Scoundrel
To Love a Thief (a novella)
Never Love a Scoundrel
Scoundrel Ever After

Legendary Rogues

Lady of Desire
Romancing the Earl
Lord of Fortune
Captivating the Scoundrel

Contemporary Romance

Ribbon Ridge

Where the Heart Is (a prequel novella)

Only in My Dreams

Yours to Hold

When Love Happens

The Idea of You

When We Kiss

You're Still the One

Ribbon Ridge: So Hot

So Good

So Right

So Wrong

A DUKE WILL NEVER DO

"I have wanted to see Anthony's story since we first met him in The Duke of Distraction from the Untouchables series. He just begged to have a warm, loving, and very caring lady to heal his heart and soul, and he certainly found her in Jane."

– Flippin' Pages Book Reviews

"How they care for each other, how they heal each other and hurt each other simultaneously is the very heart and soul of this intriguing story."

– The Reading Café

THE UNTOUCHABLES SERIES

THE FORBIDDEN DUKE

"I LOVED this story!!" 5 Stars

-Historical Romance Lover

"This is a wonderful read and I can't wait to see what comes next in this amazing series..." 5 Stars

-Teatime and Books

THE DUKE of DARING

"You will not be able to put it down once you start. Such a good read."

-Books Need TLC

"An unconventional beauty set on life as a spinster

meets the one man who might change her mind, only to find his painful past makes it impossible to love. A wonderfully emotional journey from attraction, to friendship, to a love that conquers all."

-Bronwen Evans, *USA Today* Bestselling Author

THE DUKE of DECEPTION

"...an enjoyable, well-paced story ... Ned and Aquilla are an engaging, well-matched couple – strong, caring and compassionate; and ...it's easy to believe that they will continue to be happy together long after the book is ended."

-*All About Romance*

"This is my favorite so far in the series! They had chemistry from the moment they met...their passion leaps off the pages."

-*Sassy Book Lover*

THE DUKE of DESIRE

"Masterfully written with great characterization...with a flourish toward characters, secrets, and romance... Must read addition to "The Untouchables" series!"

-*My Book Addiction and More*

"If you are looking for a truly endearing story about two people who take the path least travelled to find the other, with a side of 'YAH THAT'S HOT!' then this book is absolutely for you!"

THE DUKE of DEFIANCE

THE DUKE of DANGER

THE DUKE of ICE

"An incredibly emotional story...I dare anyone to stop reading once the second half gets under way because this is intense!"

THE DUKE of RUIN

"This is a fast paced novel that held me until the last page."

" ...everything I could ask for in a historical romance... impossible to stop reading."

THE DUKE of LIES

"THE DUKE OF LIES is a work of genius! The characters are wonderfully complex, engaging; there is much mystery, and so many, many lies from so many people; I couldn't wait to see it all uncovered."

"..the epitome of romantic [with]...a bit of danger/action. The main characters are mature, fierce, passionate, and full of surprises. If you are a hopeless romantic and you love reading stories that'll leave you feeling like you're walking on clouds then you need to read this book or maybe even this entire series."

THE DUKE of SEDUCTION

"There were tears in my eyes for much of the last 10% of this book. So good!"

"An absolute joy to read... I always recommend Darcy!"

THE DUKE of KISSES

"Don't miss this magnificent read. It has some comedic fun, heartfelt relationships, heartbreaking moments, and horrifying danger."

"...my favorite story in the series. Fans of Regency romances will definitely enjoy this book."

THE DUKE of DISTRACTION

"Count on Burke to break a heart as only she can. This couple will get under the skin before they steal your heart."

"Darcy Burke never disappoints. Her storytelling is

just so magical and filled with passion. You will fall in love with the characters and the world she creates!"

LOVE IS ALL AROUND SERIES

THE RED HOT EARL

"Ash and Bianca were such absolutely loveable characters who were perfect for one another and so deserving of love... an un-put-downable, sensitive, and beautiful romance with the perfect combination of heart and heat."

"Everyone loves a good underdog story and . . . Burke sets out to inspire the soul with a powerful tale of heartwarming proportions. Words fail me but emotions drown me in the most delightful way."

THE GIFT OF THE MARQUESS
"This is a truly heartwarming and emotional story from beginning to end!"

"You could see how much they loved each other and watching them realizing their dreams was joyful to watch!!"

JOY TO THE DUKE

"…I had to wonder how this author could possibly redeem and reform Calder. Never fear – his story was wonderfully written and his redemption was heartwarming."

– *Flippin' Pages Book Reviews*

"I think this may be my favorite in this series! We finally find out what turned Calder so cold and the extent of that will surprise you."

– *Sassy Booklover*

WICKED DUKES CLUB SERIES

ONE NIGHT OF SURRENDER

"Together, Burke and Ridley have crafted a delightful "world" with swoon-worthy men, whip-smart ladies, and the perfect amount of steam for this romance reader."

–*Dream Come Review*

"…Burke makes this wonderfully entertaining tale of fated lovers a great and rocky ride."

–*The Reading Café*

ONE NIGHT OF SCANDAL

"… a well-written, engaging romance that kept me on my toes from beginning to end."

–*Keeper Bookshelf*

"Oh lord I read this book in one sitting because I

was too invested."

–*Beneath the Covers Blog*

ONE NIGHT OF TEMPTATION

"One Night of Temptation is a reminder of why I continue to be a Darcy Burke fan. Burke doesn't write damsels in distress."

– *Hopeless Romantic*

"Darcy has done something I've not seen before and made the hero a rector and she now has me wanting more! Hugh is nothing like you expect him to be and you will love him the minute he winks."

– *Sassy Booklover*

SECRETS & SCANDALS SERIES

HER WICKED WAYS

"A bad girl heroine steals both the show and a high-wayman's heart in Darcy Burke's deliciously wicked debut."

–Courtney Milan, *NYT* Bestselling Author

"...fast paced, very sexy, with engaging characters."

–*Smexybooks*

HIS WICKED HEART

"Intense and intriguing. Cinderella meets *Fight Club*

in a historical romance packed with passion, action and secrets."

"A romance...to make you smile and sigh...a wonderful read!"

TO SEDUCE a SCOUNDREL

"Darcy Burke pulls no punches with this sexy, romantic page-turner. Sevrin and Philippa's story grabs you from the first scene and doesn't let go. *To Seduce a Scoundrel* is simply delicious!"

"I was captivated on the first page and didn't let go until this glorious book was finished!"

TO LOVE a THIEF

"With refreshing circumstances surrounding both the hero and the heroine, a nice little mystery, and a touch of heat, this novella was a perfect way to pass the day."

"A refreshing read with a dash of danger and a little heat. For fans of honorable heroes and fun heroines who know what they want and take it."

NEVER LOVE a SCOUNDREL

"I loved the story of these two misfits thumbing their noses at society and finding love." Five stars.

–A Lust for Reading

"A nice mix of intrigue and passion...wonderfully complex characters, with flaws and quirks that will draw you in and steal your heart."

–BookTrib

SCOUNDREL EVER AFTER

"There is something so delicious about a bad boy, no matter what era he is from, and Ethan was definitely delicious."

-A Lust for Reading

"I loved the chemistry between the two main characters...Jagger/Ethan is not what he seems at all and neither is sweet society Miss Audrey. They are believably compatible."

-Confessions of a College Angel

LEGENDARY ROGUES SERIES

LADY of DESIRE

"A fast-paced mixture of adventure and romance, very much in the mould of *Romancing the Stone* or *Indiana Jones*."

Daphne stole all of my heart and then some. This book was such a delight to read."

"Darcy knows how to end a series with a bang! Daphne and Gideon are a mix of enemies and allies turned lovers that will have you on the edge of your seat at every turn."

Contemporary Romance

RIBBON RIDGE SERIES

A contemporary family saga featuring the Archer family of sextuplets who return to their small Oregon wine country town to confront tragedy and find love...

The "multilayered plot keeps readers invested in the story line, and the explicit sensuality adds to the excitement that will have readers craving the next Ribbon Ridge offering."

"Darcy Burke writes a uniquely touching and heartwarming series about the love, pain, and joys of family as well as the love that feeds your soul when you meet "the one.""

I can't tell you how much I love this series. Each book gets better and better.

"Darcy Burke's Ribbon Ridge series is one of my all-time favorites. Fall in love with the Archer family, I know I did."

RIBBON RIDGE: SO HOT

SO GOOD

" ...worth the read with its well-written words, beautiful descriptions, and likeable characters...they are flirty, sexy and a match made in wine heaven."

"I absolutely love the characters in this book and the families. I honestly could not put it down and finished it in a day."

SO RIGHT

"This is another great story by Darcy Burke. Painting pictures with her words that make you want to sit and stare at them for hours. I love the banter between the characters and the general sense of fun and friendliness."

" ...the romance is emotional; the characters are spirited and passionate... "

SO WRONG

"As usual, Ms. Burke brings you fun characters and witty banter in this sweet hometown series. I loved the dance between Crystal and Jamie as they fought their attraction."

-The Many Faces of Romance

"I really love both this series and the Ribbon Ridge series from Darcy Burke. She has this way of taking your heart and ripping it right out of your chest one second and then the next you are laughing at something the characters are doing."

-Romancing the Readers

ABOUT THE AUTHOR

Darcy Burke is the USA Today Bestselling Author of sexy, emotional historical and contemporary romance. Darcy wrote her first book at age 11, a happily ever after about a swan addicted to magic and the female swan who loved him, with exceedingly poor illustrations. Join her Reader Club newsletter at http://www.darcyburke.com/readerclub.

A native Oregonian, Darcy lives on the edge of wine country with her guitar-strumming husband, their two hilarious kids who seem to have inherited the writing gene. They're a crazy cat family with two Bengal cats, a small, fame-seeking cat named after a fruit, and an older rescue Maine Coon who is the master of chill and five a.m. serenading. In her "spare" time Darcy is a serial volunteer enrolled in a 12-step program where one learns to say "no," but she keeps having to start over. Her happy places are Disneyland and Labor Day weekend at the Gorge. Visit Darcy online at http://www.darcyburke.com and follow her on social media.